CONVICTION

BY D. A. MISHANI

The Inspector Avraham Avraham Mysteries
The Missing File
A Possibility of Violence
The Man Who Wanted to Know

Three

CONVICTION

D. A. Mishani

Translated by Jessica Cohen

riverrun

First published in Hebrew in Israel in 2021 by Achuzat Bayit
First published in Great Britain in 2022 by

riverrun
An imprint of

Quercus Editions Limited
Carmelite House
50 Victoria Embankment
London EC4Y 0DZ

An Hachette UK company

A CIP catalogue record for this book is available
from the British Library

Hardback 978 1 78429 747 3
TradePaperback 978 1 78429 748 0
Ebook 978 1 78429 746 6

10 9 8 7 6 5 4 3 2 1

Typeset by CC Book Production
Printed and bound in Great Britain by Clays Ltd, Elcograf S.p.A.

Papers used by Quercus are from well-managed forests and other responsible sources.

For Marika Moisseeff
And for Michael Houseman

'Get thee out of thy country, and from thy kindred, and from thy father's house.'

(Genesis 12:1)

Part One

The Disappearance

DEPUTY COMMISSIONER BENNY SABAN, the Ayalon precinct commander, made no attempt to hide his astonishment. He yanked open his desk drawer and pulled out a blue velvet case, from which he removed a pen-shaped device made of dark glass. 'I don't believe this, Avi. You cannot be serious,' he said.

Superintendent Avraham was, however, entirely serious. Their meeting had only been arranged that morning, but he'd been planning it since the early summer and waiting for it since he came back from his holiday.

'This doesn't bother you, does it? The cigar?' asked Saban. Avraham shook his head.

Ilana Lis, the previous precinct commander, used to take a clear plastic cup out of that same drawer, pour a little water in it, place it on the desk and ask Avraham to 'light us a cigarette', even though smoking was prohibited in the station. He would light one, hand it to her, then light another for himself. Back when they'd started working together and were both young, he used to put two cigarettes in his mouth and light them at the same time.

Saban's e-cigar emitted a pink cloud, from within which he continued speaking to Avraham. 'But you've barely done two years, Avi. I don't understand you. How old are you now? Forty-six? Seven?'

'Forty-three.'

'Seriously? Even so. Where do you think you could transfer to at your age?'

He wasn't exactly sure where. He wanted to move to one of the national police units. International Investigations, or Fraud. Maybe even a different security organization. And in fact, he was almost forty-four.

'A security organization? Avi, what are you taking about? Don't tell me you're going to turn into a Shin Bet agent now.'

As he always did when he was anxious, Saban blinked a lot. And Avraham realized that he liked Saban more than he'd expected to when they'd first met in this office. Back then, Saban was the man who'd replaced Ilana when she had to go on sick leave. Just as Avraham had expected, he'd turned out to be a less inspirational boss – he mostly focused on staying within the budget and 'improving our numbers' – but he'd never lied to Avraham and was not good at hiding his tendency to become emotional and stressed, which made Avraham trust him. Still, he was not interested in sharing the reasons for his transfer request with Saban. What could he say? Was he supposed to describe that moment in the forest, when the

4

understanding that he wanted to investigate different cases had arisen from the crystalline lake?

'I really don't see the problem,' Saban persisted. 'You barely have two years under your belt overseeing the Investigation and Intelligence branch, you're doing good work — really quite good, even. Give it another year, eighteen months; maybe I'll move on, who knows, and you'll be promoted. You'll get chief superintendent, shoot for precinct commander. Why rock the boat now? You just got married. Do you really need more changes?'

Had it been Ilana sitting in that seat, they would have talked at length about everything Avraham had been through that summer. But Ilana was not there. Or at least not in the way she used to be, because, for a fleeting moment, Avraham did see her get up to open the window for him, her presence wafting translucently, and he shut his eyes, as if to capture the scene behind his eyelids before it could vanish.

ILANA HAD DIED AT the beginning of the summer, and Avraham's profound grief was compounded by his anger at her refusal to see him before her death and his guilt at having missed the funeral.

She had shut herself up at home since Passover, seeing no one except family and a handful of friends that did not include him. She had decided that Avraham would not be one of the close few who would be with her through her illness and death, and so he had given up, stopped phoning and sending messages, only calling Gary every so often for an update.

He told Marianka that he understood Ilana, but the truth was that he didn't. What was he being punished for? Why were colleagues who didn't know her as well as he did allowed to see her, while Avraham was denied even a single visit? He knew, of course, that she hadn't timed the moment her heart stopped beating to make it impossible for him to be at the funeral, yet he felt that her death at home in Ramat Hasharon while he was on his honeymoon in Slovenia was further evidence of her desire to hurt him.

Just like the farewell letter.

When Eliyahu Ma'alul had told Avraham of Ilana's death, he'd immediately phoned Gary to express his condolences and apologize for not being able to come to the funeral. Gary told Avraham that Ilana had left him a letter, which he was welcome to pick up when he got back to Israel.

During the honeymoon, Avraham kept wondering what Ilana might have written. He and Marianka got married twice, once at the municipality of Koper, the town where she was born, and once in a small church in town, on the shores of the Black Sea. The only wedding guests were Bojan and Anika Milanich, Marianka's parents, who did little to conceal their sorrow whenever they had to hug the man who was taking their daughter away from them; a few relatives whose names Avraham was unable to learn; and two of Marianka's childhood friends, Eva and Monika, who told him admiringly that he reminded them of the main character from *Fauda*. At the luncheon after the wedding, they asked Avraham if he also dressed up as an Arab and fought terrorist organizations as part of his job. That night,

Eva and Monika insisted on invading his dream, and since his attempts to banish them fell short, Avraham was forced to accept their thrilling presence in a short dream, which, fortunately, was soon replaced by a different one, in which he was a teenager driving a white Subaru with his father on the highway to Jerusalem. In that dream, his father was around Avraham's own age now, and he smoked the whole way and told Avraham a long story which Avraham could not remember in the morning. That seemed to have been his way of sharing his wedding day with his father, who had been too unwell to travel.

They stayed in Koper for five nights and then drove to the woods in an old Fiat without air-conditioning which Marianka's uncle had insisted on lending them. They read books and went for walks, from which Marianka returned with baskets full of blueberries and moist mushrooms. At times Avraham still had trouble believing that this woman had come to live with him in Holon. She'd started working in Israel for a private investigation firm that specialized in surveillance services for women going through divorces, and she was sometimes hired by the police to interpret at tourists' interrogations or online questionings of overseas witnesses. Avraham saw nothing sad about getting married thousands of kilometres from his home, his parents and his friends because the wedding was just for the two of them, not for anyone else. The priest spoke in English, and when Avraham wasn't sure what to do, Marianka whispered in his ear.

In the early evening, they sat by the lake, and the surrounding treetops were painted on the water in dark colours. Marianka sat on the wooden bench outside the cabin they'd rented, with her knees

7

folded up, and wrote in pencil in a red notebook, using words in a language he would never understand. Avraham read about the latest Kurt Wallander case, which led his beloved detective into the Swedish intelligence service's vaults and into nuclear submarines, where he exposed dark secrets from the Cold War era. When Marianka asked him, 'What are you thinking about?' he said nothing because that's what he was used to saying.

But then he changed his mind. 'I don't know if I can go back,' he said, and when she asked if he meant to Holon, he said, 'To work. To the usual investigations.' Of course it was related to Ilana, as Marianka assumed, but that wasn't the only reason.

Most of the cases he'd handled in recent years—he explained to Marianka—were tragically violent, and solving them had done no good for anyone. Who was helped by him finding out that Rafael Sharabi had killed his son, Ofer? Or that Chaim Sara had strangled his wife, Jennifer, and buried her in the yard? It was as if he were constantly fighting meaningless wars in which there could never be a winner – all they had was losers.

'How can you say those cases were meaningless?' Marianka asked.

He answered, 'Of course they're meaningful to the people involved in them, but solving them doesn't change the bigger picture. It doesn't even help the victims or their relatives.' It certainly hadn't helped Ofer Sharabi or Jennifer Salazar that he'd found out who murdered them, and it hadn't given their families anything either. Hannah Sharabi was left not only without her son but also without a husband. Jennifer Salazar's children were now living not

8

just without their mother but without their father, too. 'I think the most important thing I've done in the past few years is catching that chimpanzee, don't you?'

Marianka reminded him that it was an orang-utan.

Besides, Avraham hadn't really caught the ape; he'd spotted it crouching on a stone wall in an upmarket neighbourhood near the beach and radioed its location. He'd been on his way back to the station after visiting Ashdod port to investigate a fake Viagra smuggling operation when he'd heard over the police radio that a dangerous ape had escaped from the zoo, and drove off the highway to help with the search. The next day his picture was on the back page of *Israel Today*, and the police spokespeople made him go on one of the morning TV shows, where he was interviewed along with a zoologist. 'Weren't you afraid?' the interviewer asked him, 'The ape could have attacked you!' Avraham replied that he wasn't.

The ape hadn't moved, after all. He seemed to have understood that his escape attempt had failed, and had become filled with despair. Instead of resisting when the vet approached him, he simply hopped off the wall into her arms, at which point they got into the van together and disappeared. Still, the interviewer thanked Avraham for his courage.

SABAN TRIED IN VAIN to turn off his e-cigar, and finally put it back in the open case, still buzzing and discharging dark vapours.

'Look, Avi,' he said with a sigh, 'I'll forward your request. I have no choice, but you know it could take weeks, even months, right? And do you have any thoughts on who could replace you? Do you think we'll have to bring in someone from outside or is Vahaba seasoned enough?'

Avraham said he thought Vahaba would do an excellent job. When Saban asked if he knew Chief Inspector Orna Ben-Hamo, who'd tracked down the lawyer from Givatayim who'd murdered two women and staged their deaths as suicides, Avraham said he hadn't met her but had heard good things about her from Ilana Lis.

Saban walked to the door, then stopped and put his hand – with its glossy, manicured fingernails – on Avraham's shoulder. 'I think I get what you're going through,' he said, 'even if you're convinced I can't see it. You think the precinct and its cases are beneath you, right, Avi? You're always kind of quiet and make yourself out to be modest, but really, you're convinced you're headed for the big leagues. And I know the stories about how you're sure all the detectives on TV and in books are always wrong and you're the only one who knows the real solution. Isn't that what this is about?'

Avraham smiled and said no, and Saban abruptly closed the open door, as if what he was about to say was a secret. 'But I want you to know that you're making a big mistake in how you think about what we do here. There's a reason they changed the name to "Ministry of Public Security". It's not the "Ministry of Police" any more. We're part of the country's security apparatus, and what we do here is no less meaningful than what they do in other organizations. Besides, don't forget that this is your home. How many years have you been here? Fifteen, at least?'

Walking back to his office, Avraham saw Eliyahu Ma'alul making his fourth or fifth Turkish coffee of the day in the open kitchenette down the hallway, and thought perhaps he should have asked Saban to keep his request confidential. Ilanit wasn't at her desk, and although he assumed she'd taken a lunch break, he called her to find out if there was any news. 'Just the things from the morning. Nothing else,' Ilanit said.

'The things from the morning' were exactly the kind of cases he'd been handling for about a decade, since joining the precinct. *9:07 a.m. — Avi, message from intensive care at Wolfson, newborn baby found outside the hospital, no identifying marks. Should I send Vahaba? 9:53 a.m. — 36-year-old mentally ill male tried to set his mother on fire in her apartment on Aharonowitz St and attacked a social worker with a kitchen knife. 10:37 a.m. — lawyer for suspect in fake Viagra smuggling wants to talk to you urgently. When can you get back to her? 11:19 a.m. — manager of hotel in Bat Yam reported that a tourist disappeared without paying his bill. 11:22 a.m. — 3-year-old boy was left in car at Zahav Mall parking lot, arrived at A&E severely dehydrated and died an hour later. Do you want to bring the parents in today or wait till after the funeral?*

Outside of what Saban had called 'your home', there were entities engaged in elaborate operations to stop the Iranians from building a nuclear bomb, heroically thwarting terrorist attacks, investigating presidents and prime ministers and other politicians. Behind all these were people whose work was genuinely valuable, who were fighting important wars. Wars in which there was not only a losing side but a winning side, and a just side. And now Avraham was supposed to bring in a pair of grief-stricken parents to be questioned because they'd left their son in the car while they went to buy a dishwasher. Or to question a mentally ill man who'd tried to murder his mother in a fit of fury, and understand his motives. Saban was wrong. Avraham didn't think these investigations were beneath him. It was just that he wanted to fulfil his dream from way back when he'd joined the police, which he'd only revealed to Ilana.

It was at his job interview for the precinct, which was the first time they'd met, and he'd told her he wanted to save lives and fight against cruelty, violence and evil. Ilana had flashed the smile he'd come to know over the years, and asked him, 'Do you think the police is the right place to do that?' When Avraham replied that he did, she'd said, 'I wish I could say you're right.'

He called Ilanit and asked her to bring him a lunch of rice and beans from the cafeteria. He texted Marianka to say he'd be home early and asked if she wanted to go for a run on the beach with him, but she responded saying she had karate practice and wouldn't be back before nine. Ilanit brought him a salad with avocado and hard-boiled egg because they were out of beans. She said the fake Viagra smuggler's lawyer wanted to postpone her client's questioning because he'd just had his appendix out.

He could have gone home.

Esty Vahaba was at Wolfson, gathering information about the baby who'd been abandoned at the hospital, and collecting testimony from the doctors who'd cared for the boy who was left in the car and died. Eliyahu Ma'alul was waiting for the social worker who'd been attacked by the mentally ill man who'd tried to murder his mother, and meanwhile he was questioning the young man's psychiatrist on the phone.

Avraham called Gary to ask if he could pick up the letter from Ilana, but as usual, there was no answer. When he got into his white Hyundai, he still wasn't sure where he was heading, but he ended up driving to the hotel in Bat Yam because there was no one else to send there. On the radio they were talking about another mysterious poisoning of a Russian dissident, allegedly by Vladimir Putin's secret service, and Avraham couldn't help imagining himself being recruited by the CIA or MI6 to solve the case: *Inspector Avraham? This is Langley. We know you've been expecting our call.*

The sight of the Palace Hotel building reminded him that he was on Ben Gurion Boulevard in Bat Yam. Although the sign hanging from one of the windows declared it a 'Luxury Suite Hotel', the Palace looked more like a dilapidated apartment building. The walls were peeling from the sea air, and years of neglect had knocked down most of the blinds and coloured the remaining ones in shades of dirt. Its only advantage was the location. The beachfront balconies overlooked the promenade and the sea, which was the same sea everywhere, and which made Avraham happy every time he saw it. Three shirtless young men stood smoking on one of the balconies, and when they saw Avraham walking in, they hurried inside.

The Palace was not the only incongruously named establishment in the area. Next to the hotel, along the promenade, Avraham spotted a restaurant named 'Elegance', with oilcloths on the plastic tables set out on the pavement; a shuttered fish restaurant named 'Venice'; and the former 'Deluxe Delicatessen', now a convenience store selling cigarettes and cheap alcohol. The hotel adjacent to the Palace was an even more decrepit building, and its name offered stiff competition: 'Monaco Hotel Seashore Luxury & More.'

But wasn't this exactly Avraham's story? The plaque next to his office door read 'Investigations and Intelligence Branch Commander'. On the desk in the middle of his room sat the brown wooden pipe that Marianka had bought him at the Armenian market in Jerusalem's Old City. Avraham was a 'detective'.

Just like Kurt Wallander, except with peeling walls and stained oilcloths and broken blinds. A detective for grief-stricken parents and wounded children and sad little investigations whose resolutions only added more sorrow to the world.

The Palace lobby, though, did surprise him.

It was open, with no inner door separating it from the street, and the décor was Far Eastern. Two massive porcelain vases stood on the marble floor, each a head taller than Avraham and painted with women in kimonos and Japanese or Chinese lettering. The vases sprouted colourful plastic flowers on long stems. There was also a likely-fake cherry tree in a huge container. The front-desk clerk sat reading a book, his fair hair just visible behind the high wooden counter. It took the young man some time to understand why Avraham was there, but when he did, a grin spread over his face and he said, 'Oh, that's all fine now. No problems with that guy.' That afternoon, a few hours after the hotel manager had called the police, the tourist's relatives had turned up, explained that he'd be staying with them from now on, taken his belongings and paid the bill. Oleg, the clerk, hadn't informed the police because he didn't think they'd send anyone to handle the complaint anyway.

This seemed to be an appropriate ending to Avraham's day.

He could have sat down at the Elegance, ordered a khinkali or khachapuri, which looked seductively greasy in the photographs displayed in the window, and waited for Marianka to finish her karate practice. 'How do you know they were his relatives?' he asked Oleg.

'Well, that's what they said. And they paid his bill.'

'So?'

'What do you mean, so? So why would someone pay for a guy they're not related to?'

'So essentially, you allowed these people you did not know to take a guest's luggage, simply because they asked to?'

Oleg looked uncomfortable. 'Okay,' he said, 'but the guest hasn't been here for two days. He left two or three hours after he checked in and never came back. And anyway, the suitcases were empty.' When Avraham asked how he knew this, the clerk's face turned red: 'That's what I saw. They looked totally empty.'

'Did you open them in his room?'

'Of course not. Why would I open his suitcases?'

When Oleg stood up, Avraham realized why he'd been hired as the front-desk clerk. He was tall and brawny, and if there was ever any trouble with guests at the Palace – and Avraham had the feeling there was – Oleg would know how to solve it.

'Did they leave you a name? A phone number?' he asked, and the clerk looked even more uneasy.

'A number for who?'

'For the relatives. That's what they told you, isn't it? That they were his family?'

'Yes. But they didn't give a number.'

'Do you have the guest's phone number?'

'No. He didn't give it.'

'And how did they pay?'

'Cash. Six hundred shekels in bills of two hundred. Four hundred for the two nights he was supposed to have already stayed, and two hundred for the other night he'd booked. He booked three nights in total.'

'Is there a camera here? Can I see?'

'Sure. It's right there, on the ceiling.'

'I don't mean the camera. The relatives. In the video footage.'

'Oh, sure. Do you want to see it now?'

'Not yet.' He wanted to go up to the room first. 'Do you remember what they knew about him?' he asked.

'What they knew? They said they were relatives of the tourist who'd stayed here, and that they'd come to pay. That's it.'

'So they didn't know his name? Or show you his passport or any other papers?'

Now Oleg looked decidedly embarrassed. 'Do you think they're not related to him? That he might come back all of a sudden and his luggage will be gone?'

Avraham said, 'I have no idea. Let's go up to his room.'

THE ROOM WAS ON the second floor.

It was large, perhaps because the building was not intended to be a hotel, and dark because the big window, which was shut when they went in, did not face the sea but the back yard and a neglected building that blocked out the sunlight. Avraham pulled back a dusty curtain that used to be cream-coloured, rolled up a blind that hadn't been washed in years, and looked out. There was a name written by someone's finger in the dust on the window-pane: *Yaakov Ben-Hayat*. Whoever designed the room must have envisioned a palatial theme: the ceiling had floral reliefs in plaster, and the walls were hung with giant paintings in faux-gold frames, as if it were a museum in Florence. Two details immediately drew Avraham's attention: the minibar, and a ceramic mug by the bathroom sink.

'Has anyone cleaned the room since they were here?' he asked.

Oleg shook his head. 'The cleaner will be here the day after tomorrow.'

'Did you restock the minibar, or was it full?'

'The cleaner does that, too.'

During the hours the tourist had spent in the room, he seemed not to have had any alcohol. But he had made coffee with the electric kettle, and if they needed to collect his fingerprints, they might be able to get them.

'Were you with them when they came up to the room?' asked Avraham, and Oleg shook his head. He had been alone at reception and hadn't been able to leave the front desk. 'And how did you know he was really a tourist?'

'Who?'

'The man who took the room. And disappeared. What language did he speak?'

'English, but he had an accent. French, I think. And he showed me his passport, too. I can check for you.'

'You were here when he checked in?'

'I'm here every day, I do the night shift.'

'What did he say?'

'Nothing much. But he arrived in an airport taxi. I saw it.'

Avraham asked Oleg to lock the door to the room and not let anyone in. On their way downstairs he asked how many guests were currently staying in the hotel, and Oleg said there were only two occupied rooms at the moment, but some rooms were rented by the hour. 'Like, you know, couples, married ones, and other people. But tourists only stay in the suites. And there are some Chinese guys on the fourth floor. They're here to work on the light railway. Engineers.'

Why, then, had the tourist, whose name Avraham hadn't yet asked for, been given a room facing the back yard and not the sea?

Oleg said that's what he'd asked for. A room that didn't face the street.

Back at the front desk, Avraham asked Oleg to check the tourist's name and how he'd booked the room. Oleg switched on an old desktop computer and waited almost five minutes for it to start up. The guest's name was Jacques Bertoldi. He hadn't reserved the room, but had walked into the hotel, asked if they had a room available, and booked it for three nights. He hadn't left a phone number, but had given Oleg a Swiss passport number, which Avraham wrote in his notebook. Until he could see Bertoldi on the security camera footage, Avraham had to make do with what Oleg remembered. He took a blue pen out of his shirt pocket and wrote in the black notebook that Marianka had bought him in Slovenia: *Approx. 60, tall, at least 1.85, very thin, fairly dark skin, full head of silver hair. Wore brown trousers and brown jacket when he arrived at the hotel at night and when he left the next morning at five or six.*

'When he left in the morning, did he say anything to you?' Avraham asked, and Oleg looked like he was trying to remember.

'Oh, yeah. That's another reason why we called. He asked if I could recommend a restaurant, and when I said yes, he asked if I'd be in the hotel when he got back that evening so I could give him directions. I told him not to worry, I was here every evening, and he said, "Great, then I'll see you in a few hours." In English. See? So that's why we were positive he'd be back.'

ON THE WAY HOME, Avraham did not turn the radio on.

The Palace security camera was on the passenger seat next to him, but Avraham could already see in his mind's eye a sixty-year-old man, tall and thin, getting out of a taxi in the middle of the night at a promenade hotel in Bat Yam, asking in French-accented English for a room that did not face the street, not going to sleep and not even lying down, but making himself a cup of coffee, leaving his room in the morning, promising to return in the evening – but not returning. Two men had taken his belongings before Avraham had been able to get to the Palace himself or send an officer to look into the complaint. Why did Avraham sense that he would regret not coming sooner? After all, at this point he had no reason to think the tourist was in any danger, perhaps other than his promise to Oleg that he'd be back in the evening.

And there was also the desk clerk's response to Avraham's final question.

'The people who came to pick up the luggage, did they look like him?' he'd asked, and Oleg had turned red again and said, 'I don't remember exactly what they looked like. One of them was short, actually. Blond. You can see it on the camera. But relatives don't always look alike, do they?'

2

THE POLICE ARRIVED AT quarter past five.

They must have assumed they'd be waking her, but Liora was already loading the washing machine on the utility porch, so she didn't hear them coming up to her third-floor flat. When she heard someone banging on the door and shouting, 'Police! Open up!' she did get startled, but they had no chance of finding what they were looking for.

She was thoroughly prepared, and the flat was as gleaming as it would be after a spring clean. Thirty-odd years of housework had made her an expert in covering her tracks.

THE POLICEMAN WAS FAT and sweaty and smelled of tinned tuna. He walked around the flat, asked Liora if she was alone and, when he caught sight of the basket in front of the washing machine, asked her to empty the machine and went through the dirty clothes, one by one. He called to the Ethiopian policewoman, whispered something in her ear and she proceeded to sift through the panties and bras and sniff them like a hungry dog. They moved on to the girls' room, where they emptied cupboards and drawers, then they searched the bathroom and the toilet, and climbed up the ladder to the storage attic, which was the only place Liora never cleaned because it contained David's tools and construction materials.

'Can you explain to me what you want? What are you looking for?' she asked.

The policeman said, 'Where are your daughters?'

'They're sleeping over with someone. Why, did my girls do something to you? Are you here to arrest them?'

They were becoming increasingly frustrated.

She considered calling Avi Edry again and decided not to, but she did take out her phone to document the search: clothes tossed on the beds, pillows pulled off the living room couches, drawers overturned and emptied out on the floor. In Danielle's room, the Ethiopian policewoman shone a torch under the bed and dragged out a maroon sheet. Liora panicked for a moment, but when she saw the dust on it, she realized it had clearly been there for weeks.

'Please put back everything you moved,' she said.

'No problem, we will,' the policeman said.

She aimed the camera at him because he was obviously someone who didn't like to have his photo taken, and she said, 'Can you tell me your name? I can't see your name. And tell the camera what you're looking for – because I don't understand.'

He was ready to leave, but the policewoman was still searching the kitchen – fridge, freezer, cupboards, cutlery drawers. They were like a pair of exasperated criminals who'd broken into a flat with a safe and found it empty. In the end, they put a few towels and kids' clothes into a crate they'd brought.

Liora kept recording them when they told her she was being detained and had to come to the station with them. She asked, 'Why do I have to? Can you tell me what this is about?'

The policeman replied, 'At the moment it's about leaving a minor unsupervised and harming minors and defenceless individuals. Beyond that, they'll tell you at the station.'

Liora said, 'But my girls are staying with my older daughter – talk to her. How can you call that unsupervised?'

All this was part of the plan she'd devised in case the police turned up, even though she hadn't thought it would happen so soon.

The street was dark and empty when she was put into the police car.

The neighbours did not look out of their windows, despite the fact they'd all heard the banging on the door and the shouting, but that wasn't anything unusual in this neighbourhood, and whoever had woken up might have gone back to sleep.

Liora didn't know how the police had managed to identify her – although she had her suspicions – but she wasn't afraid, not even when they drove past the hospital, whether they did so coincidentally or deliberately in order to scare her. The policewoman drove and the policeman sat next to her, typing on a tablet with one hand and clutching his half-eaten tuna sandwich in the other, as if someone was threatening to steal it. Since the car windows were tinted, Liora couldn't see if the guard sitting at the entrance to the mall adjacent to the hospital was the woman or the old man, and whether there were more police or police cars there.

If you could see me now, you wouldn't recognize me, she said to David silently. *You'd be so impressed by how I'm not letting them scare me. You're with me, and so is God, and this time I know what has to be done.*

IT HAD BEEN THAT way since the moment the doctor had left. Everything she did had been planned.

She'd taken a reconnaissance tour of the hospital. It had two entryways – one for cars, through the car park, and another for pedestrians, through the shopping centre. Liora realized it would be riskier for her to arrive by car because the security guards at the car park made a point of checking each vehicle and she wanted to avoid any delays on her way out. If a car was stopped for any reason at the exit, she might get stuck behind it, and she needed to get out of the hospital grounds as soon as possible. There were also more security cameras in the car-park area, and she had a feeling there were other pairs of eyes she hadn't spotted. At the shopping centre entrance, on the other hand, there was one camera at the guard's booth, and if she wore a head covering or hid her face at the right moment, it would be impossible to identify her. The elderly guard didn't make anyone open their bags, and that was the most important thing. He just used his metal-detector wand, which probably didn't work anyway, and barely glanced at anyone. Even if he asked her to open her bag, she would have time to retreat. She could say she'd forgotten something and she'd be right back.

Café Roladin was just inside the entrance. She ordered a latté and a cheese-and-raisin Danish fresh from the oven, then sat down facing the guard station and the street exit.

A bus arrived every minute. Number 140, number 26, number 12. Another 140. Sometimes two or three came together. The distance from her café table to the station was no more than fifty metres, which she could walk in thirty or forty seconds. She'd be sitting on a moving bus within a minute, or just over, without anyone having noticed the bag she'd left under the table. And even if someone did notice and called after her, 'Lady, you forgot your bag!' Liora could go back and thank them and try another time.

At first, she thought the ideal time would be early morning, or perhaps late at night, just before the buses stopped running, but then she realized there were fewer people in the mall and the buses were less frequent. It would be better if the café was busy and the guard had to deal with a crowd. And wasn't that the right way to commit a crime in Israel – in broad daylight with as many people around as possible? Burglars who broke into homes at night sometimes got caught and punished, but people who committed really serious crimes, in plain sight, never got caught, and even if they did, they had lawyers who helped them get off.

This was the first time she'd taken the back door into the Holon police station, through the car park. She was not handcuffed while the fat policeman walked her up the stairs to the second floor. He put her in a small, windowless interrogation room, where the air-conditioner was off, and she could feel her shirt clinging to her chest and neck. But none of that affected her. It was more than an hour before anything happened, but she had a Bible in her bag, and reading it calmed her: it put some weight into her body, giving it inner stability.

When the detective came into the room, at first she acted as if Liora wasn't there. She sat down at the computer and typed, with her eyes too close to the screen. Only when she introduced herself and had to look at Liora did Liora realize why the woman had tried to hide her eyes. She was cross-eyed, so that when she looked at something, her gaze fell a couple of centimetres away from what she wanted to see. Her eyes were also red and watery, as if coated with a wet membrane.

Chief Inspector Esty Vahaba asked Liora to state her name and identity number, and Liora said them out loud, in a voice she hoped indicated that she was not afraid: 'Liora Talyas. ID number 35655131.'

A camera in the corner of the room was recording them.

'Date of birth?'

'Third of Tevet.'

The detective looked up with her rheumy eyes, and Liora felt herself gaining confidence.

'What's the Gregorian date?' she asked.

'Why, what's wrong with the Hebrew date?' Liora said, but then she added, 'December twenty-third, nineteen seventy-nine.' When she was asked for her address, she said, 'But you already know my address. You sent the two cops there to bring me in, didn't you? It was so important for them to bang on the door and kick up a fuss at five a.m., like we're some criminal organization. And what did they find? They found shit.'

Chief Inspector Vahaba tried to look at Liora as directly as possible. 'Your home address?' she repeated, and Liora answered, 'Two Ha'giborim Street. Bat Yam.'

'Thank you. I am beginning the interview. You should be aware that it is being recorded and videotaped. It is now eight-forty a.m., Tuesday, August twenty-sixth. And this is a questioning under caution. Can you explain to me why you left the baby?'

Liora immediately replied, 'I didn't leave any baby. I don't know what you want.'

'Yesterday, on Monday, August twenty-fifth, you left a baby in a black bag at Wolfson Hospital. Or rather, not in the hospital but in the shopping centre adjacent to the hospital. You entered with a black bag and left without it.'

For an instant she was back outside the shopping centre.

She'd noticed from a distance that the elderly guard wasn't there, and instead there was a young female guard who was searching people's bags. She'd hesitated for a moment or two, no longer. The guard wasn't making everyone open their bags, and she wasn't putting her hands inside them. She just glanced in and ran the metal detector around the outside of the bags.

Liora told the detective, 'I have no idea what you're talking about.

Where would I get a baby to leave? And if I had one, why would I put it in a bag?'

'I think you had a baby. And that you abandoned her.'

'Then you're wrong.'

Liora was suddenly positive that the hour she'd spent alone in the interrogation room had helped her, rather than increasing her anxiety. She'd grown accustomed to the room, to being in it. The previous conversations she'd had in interrogation rooms – perhaps even in this one – had infused her with more power. *If only there was a way for you to see me now*, she told David soundlessly.

'There is footage from the mall's security camera showing you walking in with the bag in which the baby was found and leaving the mall without it. You can clearly see the bag and you can clearly see that *you* are holding it. I'm not saying it was intentional. You might have forgotten it by mistake. Perhaps you forgot the baby and realized a few hours later and panicked. Could that be what happened?'

Liora smiled and the detective's gaze grew shorter again. This was the point at which she was assuming Liora was stupid and would confess in response to her lies. Liora said, 'Do you think if you tell me I forgot it by accident, I'll tell you it was mine?'

'Do you want to see her? Maybe that'll help you remember?'

Liora raised her voice: 'Are you for real? You think if you show me some baby, I'll tell you I abandoned her? You send two cops into an ordinary family's house at five a.m. with a search warrant and an arrest warrant because of a baby who doesn't exist, and now you want me to go and see her with you? I can't understand if you're putting on an act or if you're for real.' Liora thought the detective was taken aback, perhaps not so much by what she'd said, but by her tone. And now she knew for sure that the baby was alive. Not that she'd had any doubt – she'd assumed the baby would be found within minutes and be cared for immediately. Still, in the news Liora had read online about the baby found at Wolfson there was no information on her condition, but now she knew that she'd been right, and the baby would be fine.

The detective wouldn't give in, but the more time went by, the more confident Liora felt in herself and in her own strength, and she wasn't fazed even when the detective denigrated her.

'I'm not alarmed by the tone you're taking with me,' she told Liora. 'I've sat in this room with people who are a little bit more threatening than you. I suggest you change course and understand that I can help you. And at this point I *want* to help you, but that might not last much longer. We know you left the baby, not only because of the camera and the bag. Believe me, I wouldn't be sitting here telling you the baby was yours if I'd only seen something on the camera. You have a window of opportunity right now, when I'm giving you the right to say: "I was wrong, I had postnatal depression." Or whatever. "Now I'm well, give me back the baby and we'll call it a day." It won't be straightforward – there will be a welfare investigation; the case for neglect won't be closed easily – but it might end there. That depends on the baby's condition. If you keep talking to me the way you have been, you'll just be digging yourself into a deeper hole.'

Do you understand how blind she is, David? How she believes the stories she's telling herself?

Liora made it clear that she was not going to answer, but Detective Esty Vahaba made one more attempt. 'Liora, listen to me for a minute. I'm on your side. I'm sure you didn't do what you did out of malice. You woke up in the morning, maybe you hadn't got any sleep, the baby was screaming and screaming, maybe she vomited, maybe she wasn't eating, and you couldn't take it any more. Or you got scared because you thought the baby was sick and you hadn't taken proper care of her. And no one was there to help you. It could happen to anyone, and no one's going to judge you for it.'

Liora could see her own smile reflected in the despairing look of the detective, who now gave up. 'Can I ask who the lawyer you consulted before coming in here is?' she asked.

'Avi Edry.'

'And did Avi Edry advise you to deny everything?'

'Avi Edry didn't advise me to do anything. I don't need advice. People who tell the truth don't need lawyers. Only liars do.'

'Does your husband know? Or was that why you put the baby there? To hide it from him?'

That was the only one of the detective's questions that surprised Liora, and her answer burst out with unexpected fury. 'If you'd done your job, you'd know that my husband, David, died. No, sorry, he didn't die; he was murdered. Didn't you research who you were bringing in? So *you* tell *me* now: where would I get a baby?'

The detective stood up.

Liora said, 'I want to leave now. I have to get to work.'

'I'll find out what's going to happen and let you know,' replied Vahaba. 'Until then, you're staying here. Would you like me to give a message to Avi Edry?'

ODDLY, IT WAS ONLY once the detective had left that, for the first time that day, Liora felt some fear inside her that needed to be destroyed. Perhaps because the confrontation had demanded all her strength, or perhaps because every time she mentioned David's murder she felt weak. She thought about the baby and the ridiculous things the policewoman had said about her. The baby hadn't screamed or thrown up, and she'd eaten well. And despite what she'd been through, she'd slept more peacefully than any other baby because God must have wanted her to live.

Liora took out her Bible and reread the verses that had fortified her from the moment she'd understood what she must do. *And the woman conceived, and bore a son; and when she saw that he was a goodly child, she hid him three months. And when she could no longer hide him, she took for him an ark of bulrushes, and daubed it with slime and with pitch; and she put the child therein and laid it in the flags by the river's brink.* She had read these verses on the number 140 bus, too, which she'd just managed to hop on to a second before the driver closed the door. But unlike Miriam, who had stayed to watch the ark of bulrushes until Pharaoh's daughter fished it out of the river, she couldn't stay. She had sat in the back of the bus, near the window, and although she'd planned to get off after one or two stops, she stayed for a long time. The bus drove on to Ayalon Highway North, then took Menachem Begin Road towards Azrieli Towers, and turned east to the diamond-exchange area. By then it was full. A tall, thin Sudanese man sat down next to her, and afterwards a woman of sixty-five or seventy with a head covering, who read the newspaper. No one looked at Liora, and the driver didn't see where or when she got off.

Would anyone have told Miriam she'd been wrong to leave Moses to be gathered from the river? She'd also done something that was against the law. And could anyone have punished the two midwives who had broken the law and *did not as the king of Egypt commanded them, but saved the men-children alive*? Mordechai had agreed with Liora that what she was planning was not a crime. He'd told her, 'It's just like the story of Moses, where the criminal is the one who decides the law.' That was the true criminal – whoever did things in daylight without hiding because they were in control and he himself determined what was allowed and what wasn't.

When ye do the office of a midwife to the Hebrew women, ye shall look upon the birthstool: if it be a son, then ye shall kill him; but if it be a daughter, then she shall live. That was the law of the land.

The detective came back into the room two hours later, with a bottle of water. She was followed by a policeman who looked more senior, and he stood in the corner and watched the two of them while the detective asked Liora to sit down. 'Your lawyer is on his way and you might be released today. We'll see,' Vahaba said.

'What do you mean, "we'll see"?' asked Liora. 'I have to get to work, and I want to talk to my daughters.'

Vahaba nodded and then asked Liora the question she'd been expecting and which she knew how to answer. 'Are you prepared to give us a saliva sample for a DNA test? If you consent willingly, we might be able to let you go after the test. We want to confirm what you say, that the baby isn't yours.'

3

THE NEXT MORNING, ILANIT was uncharacteristically sitting at her desk outside Avraham's office. And although there was no official cause to continue looking into Jacques Bertoldi, Avraham asked her what would be the fastest way to find the phone number of a tourist who had left no contact information at the hotel. She immediately answered, 'What do you mean? We contact the airline. Do you know if he flew El Al?'

One of the advantages of the first secretary Avraham had ever had was that there was no information she could not obtain. 'So can you tie up that loose end for me?' he asked.

'I'm on it,' Ilanit replied.

Avraham then called the Palace Hotel, and the phone was answered by the manager, Simcha Hozez. Avraham introduced himself, and asked, 'Did he come back, by any chance?'

'Who?' asked Hozez. 'Did who come back?'

'The tourist who disappeared without paying. Bertoldi. You called to report him missing, didn't you?'

'Yes, but you sent a policeman yesterday and someone explained to him that the problem was solved. Don't you know about that? He took our security camera, and we need it back urgently.' Hozez was surprised when Avraham explained that *he* was the policeman who'd visited the hotel. 'In that case,' he said, 'I don't understand. Why would you think he'd come back?'

Avraham didn't, but he had a hunch that Bertoldi's promise to Oleg, and the peculiar circumstances of his relatives' appearance, might indicate that someone had forcibly prevented him from returning to the Palace.

IN THE REPORTS OF unidentified bodies found in Israel in the past week, Avraham could not find a single one who might have been Bertoldi. The body of a woman in her thirties had been found with a plastic bag over her head in the woods between Tel Aviv and Ramat Gan. The list of incidents from the previous night included mostly complaints about noise, fights, burglaries and car thefts, and there was a report by Eliyahu Ma'alul on his investigation of the mentally ill man who'd tried to set his mother on fire. *According to the psychiatrist, the mother is also apparently mentally unstable. The father has never been in the picture. The assailant is thirty-six and has had various long-term hospitalizations since the age of fourteen.* Ma'alul had also interviewed the parents of the boy who got dehydrated in the car, and Avraham quickly read through the report: each of them took responsibility, claimed they were at fault for forgetting the boy in the car, and tried to absolve the other. Avraham wrote in the margins: *Make sure they're both under supervision because the mother's testimony indicates a risk that she might harm herself, no?* In the second-floor interrogation room, Vahaba was conducting a questioning under caution with the suspect in the abandoned-baby case. Avraham had offered to join her, but Vahaba had said she could manage on her own, so he hooked up the Palace security camera to his computer and watched as the oriental-style lobby flickered onto the screen.

The date was August the twenty-second, and the time at the beginning of the footage was 21.50.

For most of the evening, nothing happened at the Palace that required Oleg to stop reading. At 22.13, a well-dressed woman of about fifty walked in, followed by a short man several years younger, and since Oleg merely said hello to them when they walked past, Avraham assumed they were the tourists he'd said were staying in a suite, not a couple renting a room by the hour. Two Chinese men came in at 22.47, and a short while later a third Chinese man entered, presumably their co-worker. He stopped at the desk and talked with Oleg for roughly ten minutes, at which point the clerk showed him something on his phone. When the man disappeared up the staircase, Oleg went back to his book. The date on the screen switched to the twenty-third of August and Jacques Bertoldi walked into the hotel. 01.52.

His brown suit struck Avraham as shabby, almost threadbare.

Perhaps the suit of someone who had been a successful businessman ten years ago and could no longer afford new clothes. And he looked older than Avraham had pictured him. Sixty-three or sixty-five. His conversation with Oleg was brief. Bertoldi showed his passport, and Oleg copied down the number and handed him a key. It was impossible to hear what the tourist was saying, or in which language he spoke and with what sort of accent. When Avraham had asked Oleg why he hadn't photocopied the passport and whether he'd taken Bertoldi's credit-card number, Oleg had explained that the hotel was being 'more discreet' lately and that his instructions from Simcha Hozez were to take a passport number and not ask for a credit card or payment in advance because guests might be put off.

Bertoldi went up to his room at 01.59. When he stepped out of the camera's range, he was carrying his two suitcases himself, quite easily, as if they really were empty. Avraham pictured Bertoldi stopping outside room 203 and opening the door with his key. Turning the light on, looking at the ancient bedspread, the night-light, the old fridge under the desk. Drawing the curtains that used to be cream-coloured and looking at the building across the way. A gloomy building engulfed in darkness – because that was the view he'd asked for. There might have been a light on here and there in a flat where someone couldn't fall asleep. Perhaps a window was open because these last days of summer were hot and humid. If he needed to pursue the investigation, he could question neighbours in the building: someone might have been awake and seen Bertoldi through the window. *Maybe he requested a rear room so that he could communicate with someone who was waiting for him behind one of those windows?* Avraham wrote in his black notebook.

Bertoldi did not go to sleep, as one might expect of a tourist his age who'd just arrived in Israel on a night flight. The sheets were untouched, unless Oleg had been wrong or lying and someone had made the bed. What had he done until 5.12 a.m., at which point he was captured by the camera again, asking Oleg for a restaurant recommendation and promising him they would meet that evening, then leaving the hotel, walking quickly and turning right, as if he knew where he was going?

If Avraham had been convinced it was justified, he could have had security footage collected from the businesses and traffic lights on the streets Bertoldi might have walked down in the early morning, to try and retrace his steps. But other than the tourist's assurance to Oleg, which aroused vague apprehension in Avraham, there was no reason to do so. And he had to turn his attention to other cases. The lawyer for the parents who'd left their boy in the car phoned, and Avraham stopped the video to talk to him. Shortly before noon, Vahaba called and asked Avraham to meet her in the hallway outside the interrogation room. She looked rattled when she asked him for authorization to run a DNA test on the suspect to find out if she really was the baby's mother.

Avraham said, 'No problem, Esty. If you can get her to give us a sample voluntarily, it'll save us having to get a court order. But did you ask the neighbours and relatives if she was even pregnant? You might be able to find out if she's the mother without a test, don't you think?'

When Vahaba blushed, he realized she hadn't thought of that.

At the search in the suspect's flat, Vahaba said, they'd found nothing to indicate that there'd been a baby there up until a few hours ago. No baby food, no nappies, no sheets or clothes soiled with milk or spit-up, as she'd hoped to find. On the other hand, when news about the baby was made public, a call had come in from one of the suspect's neighbours, who said she'd heard crying and screaming from the flat, which had stopped suddenly two days ago. That was how she'd tracked down the suspect, who did look exactly like the woman seen on camera entering the mall with a bag and leaving without it.

'Is everything okay, Esty?' Avraham asked, sensing she was distraught.

'Absolutely. Everything's fine, Avi. There's something violent about her, but I'll talk her down.' Still, when he reiterated his offer to sit in on the interrogation, she said, 'You know what? Maybe just come in for a second. Look at her and tell me if she seems familiar from an investigation into a work accident her husband was in. I didn't know about it before, and I just looked into it. He died after falling off a crane at a construction site not far from here, five years ago. Does that ring a bell for you? His name was David Talyas. Remember anything like that?'

ILANIT PHONED WHEN HE was back in his office – four steps and one plaster wall away. 'Were you at lunch earlier?' she questioned him, and Avraham came clean. He still did not know that this would be the moment that would change the nature of his search for the missing tourist. 'Good for you. And what do you think about Esty's suspect? Is she the one or not?'

In his view, there was no doubt that the woman he'd seen in the interrogation room was the woman on camera from the hospital. He recognized her straight hair tied back with a band, dyed or bleached, and the black tank top that emphasized her short, strong arms and thick hands, which had been visible in the footage. She hadn't stood up while Avraham was in the room, but it was clear that Liora Talyas, like the woman carrying the bag, was very short — less than one metre fifty.

Ilanit agreed. And then she said, 'Okay, listen, I want to tell you about the tourist whose phone number you asked for. Remember him? There's no record of him coming in. No such person entered Israel. We tried with his name and his passport number. Could he have another passport?'

Avraham immediately tensed up. When Ilanit said, 'Or maybe you have his flight number?' he pointed out that that was exactly what she'd promised to find out for him.

He thought for a moment and then asked her to get the passenger lists for all flights from Switzerland that had landed on the night between the twenty-second and twenty-third of August. 'And if he's not there, let's search all flights that landed in Ben Gurion between eleven and one. Doesn't matter where from.'

'No problem, Avi. But which name am I looking for?'

That was an excellent question, to which he had no answer. When he'd checked in at the hotel, the tourist had shown a Swiss passport with the name Jacques Bertoldi, but he must have entered Israel under a different name. Unless he hadn't landed that night at all, and Oleg had been wrong about him arriving in an airport taxi.

'Do you think there's any way to see everyone who came into Ben Gurion that night, say between eleven and one? How many people could that be? Adult men.' He doubted it was possible, but Ilanit thought otherwise, since she'd done her military service in the Border Patrol, partly at Ben Gurion Airport. Within minutes she'd sent a photograph of the tourist to a border agent with a request to search for him among incoming passengers.

Avraham made his fourth cup of coffee and ate too many chocolate cream cookies from an open packet he found in the kitchenette. He went back to his office and kept watching, now with greater interest, the security footage from the Palace. The date on the screen was the twenty-fifth of August. The time: 14.43. Just over three hours earlier, Simcha Hozez had called the police to report a tourist who'd disappeared from the hotel without taking his luggage or paying his bill. Avraham had read the report because it had been on Ilanit's notes, which she'd given him after his meeting with Benny Saban. But at the time he'd had lots of matters to attend to and hadn't thought the complaint was urgent. He might have been wrong. If he'd sent a patrol cop to the Palace, he would have had the suitcases in his possession, and he would likely have known more about the reason for the tourist's arrival and the circumstances of his disappearance.

42

The two men now visible on the computer screen had beaten him to it.

Only one of them – short and stocky, blond, roughly thirty, wearing a tight white T-shirt tucked into light jeans – spoke with Oleg. The other man – older, taller, bald, floral button-down shirt – stood behind him without saying a word. But he was the one who took a wallet out of his back pocket and paid Oleg, in cash. Oleg handed them the key to room 203 and watched them disappear up the staircase. The next time they were on camera was at 15.02, which meant they'd spent approximately fifteen minutes in the room.

Oleg had not told him that.

There was no reason for them to spend so long in the room, unless they were looking for something other than the suitcases.

At the top of the page in the black notebook it still said *Jacques Bertoldi*, even though Avraham was now assuming that was not his real name. Underneath, he added more questions: *What was in the suitcases? What were they looking for in the room?* Next to those he wrote, in larger letters: *Go back to the hotel asap and search the room again. Maybe they didn't find what they wanted.*

Vahaba knocked on his door to update him on the medical report from the doctors who'd examined the baby. They estimated she had been born ten days ago, prematurely, at week thirty or perhaps thirty-one of the pregnancy, and although she'd been fed, she had not been given the medical care she required. She was in the NICU at Wolfson, suffering from respiratory distress, and was still not out of danger. Furthermore, Vahaba said, she wasn't convinced Liora

Talyas was the right person. Both because the preschool teacher where Talyas worked had testified that she wasn't pregnant, and because she'd agreed to give a DNA sample. 'Although, I do have a different neighbour who says he thinks she was pregnant, so I'm not sure.' When she told Avraham that Marianka had invited her for dinner and she was going straight to his place from work, he wondered if he should join her, but decided to stay in the office because he felt he should not put off the Bertoldi case any longer. And he was right.

Ilanit phoned half an hour later, from home. 'Are you writing this down?' He could hear the television in the background, and her children's voices also distracted him, but he wrote down what she said. 'The person you're looking for isn't named Bertoli. Or at least that's not the name he used to enter the country. He's called Rafael Chouchani. And he entered on a French passport, not Swiss. Who told you he was Swiss, anyway?'

Avraham wrote down *Rafael Chouchani* at the top of the first page in the notebook. Next to *Bertoldi*, not instead of it.

'Are you sure it's the same guy? His name is Bertoldi, not Bertoli.'

'I'm sure. Shelly compared our photograph with their camera footage and she says it's the same clothes, same height. There's no mistaking him. Besides, he talked with the border-crossing agent who stamped his passport. Shelly phoned her, and this woman remembered him almost immediately. Her name is Aflalo, and Chouchani asked if she knew where her name came from and if she'd ever been to Morocco. And then he said, "Thanks, and I promise I'll remember you, Ms Noa Aflalo. Do you think you'll remember me?" Something

44

cute like that, nothing lurid or flirty. Anyway, she can send over a photocopy of his passport. And you know what else, Avi? He arrived on an Air France flight from Paris, so we can talk to them tomorrow morning and get his details.'

Having realized that not sending a cop to the hotel in time had cost him the suitcases, Avraham wasn't about to delay it again. Not even till morning. It was just after seven, which was after six in Paris, but there was no answer at Air France; the recorded message, in English, said to call back the next day between nine and five. Avraham phoned the headquarters of the international-relations unit in the police, apologized for the late hour and asked for help conducting a brief inquiry with the French police. The woman who answered the phone said, 'Why don't you ask the French representative directly? I'll send you her number. Don't you know her?'

He didn't, but Chief Superintendent Idit Gerti did know him.

'You're Avraham who worked with Ilana Lis in Holon for years, aren't you?' she asked, and he said he was – both because it was true and because he sensed it would encourage her to help. She promised she would, and when she got back to him a few moments later she said she'd pulled some strings and he'd soon be getting a call from someone at the French police's information bureau who would help him get anything he needed. Avraham thanked her warmly, partly because before they hung up, Gerti said, 'Ilana was so fond of you. She talked about you all the time.'

Darkness fell. The air-conditioning had been on in the room since morning, and Avraham turned it off and opened a window that faced the densely built high-rises that had sprouted up opposite the station. Marianka could have helped him with the French, but she was in their flat in an old building in Kiryat Sharet, which was hidden behind enormous towers. Having dinner with Esty Vahaba. They'd struck up a friendship recently, and Esty seemed to be Marianka's best friend in Israel – perhaps a sad sort of substitute, or at least so Avraham thought, for Eva and Monika back in Koper.

The representative from the French police information bureau was a man with a gentle, young voice. 'Is this Inspector Avraham?' he asked in English, and for some reason Avraham answered, '*Oui*,' although it was one of the only French words he knew and it over-stated his command of the language. Avraham apologized, in English, thanked the representative for agreeing to help and briefly explained about the tourist with the French passport who had arrived on an Air France flight and disappeared, and about his relatives, who'd paid his bill and taken his luggage.

'We want to make sure he's okay,' Avraham said, and he thought the man was impressed with the Israel Police's concern not only for its own citizens, but for visitors. Avraham did not mention anything about the name the tourist had given at the hotel, but asked for the phone number of Rafael Chouchani or any of his relatives living in France.

The Frenchman asked Avraham to hold, and Avraham heard his fingers tapping on a keyboard and some voices on other phone calls being held in the same room. Could the information bureau be in the same building where Inspector Jules Maigret worked, on Quai des Orfèvres? The question filled him with delight, although the answer was probably not. And what would happen if he addressed the representative, who had not given his name, as Lucas or Janvier? Would the young man even know that those were two of the devoted assistants to the rotund, beer- and sandwich-loving police inspector, thanks to whose investigations Avraham had dreamed of joining the police? Before he could find out, the representative's soft voice asked if he had a pen.

On the second page of the black notebook, Avraham wrote: *Rafael Chouchani left France for Israel four days ago. He lives in Paris, at 89 Boulevard de Picpus.* The representative gave him Chouchani's home number and a mobile-phone number, and then he said, 'I'll also give you his daughter's number. Her name is Annette M-a-l-l-o-t. If he doesn't answer, you can talk to her. And we'd be happy if you could update us on any news regarding his case, or to help you if you need further assistance.'

When the young man gave his name, Avraham could not believe his ears: it was not Lucas or Janvier, but Jules!

THE PHONE AT CHOUCHANI'S house rang for a long time. And his mobile phone was off.

Avraham called Chouchani's daughter, and while he waited for an answer, he typed his address into Google Maps, although it was of little significance. Judging by the images, Rafael Chouchani lived in a restored building at the intersection of a wide, busy boulevard and a small lane, and on its ground floor there was a café or restaurant named Capone. On Google Maps he could see a row of red, round tables set out on the pavement, and the street was wet, as if the picture had been taken in the rain. When he heard Annette Mallot's voice, Avraham realized he hadn't prepared for the conversation and wasn't sure how to say what he wanted to ask without frightening her. When he introduced himself, she immediately asked, in English, 'Has something happened?' Avraham said no.

'Then why are you calling me?'

That was the first surprise in their conversation.

Annette Mallot didn't know that her father had gone to Israel.

They spoke on the phone every three or four weeks, certainly not daily, and met no more than twice or three times a year because Mallot lived in Strasbourg, a three-hour train ride from Paris. The last time they'd talked, her father hadn't mentioned an upcoming trip to Tel Aviv. Sometimes, she added, they didn't talk for more than a month, and the fact that he'd travelled without letting her know wasn't unusual.

Avraham made a slight change to the story so as not to alarm her. He said that her father had stayed at a hotel in Bat Yam and left with two relatives, but he'd left some of his belongings in the room. And since he hadn't given a phone number, the hotel had no way to get hold of him.

He heard a man whisper something in German to Annette Mallot. The information Avraham had given in order to reassure her had only startled her more. She told Avraham that as far as she knew,

48

they had no family in Israel close enough for her father to stay with. 'He has distant cousins, I think, but I'm not sure they're in touch. I don't understand what relatives he could have gone to.'

That was the second surprise.

Avraham asked her to look for the cousins' phone numbers, and then he said, 'Could I send you a picture of the two men in the meantime, so you can tell me if you recognize them as your relatives?'

While the photograph showing the stocky blond man and the tall taciturn man was on its way to Annette Mallot's inbox, Avraham said, 'You mentioned your father disappears sometimes. Travels without letting you know. That's what you said before, isn't it?'

'He doesn't go missing for months, but yes, Father used to travel a lot. He has business matters, or he used to, and sometimes he doesn't get in touch for a while. But he's not a young man, so I'm worried. Could those two men have kidnapped him? Could they be holding him and planning to hurt him?'

Avraham hadn't considered that possibility. Or hadn't formulated it to himself in those words. 'I don't think there's any cause to jump to that conclusion. We have no reason to think anything bad has happened. Can you tell me how old your father is?'

'Sixty-two now. Yes, he turns sixty-three in November.'

She must have been in her thirties, and judging by the voice in the background – a man who kept whispering in German – she might have been married. There were no sounds of children, perhaps because it was late.

'Is he in good health?'

'What do you mean?'

'Does he have any medical issues? Heart trouble, for example, or perhaps early stages of Alzheimer's?'

'No. Do you think he . . . He did go through a rough patch a year or two ago, with some health problems, but I think the past year has been good. Was he feeling unwell at the hotel? Or on the flight?'

'I don't know. I'm just trying to explore different avenues. And I really have no reason to assume anything bad happened to him. Do you have any idea why he might have come to Israel? Does he have business here, or did he say anything about going to visit family when you last spoke?'

Mallot said nothing, as if she were trying to remember. Or debating whether to answer?

'And why did he choose that hotel in Bat Yam, and not somewhere in Jerusalem or Tel Aviv – do you know?'

'I assume that if he went to Israel, it would have been for work, don't you think?' Annette replied with a question.

Avraham said, 'I don't know. What exactly does your father do?'

'You're supposed to know that, aren't you?' said Annette.

That was the third surprise. Because Annette went on to say, 'I don't know the details because he didn't talk about it with me, and also I'm not sure what I'm allowed to say, but he was working for the Mossad. Don't you know about that?'

Avraham felt a sudden need to put the phone down, as if it were giving off electrical sparks. He stood up, walked to the open window and shut it, then said to Annette, 'I'll find out if he came to Israel on such business, and either way, thank you for your help. You can keep my number and phone me in a few days if he doesn't contact you by then.'

He regretted saying those last words even before they were out. Perhaps it would be better if she forgot all about his phone call and deleted his email? But Mallot was already looking at the photo and said she didn't recognize the men in the picture.

Avraham couldn't resist one more question: 'Do you know anyone named Bertoldi?'

Once again, it took her some time to answer. And while Avraham waited, he heard the man whisper in German again. Eventually she said, 'No. I don't think so.'

'Jacques Bertoldi? A Swiss citizen?'

'I don't know him. Why do you ask?'

Now it was Avraham's turn to avoid answering.

But before hanging up, Annette had another question for him: 'Do you know if he arrived in Israel alone? Or with Sara?'

Avraham didn't know who Sara was, and Annette explained that Sara Nuweima had been seeing her father for the past year, and that they should find out if she'd gone with him.

'No problem, we'll find out and let you know when we have any updates,' Avraham said. When he hung up, he added the name *Sara Nuweima* to his notebook, and underneath that he wrote: *Find out if she came in with Chouchani or before/after him.* Then he added a question mark because it might not be his business at all, but something best left to the Institute for Intelligence and Special Operations – the Mossad.

4

FROM THE MOMENT THEY took her sample for the DNA test,
she waited for a phone call from the police. And planned how
she was going to explain the results. She learned nothing new from
what Avi Edry had to say about her release conditions and how the
investigation could be expected to proceed. Until the test results came
in, the police were going to talk to her neighbours, the preschool,
the health clinic, her relatives. They'd try to find out if Liora had
been pregnant, if she'd told anyone she was having a baby. All this
was predictable and had been taken into account in the plan she'd
hatched when the baby was still at home.

Nor was there any need for the rules Edry kept repeating: 'No
more phone calls, no WhatsApp, no status updates or messages
on any device or app. You don't tell anyone anything and you
don't write anything anywhere.' He wanted Liora to go over
all her correspondence, 'on every possible medium', to look for

'conversations or pictures that we should be aware of'. She'd already done that, too.

Detective Vahaba called at 11 p.m., to give her as little time as possible to prepare, and the phone woke Mordechai, who was asleep on the closed-in balcony. She asked Liora to come to the station at half past eight in the morning because the results had come in. Liora said, 'We're getting the preschool ready for the beginning of the school year. Can't I come in the afternoon?' She could hear the anger frothing in the policewoman's voice when she said no, she couldn't. 'Then maybe now over the phone?' Liora suggested, and the policewoman said, 'I did you a favour by letting you go home. If you keep this up, I'll make sure you spend two or three nights with the rats in the detention centre at Abu Kabir instead of at the preschool. Would you prefer that?'

Abu Kabir didn't scare her. On the contrary: her hell was already behind her.

It might even have been an opportunity to appear in court and say out loud what she wanted to say.

IT WAS THE NIGHT before the second interrogation: her last night at home without the girls.

After a long day at work, she didn't have the energy to cook, so she'd asked Mordechai to bring some food, and he'd arrived with a pot of rice, nicely burned on the bottom, and fish cakes in sauce. He'd wanted to sleep in the bedroom but Liora was tired and preferred that he stayed on the balcony. While they had dinner, she'd told him about the preparations. As usual, Alice was anxious about the preschool not being clean and decorated, and she'd made Liora disinfect everything with bleach and then cut out stars from coloured card, glue pictures of the children onto the stars, labelled with their names and birthdays, and hang them on the 'wall of stars' that Alice's husband, Yakir, had painted in an ugly shade of light blue. Among the new stars, Liora had also put up the pair of worn clouds from two years ago, with pictures of her and Alice and their birthdays.

Mordechai had eaten slowly and quietly. He washed the dishes after they'd finished. And the crime reporter, whom Liora was assuming she would need to contact, had a segment on TV about a lawyer from Haifa who'd forged a power of attorney and transferred money from an elderly couple he was representing into his bank account. The lawyer denied the accusations, claimed the sums he'd taken were his fees and threatened the reporter with a defamation suit. The police response, as always, was that 'there will be a full investigation into the matter'.

Mordechai had fallen asleep on the couch, and Liora had woken him and helped him move to the mattress on the balcony. She opened the blinds so he'd have some fresh air at night. Then she'd phoned Michal, who told her the girls were fine. Eden had played with the baby all day and helped Michal around the house, and Ofrit was on her screens.

She wasn't looking forward to the girls coming back.

She liked the quiet at home since Eden and Ofrit had gone to stay with their older sister, but the new year was starting soon and they had to go to school, and now, once the results had arrived, there would be no reason to hide anything from them, nor would it be possible. She could tell Michal, too, since she'd probably be called in for questioning, but she'd decided to wait because as soon as Michal heard what had happened, she would tell her husband, Maxim, and the two of them would pressure Liora to do what they thought was right. When Michal had asked how Danielle was, Liora had said, 'She's fine. Recovering.' 'Recovering from what?' Michal wanted to know, and Liora had replied, 'How should I know? Don't you remember what it's like to be an adolescent?'

When Vahaba called to ask her to come to the station, Liora was almost asleep, but after the phone call she wasn't able to shut her eyes until 1 or 2 a.m. because of the adrenaline and because she was trying to imagine what she would be asked at the second interrogation and how she would answer. She would tell the detective: you can't understand because you haven't been through what I've been through. I don't know why I did it, but I had no choice. Could you support a family on your own, on a preschool assistant's salary and with no help? I have no money to raise another child and I wanted her to have a better life than ours. That's why I put her there. I thought she would end up with parents who could give her all the things I couldn't. Do you really think that's such a terrible crime?

MORDECHAI HAD ALREADY LEFT for synagogue when Liora woke up, so she had her first coffee without him. She felt happy that he would be back soon, and he would bring some cheese bourekas and drink a second cup of coffee with her. He'd stay with her until she went to Holon.

56

On the day she told him about Danielle, Mordechai had suggested reading together about how Joseph was sent to prison after Pharaoh's wife accused him of raping her, and on the morning of the second interrogation she reread the chapter because it gave her strength. Mordechai said it was a story about the distortion of justice: Joseph was not sent to prison because he had raped Potiphar's wife, as she claimed, but because he'd refused to sleep with her since she was not an Israelite. Liora's interest in the story lay elsewhere: only good things had come of Joseph's sentence. If Potiphar's wife hadn't accused him of rape, Joseph wouldn't have met Pharaoh's ministers in prison and interpreted their dreams, and he wouldn't have been brought to the palace to interpret Pharaoh's dreams and risen to greatness so that he could go on to save his brethren, the sons of Jacob, from the terrible famine that beset the land.

Because the Lord was with him; and that which he did, the Lord made it to prosper.

She hoped that verse would apply to her, this time. If not for her sake, then for David, or for the baby, whom God had clearly been with since the moment she was born.

Mordechai offered to accompany her to the police station and wait until the questioning was over. She refused. She told him to go back to his flat and promised to call. When she got to the station, Vahaba walked her to the same room where she'd been questioned the first time, but this time the air-conditioner was on and there was a bottle of water and some plastic cups on the table. Vahaba offered Liora coffee before she started, perhaps hoping the atmosphere would be different from the previous day. 'You know what we found out from the test, don't you?' was her first question.

Liora answered without thinking, 'That man is descended from apes?'

The detective's eyes were even more bloodshot and watery than the last time. There were grey flecks on her eyelids, probably dried-up remnants of some ointment she'd applied overnight.

'It showed that you're not the mother of the baby you left outside the hospital.'

'Like I told you. Eventually, you'll also find out that I didn't leave her.'

'That's not going to happen. Because the test showed that you are related. I'm guessing the baby is your granddaughter.'

Liora smiled.

Up until this moment I hadn't thought about her that way, you know, David? As our granddaughter. You would have enjoyed grandchildren, if you'd been given the chance. I didn't think of her as my granddaughter when I fed her from a bottle, or when I changed her nappy, or when I wet her mouth with water, or when I put her to sleep on our bed. She had downy black hair on the back of her neck, which our girls didn't have.

'I only have a grandson,' she said, 'he's at home with his mother. You can check.'

Vahaba slid the keyboard to the corner of the desk, as if to remove a barrier between them, and said softly, 'I've tried to figure out why you're wasting time, Liora. What you think you're getting out of it. I don't have an answer. I understand that you don't like the police or that you don't like me personally and don't want to help me, but don't you want to help your daughters? Your granddaughter?' She paused for a moment, perhaps to sense whether her words were penetrating Liora, before pressing on with the speech she'd prepared, hoping it would make Liora cooperate. 'We have two possible roads, and you get to choose which one we take. One is for you to tell me which of your daughters is the baby's mother and what exactly happened. Why she was born prematurely and why you didn't go to the hospital properly but left her in a bag and ran away. The second is for us to take you to Abu Kabir—they've got a comfortable bed ready for you there, and there are some girls who will be happy to welcome you—and while you're staying there, I'll bring your daughters in. We'll sit them down in an interrogation room with police detectives who will ask them what they saw and what they know, and will threaten them and take saliva samples like they did from you. Which do you prefer?'

Liora knew what she was going to answer as soon as Vahaba started talking: 'I have to ask, have you thought of seeing an eye doctor? Because it's awful, what you have going on. It's really disgusting. I hope it's not contagious.'

THERE WAS A LONG ringing sound from the other side of the door. Liora assumed the detective was in the hallway, perhaps consulting with a colleague on the phone. Or was she outside alone? Steadying her breath, trying to regain her composure after Liora had knocked the wind out of her sails with a line she hadn't known she'd be brave enough to say until a second before she'd said it?

When she came back into the room, the blind detective was sweating. She turned up the air-conditioning.

For fifteen minutes she did things on the computer without saying a word to Liora, probably to show that she was in control of the situation, and then she left again. When the interrogation resumed, it was clear that she'd decided to ask questions dryly and without looking at Liora, so as not to disclose her emotional turmoil and to prevent Liora from getting stronger. Vahaba said, 'I'm continuing the interview. Another detective may join me later, but for now I would like you to answer to the point, without any of your wisecracks, so we can finish this up as soon as possible.'

Liora answered, 'I'm all for that. I also have work to do.'

'You have four daughters?'

'Yes.'

'Your oldest is twenty-four, right? Michal Kalimi. Married with one son?'

'That's right.'

'Does the baby you left in a bag outside Wolfson Hospital in Holon, on August twenty-fifth at ten twenty-five a.m., belong to her? Is your daughter, Michal Kalimi, the mother of the baby?'

'Why don't you ask her? Or you could get a DNA sample from her, you—'

'I've already talked to her. She didn't know you were here. Why didn't you tell her?'

That was the first time in the interrogation that the detective had interrupted her, perhaps upon the advice of the person she must have talked to on the phone when she left the room. Liora said, 'What was I supposed to tell her? That a policewoman who's blind as a bat is convinced I gave birth to a baby, apparently without noticing it?' Vahaba looked up at her, and for a moment Liora was startled by her own courage, and quickly said, 'Why do you think Michal would give up her own baby? Where's the logic in that? She's young and wants to have children.'

The detective gazed back at the screen, again trying not to look straight at Liora. 'There could be all sorts of reasons,' she said. 'Maybe her husband didn't want a baby. Or didn't know she was pregnant. Maybe she wanted to hide the baby from him?'

'You can't be serious. Honestly, the stories you come up with. One thousand and one nights. Why don't you bring them in and ask them about it? I'd like to see Maxim's reaction when you ask him if Michal had a baby from another man. I wouldn't recommend that you be in a room alone with him.'

'I did ask them. And he is coming in. Michal says she can't come today because your two little girls are with her. Can you explain to me why they're there?'

'Summer holidays. I needed a break from the kids. Starting on September first I'll have thirty-something of them on my hands every day.'

The bat couldn't restrain herself: 'If things go on this way, you're going to lose your freedom for a very long time. But at least you'll get a break from the kids.'

Liora smiled. 'You're finally loosening up a bit. Now you just have to take care of your eyes and wash your face in the morning and you'll be almost human.'

From moment to moment she felt she was gaining more power. *Do you hear the way I'm talking to her, David? Just like I talk to the girls at home, without being afraid of anything.*

The detective did not respond to what Liora said. 'How old are your girls, the ones who are at Michal's?'

'Nine and twelve. Would you like to know if the babies are theirs?'

Vahaba immediately asked, 'And where is Danielle?'

'I don't know.'

'I'm asking you again, Liora. And I demand an answer. Where is your daughter Danielle? She's a minor and you are responsible for her. You should know where she is.'

'I'm giving you an answer. Are your ears stopped up, too? I don't know where she is.'

'Is your daughter Danielle the mother of the baby you left at the hospital?'

Liora stopped answering because the transition to the next stage was close, and she had to find the right moment. And perhaps also because she was temporarily unsure about the timing. She was overcome with exhaustion, having slept only three hours, and felt that the sleep deprivation was diminishing her strength, allowing the apprehension to weaken her from the inside. But she put a stop to that and reminded herself to imagine that she was talking to David.

The perfect moment came at midday, which, paradoxically, was when she was most tired.

No other detective had joined the blind one. She was only asking about Danielle now. Liora refused to answer most of the questions and demanded to end the interrogation and go home. She said, 'I don't want to talk about that baby any more. And anyway, it's not like anything terrible happened. You found a healthy baby, she was taken good care of, so find her a home and move on. Sixty years ago the state stole Yemenite babies from their parents and told them they'd died so they could give them to Ashkenazis who didn't have children – and that wasn't against the law. On the contrary, it was the state that did that, for the babies' benefit, right? And now, all of a sudden, it's a criminal offence? You got a baby – be thankful, and that's that.'

'But this baby was born prematurely and needed medical care. Chances are she's not going to survive, Liora.'

Liora knew these were lies. The baby *had* received care. And she *would* survive. Someone was watching over her, otherwise she would have died long ago.

'But what do you want from me? How is this connected to me?' Liora said.

'I want you to tell me where your daughter Danielle is.'

'She's not home.'

'Do you know where she is?'

'Right now? No.'

'Is she in Israel?'

'I don't know. I haven't talked to her for a few days.'

Perhaps her exhaustion was not only because of the sleepless night and the tension ahead of moving to the next stage. Perhaps it was the result of everything she'd been through in the past few days, all of which was now surfacing in her memory because of the questions.

Danielle's screams, which Liora had muffled with her hands so that no one would hear.

The bite marks Danielle had left on Liora's hand and the scratches all along her arm.

The blood on the sheets that Liora had laundered twice before throwing them in the rubbish skip.

Danielle crying for two days after the birth and the anxiety before she went away. The worry that someone might hear the baby, who'd insisted on living. Making sure the blinds were shut and that no one would see. Flinching every time a neighbour knocked on the door.

They had slept next to each other on the double bed, and before Liora fell asleep she could hear breaths coming from the tiny body, the body that was too tiny to be born, that should not have been born. She hardly cried at all, and after Mordechai took care of her for a few hours, he also said he'd never seen such a quiet baby in his life.

'Did something bad happen to Danielle?' Vahaba asked.

'Nothing happened. Are you worried about her?'

'If you're hiding something that happened to Danielle from us, you'll regret it. You're racking up criminal charges here.'

Liora waited for the weariness to pass. For the strength to come back to her body and mind. The bottle Vahaba had placed before her in the morning was empty, and she asked for more water. But the tiredness also helped her because it made the detective mistakenly think Liora was cracking and allowed her to disguise the next stage as an uncontrolled breakdown.

Instead of bringing Liora a bottle of water, Vahaba said, 'The truth is, I know where Danielle is,' and Liora said. 'Great, give her my regards. Tell her school starts on September first.'

'You smuggled her out of the country. That's also why I'm assuming the baby is hers and not Michal's. Right?'

'We *smuggled* her out of the country? What do you think I am?'

'Why did Danielle go to France?'

'Probably to see the Eiffel Tower. Have you ever been there?'

'We will find her without your help, but you can save us some time if you tell me where in France she is.'

'Can I leave? I'm wiped out. And you know that's not my purpose in life, to save you time.'

'Liora, if you don't tell me where Danielle is and give me a phone number where I can reach her, I'm bringing your three girls to the station now, including the two little ones, and a doctor will give them a vaginal exam to find out if they've given birth. Okay? They will never forget it as long as they live.'

That was Vahaba's mistake.

The violence of her words restored Liora's strength at once. She realized this was the moment she'd been waiting for, and she said, 'If you do anything like that, I promise you that in one hour you'll see yourself on the TV news and you'll have to explain why you sexually abused a nine-year-old girl and a twelve-year-old girl. Do you want me to tell you what happened? I'll tell you, only because I can't be bothered with you any more. I really can't. She's mine, the baby. I was pregnant with her and I gave birth to her and I left her at the hospital. All right? Happy now?'

65

Vahaba said, 'I know she's not—'

Liora interrupted: 'Will you listen to me? I'm telling you the truth now. Do you want to hear the truth or don't you?'

Vahaba moved the keyboard to the edge of the desk again and looked up at the camera that was recording them from the corner of the room. 'I want to hear it. Should I get you some more water?' Liora nodded. The weariness in her movements was an act. Vahaba left and came back after too long with two bottles of water and reiterated that another detective would join them in a few minutes. As Liora started talking, she thought of another verse from Genesis that she'd read with Mordechai, and which had helped her in recent days: *In the simplicity of my heart and the innocence of my hands have I done this.*

The verse she had whispered to herself silently when she'd hurried onto the bus, found a window seat and watched the mall where she'd left the baby, waiting for someone to run out after her with the black bag.

In the simplicity of my heart and the innocence of my hands have I done this.

No one had come after her, and the bus had started slowly driving away from the hospital.

'The truth is, I have no money. I wanted to raise the baby but I'm on my own and I don't have any way to get more money and I didn't know how we were going to manage. Don't you believe me? You can't understand it because you haven't been through what I've been through in life, but I wanted that baby to have a better future. That's why I put her there. I thought maybe that way she'd find parents who would give her things I can't give her.'

5

SUPERINTENDENT AVRAHAM SAT DOWN at his regular table – in the recesses of the basement-level space, next to the giant stainless-steel pots of simmering red soup – and when all he ordered was hummus, put off by the colour of the thick soup with shreds of dark meat floating around in it, the waitress gave him a disdainful look. He'd received Eliyahu Ma'alul's report on the hotel on his way to the restaurant in the Kerem, and now he could read it.

The Palace had opened in 1986. Its original name had been 'Riviera'. In the first few years, it had had big dreams, as well as three stars. Tourists from France and Belgium had stayed there, and groups of pilgrims from Eastern Europe, but inept management and neglect had taken their toll, and now – as Oleg had said – it served mostly mid-level Chinese workers who came to Israel for short stays, couples who rented by the hour and the occasional tourist. Simcha Hozez, the owner, a fifty-eight-year-old Bat Yam native, had bought and refurbished it seven years ago, hoping to attract East Asian tourists. He also owned a sushi place next door, Tokyo Express. Neither Hozez nor Oleg Jacobowitz, who'd been working at the hotel since 2014, had criminal records. *In terms of criminal activity,* Ma'alul wrote, *a year and a half ago there was an extremely violent attack in the hotel against a call girl by a client. In 2012, there was intelligence information on drugs smuggled through Ben Gurion Airport and a deal conducted in a nearby hotel, and the investigation covered the Palace, too, with no results. In 2001, a German tourist who'd spent a month travelling in Jerusalem and lost his mind tried to set himself and his girlfriend on fire in a fourth-floor room.* There were no complaints of theft from the hotel rooms and no intelligence information implying that the Palace attracted unlawful activity or indicating any ties to criminal organizations in the city.

What were the chances that the Mossad would have an agent stay in a hotel of that sort? Which of the organization's activities would the Palace even be suitable for? These questions were not addressed in Ma'alul's report because Eliyahu knew nothing about Avraham's late-night phone call with Rafael Chouchani's daughter. And that was precisely the reason he'd asked Ma'alul to meet him in the restaurant they went to whenever they wanted to talk out of the station's earshot and without being seen.

There was a line of people waiting for a table outside Shimon King of Soups, mostly construction workers from sites around the market area. When Avraham put down his fork and took out a pen to write in his black notebook, the waitress gave him a glare that was darker than the soup, from which Avraham inferred that he should vacate his table for other customers. He kept writing anyway. *Had*

Chouchani been to the Palace before? Must find out from the manager about previous visits, under the name Chouchani or Bertoldi – and maybe there are other names? And ask at the Swiss embassy if anyone named Bertoldi, with the passport number he gave at the hotel, even exists. Above these new questions was the one Avraham had posed yesterday, after his talk with Annette Mallot. *Is Sara Nuweima, Chouchani's girlfriend, in Israel, too? And if so – where is she?*

The reason Avraham dared to ignore the waitress's menacing look was that he knew that when Eliyahu Ma'alul arrived, all would be forgiven. And that is exactly what happened. Eliyahu sat down opposite him and the waitress hurried over, kissed his dark bald head, which was glistening with sweat, and, without asking, put down in front of him a bowl of oxtail soup, into which Eliyahu dumped two tablespoons of hot sauce. Seeing that Avraham was wearing blue sweatpants and a T-shirt, Eliyahu said, 'What's going on, Avi? Exercise day? I thought you were sick.' When Avraham explained that he'd needed a day off, Eliyahu said, 'That's what I guessed. But you have to tell me why. Is everything okay with Marianka?'

Eliyahu was almost sixty but looked far younger. And although every time Avraham saw him he was eating, he had a supple, boyish body, like a panther's. 'Did you get the report?' he asked, and when Avraham nodded, Eliyahu added, 'Who stays in that kind of place anyway? Especially if you have family here. Also, I got you the driver who picked him up at the airport. I'll get to that in a second. But what's going on? Tell me why we're here.'

In the crowded basement there was no one who seemed to take

69

any interest in their conversation. Nevertheless, Avraham spoke quietly to Ma'alul. 'There's a chance that this case has something to do with the Mossad.'

The veteran detective's hand, holding a spoonful of red liquid, was suspended in mid-air. 'Mossad? Then how did you end up with it? And why are you putting me in the middle of it?'

Apparently, he'd ended up with it by mistake. Perhaps because Simcha Hozez had been too quick to report to the police on a tourist gone missing, a moment before someone else paid the man's bill and took his belongings. Avraham explained to Ma'alul that what had aroused his suspicion was the tourist's promise that he'd be back in the evening and the fact that the relatives who'd come to take his things hadn't shown the front desk clerk any papers or even mentioned his name. At the time, Avraham still hadn't known about the two passports and the two names, but he'd become even more suspicious when he'd watched the Palace security camera footage and seen that the two men had spent a long time in room 203. When it turned out that the name and passport the tourist had used at the hotel were different from the ones he'd given at the airport, it was clear Avraham was not mistaken. Chouchani had been in Israel for four days without any sign of life. It was not just Avraham's concern that was increasing. Overnight, Annette Mallot had sent him an email urging him to contact her again because she wanted to tell him 'something else that makes me suspect someone abducted him and Sara or hurt them, and why it's connected to his work with your country'.

Ma'alul put his spoon down in the empty bowl. When the waitress headed over to refill the bowl, he motioned for her to wait. 'It could be something like that,' he said, 'but who knows? You have nothing connecting him to the Mossad except what his daughter said. Although, the cab driver's testimony might also point in that direction.'

Taxi driver, Rami Amar, resident of Lod. Thirty-three. Employed by Airport Taxis since 2014.

The driver remembered the tourist he'd picked up at the airport that night because he'd been very talkative. He'd got into the taxi alone. There had been no woman with him. At first, he'd spoken in English, asked the driver where he lived, if he was married and if he had kids, but when he found out Amar was from Lod, he'd switched to Arabic. And he had spoken excellent Arabic. He'd asked the driver questions about where his parents were born and about his wife and his four children, and wanted to see pictures of them. The tourist told Amar that he hadn't been to Israel for a few years and was here for a quick visit, to see an old friend and track down another friend – a woman who had disappeared and was likely to be in Israel. When Amar asked where his Arabic was from, the man said he spoke it growing up. He didn't give the driver a hotel name – he'd just said to drive to the Bat Yam promenade, and when they got to the Palace he'd asked him to stop. Amar remembered that when he'd offered the tourist his phone number, in case he needed a driver while he was in Israel, he'd refused, saying he wouldn't be needing him, and had physically pushed away the business card Amar held out to him, even though he could have taken it and then thrown it away. And he didn't remember whether or not the tourist had given his name.

'Did you ask him if the tourist looked frightened? If he looked out the window as if he was searching for someone?'

Eliyahu hadn't known he was supposed to ask that. And he hadn't asked if the tourist had said anything that might indicate he felt he was in danger.

'And the luggage?' asked Avraham.

Eliyahu gave him an uncomprehending look. 'What was I supposed to ask about the luggage?'

If Amar had put the tourist's suitcases in the boot and taken them out himself, he might have remembered if they were empty, as Oleg thought they were. Ma'alul wrote himself a reminder on his phone to ask the driver, and then he said, 'There was another reason he remembered him, actually. The smell.'

'What smell?'

Oleg hadn't said anything about that.

'He felt bad because the passenger was a nice guy, but he said he had a really strong smell. Something strange. Like a dead person's stench. I have no idea what that means. And because of the smell, he was glad when the guy got out of his cab.'

VAHABA HAD TRIED TO get hold of Avraham three times while he was with Ma'alul. And since Marianka had told him that morning what Esty was going through, he called her back as soon as he left and could hear that she was upset.

'I'm sure it's her daughter, Avi,' she said without any preamble.

72

'Danielle Talyas is the baby's mother, one thousand per cent. And they got her to Paris. I'm trying to find out from the older sister where exactly Danielle is and why Liora is keeping her away. The sister is cooperating but I don't think she knows much.'

This was the first time that the two cases, which had been opened on the same day, intersected. Paris: the city Chouchani had come from and which Danielle Talyas had been smuggled into.

Avraham sensed that Vahaba wanted him to join her in the interrogation room, and there was no reason for him to go home anyway because Marianka was at work and they'd arranged to meet in the evening. 'How old is Danielle?' he asked.

'Sixteen. She flew to France six days ago. And I'm sure she went so we wouldn't be able to get to her.'

'Did the suspect admit that the baby is Danielle's and explain what happened?'

'Her? Admit it? Avi, she's mentally ill. She won't even say that her daughter's abroad or that she knows where she is.'

He told Vahaba he was on his way.

But first he sat in his Hyundai for several minutes, in the car park near the Carmel Market, and wrote.

Was the conversation with the cab driver another attempt by Chouchani to imprint himself on the memory of everyone he met? And if so – did he know he might disappear? But who could have abducted him in Israel? Could a Mossad agent be kidnapped in Israel by a foreign entity? If so, he thought, I can't be the only one who knows about it. The

Mossad and Shin Bet are probably trying to locate Chouchani, too. And maybe that's what I need to find out?

When Eliyahu had asked him at the restaurant what he was planning to do, Avraham had said, 'I don't know. I have a feeling he didn't disappear voluntarily. Something happened or might happen to him. If he is Mossad, we have to pass it along, just to make sure they're aware, but I don't know how or to whom. And I don't want to get in the way if I've stumbled on something I'm not supposed to know about.'

Ma'alul had nodded. 'On the other hand, what could happen? Let's say you touched something you're not supposed to be involved in. Let's assume that, even though at this point it's too soon to know. So what's the worst that could happen? They'll tell you: this is Mossad business, pal, let it go. And from then on you heard nothing, saw nothing, knew nothing, end of story.'

'So what would you do?' Avraham had insisted. 'Forget about it? Go to the Mossad and make sure they know about the story?'

Ma'alul had laughed. 'You can try. But how are you going to get to them? You think they have a tip line?'

'I think I can find a way.'

Ma'alul had leaned forwards, and, for the only time in their conversation, lowered his voice to a whisper. 'Avi, you're not a child. I don't think anyone makes official contact with the Mossad. And what if it really is something you're not supposed to know about or mess with? Why would you even go down that road?'

'Then how do I do it?'

74

'I think you go about things differently with them. Talk to enough people, tell your story another couple of times, and if they're interested, they'll come to you. Don't you know that's how it works?'

AVRAHAM KEPT A CLEAN uniform in a cupboard in his office, and what Ma'alul had said convinced him to go straight to the station. When he knocked on Benny Saban's door, he found Saban with a young woman whom he did not introduce. Avraham asked if he was interrupting, and Saban said, 'Come in, come in. I'm leaving for the District in a few minutes, but I have a second.' The young woman got up and smiled at Avraham on her way out, as if they knew each other, although he was certain they'd never met.

'I just wanted to let you know that I might have waded into an abduction or missing-person case that might be connected to the Mossad,' Avraham said. 'I'm not sure, but I thought I'd better find out what you think I should do.'

Saban's reaction was identical to Eliyahu's. He put his e-cigar down on the desk and said, 'But how the hell does this have anything to do with us, Avi? And why would you go anywhere near things like that?' When Avraham said he hadn't, Saban asked, 'Then how did it get to you?'

He repeated the story to Saban, but tried to downplay its importance. He referred to Chouchani as 'elderly' and after explaining that Annette Mallot had told him her father worked for the Mossad, he added, 'But that could be absolute rubbish.' He told Saban about the two passports and the two names but left out Chouchani's attempts to be remembered by the people he met that night, and Saban looked relieved. 'This doesn't sound serious,' he said, and stood up, 'more like some fantasy dreamed up by a bored woman. You know how these things go. Did anyone file a complaint? If not, then why assume it's a missing person? And a Mossad-related one!' What was the chance that Saban would pass the story on? When they were at the door, the Commander added, 'If he doesn't board his flight back to Paris or if his daughter or someone else files a missing-person complaint, then we'll look into it. And if we find out it's above us, which really doesn't seem likely to me, then up there they probably know all about it already. If he is a Mossad man, then he definitely doesn't need Avi Avraham and Benny Saban to rescue him. Just forget about it and get back to your work.'

ESTY VAHABA WAS WAITING for him outside the interrogation room.

Liora Talyas refused to give any details about where her daughter Danielle was, and she'd also suddenly changed her story and claimed the baby was hers. 'Why would she lie about that?' Avraham asked.

Vahaba said, 'I'm not sure. She has some story in her head that I can't figure out, Avi. She's living in la-la land. I tried to be empathetic, but she thinks she's really clever and that she's managing to manipulate me and scare me, and I have this urge to hit her. You

76

should see the miserable baby she threw in that bag. It's a miracle she's not dead yet.'

This time, Avraham noticed that Esty's eyes were infected, but he didn't say anything about it because he'd promised Marianka not to. The evening before, Vahaba had told Marianka that she'd been diagnosed with the same eye disease that had caused her father to go blind when he was her age, and she'd asked Marianka not to tell Avraham. 'Are you telling me Esty's going blind and trying to hide it from me?' Avraham had exclaimed, but Marianka had reassured him that Esty wasn't going blind yet. She was undergoing treatment to prevent the disease from progressing, and apparently, they could delay the deterioration.

In his mind, Avraham was still at the Palace, despite Saban's advice to forget Chouchani. But in reality, he was in the interrogation room where he'd spent untold hours investigating cases like that of Liora Talyas' – the kind that had made him request a transfer.

He'd heard the story Talyas now repeated countless times, too. Since her husband had been killed in a workplace accident – she used the word 'murdered', for some reason – she was the sole provider, with a family to feed on a preschool assistant's salary and benefits. Up until two years ago, her eldest daughter, Michal, had shared the household expenses, but since she'd got married, the money she'd brought in was gone. So when she'd become pregnant, Liora hadn't thought she could support another child under the circumstances. 'Having a baby means being off work for months, and spending thousands of shekels a month that I had no way of making.' An abortion was out of the question on religious grounds, and she hadn't considered putting the baby up for adoption because of the stigma and the effect it would have on her younger daughters. When the baby was born, she thought perhaps she should keep her. But a few days after the birth she had panicked, and maybe she had also got depressed, and had decided to leave the baby at the hospital so that the welfare authorities would find her a better home.

Avraham thought Vahaba was right, and they couldn't believe a word of Liora Talyas' story because it was full of holes. He wrote to Vahaba on a piece of paper: *Then have her explain how she hid her pregnancy from everyone. And, most importantly, make her give us the father's name and say why he can't help.* But Vahaba tried a different approach. She said, 'Liora, I believe everything you're saying about your financial state. I can commiserate with you, and I understand. But I don't believe the baby is yours because the DNA test showed that you're not the mother and because everyone who knows you says you weren't pregnant. Everything you just said explains why you couldn't raise the child, so why not come clean and admit that your daughter Danielle gave birth to her?'

Liora Talyas burst out: 'But what difference does it make who gave birth to her? Explain to me why that's so important!'

Perhaps it wasn't?

Avraham felt he had to leave the stifling room, even though the air-conditioning wasn't turned on, because the short woman sitting there, lying to them for no reason, was too familiar, too close, too despicable.

He wrote another note to Vahaba: *Maybe she has a boyfriend she's covering for because he got the daughter pregnant?* When Esty didn't ask her about it, he said to Talyas himself, 'Can you please tell us the name of your boyfriend? Or the father of your baby?' The woman looked at him and said, 'I don't owe you anything. Did I ask if you can get anyone to sleep with you? Then why are you asking me?'

AT THE STOP LIGHT before Hoofien Street, Avraham debated whether to turn left, towards Marianka, who was home now and waiting for him, or right, towards the Palace, which he'd promised himself he would visit again. Just then, his phone rang. The screen said *number withheld*, and when the light changed to green, Avraham instinctively headed home and stopped the car at the first bus stop he saw.

'Is this Superintendent Avraham Avraham?'

The voice was very young and chirpy. She introduced herself as Keren from 'the Prime Minister's Office', asked if he had time for a short conversation and then said she understood he'd obtained information about a tourist who was alleged to be working for the Mossad, and that she would like him to share the details with her. She did not say how she'd understood this, but there was no doubt that Saban had done the job. And with Keren, unlike with Saban, Avraham shared all the details. From the first call from the hotel and the two passports, all the way to the home address of Rafael Chouchani, which was scribbled in the notebook that Avraham now opened and put next to him on the passenger seat. 'Boulevard de Picpus, 89. And his daughter is named Annette Mallot. She lives in Strasbourg. I'll give you her phone number. Are you writing this down?'

Keren had a soft, pleasant laugh. She did not need Mallot's number because she'd already conducted a preliminary inquiry and the tourist was definitely not a Mossad agent. 'I'm calling you because we take it very seriously when someone impersonates, or publicly claims to be, an agent within our organization,' she said, 'and so we would be very pleased if you would continue to share with us any information you find in the course of your investigation. I can tell you that, in our experience, couriers who deliver counterfeit goods or drugs often use fake passports, but I'm sure you know that better than I do. Either way, the minute you have further details, we would like to collaborate with you and investigate together why this man is pretending to work for us. And then we can make a joint decision on the course of action.'

As he merged with the heavy traffic, Avraham barely noticed he was driving again.

He felt relieved because there did not seem to be any urgency in finding Chouchani. Chouchani was not a Mossad agent in danger, as Avraham had imagined, but once again just a tourist who'd disappeared from a hotel, perhaps not even against his will. His relief might also have had something to do with having unburdened himself of the secret — like a child who finally confesses to his parents that they broke a glass and hid the pieces in a drawer in his room, even though Keren was undoubtedly younger than him. Before she hung up, she said, 'Could I be impertinent and ask you a personal question?' Avraham said she could. 'You're the officer who captured the orang-utan, aren't you? I saw you interviewed on TV that day and I thought you gave a charming performance. I just wanted you to know. I haven't seen many policemen as eloquent as you are. And I'm glad we'll be collaborating.'

HE PICKED UP MARIANKA and they drove to Tel Aviv. They saw a movie at Dizengoff Centre and ate a late dinner sitting on a bench near Ha'Bima Square, then walked all the way down Bograshov Street to the promenade and strolled along the beach.

Marianka told him about the man she'd trailed that afternoon. He was married, with two grown daughters, and had set up a fake profile on dating apps, posing as a divorcé to snare lonely women looking for a partner. Marianka had managed to film him in the early evening in a flat he'd rented in Givatayim with one of the women, and she told Avraham she was going to give the photos not only to his wife, who'd hired the investigators, but also to the women this man had misled, so they'd stop seeing him.

'How exactly did you manage to get pictures of them in the flat?' Avraham asked, and Marianka smiled because working at the private-investigation firm had enhanced her surveillance skills, which were already pretty good.

She explained that she'd gone into the building across the street and knocked on the doors of flats that were more or less opposite the man's windows. Luckily for her, a sixteen-year-old kid had opened one of the doors. 'I flashed my most charming smile and introduced myself as an estate agent who was selling a flat in the other building, and said I needed some good pictures. And thanks to the best camera lens on the market, I spent fifteen minutes documenting everything that happened in that flat.'

Avraham gave her an impressed look because he couldn't imagine himself doing something like that. And also because it was illegal. When Marianka asked why he was in such a good mood after being so tense that morning, he said it was because the Mossad agent he thought he had to save wasn't a Mossad agent and probably wasn't in any danger.

'Then who is he?' she asked.

He said he didn't know, and he'd keep investigating. Then he added, 'I guess he's smuggling goods or drugs, using a fake passport, and he disappeared because he doesn't want us to find him.' The only thing that bothered him about that theory was that if Annette Mallot had heard him, she would have been positive he was wrong.

A FEW DAYS LATER, in early September, when the cool evening air signalled the approaching holidays, it turned out his relief had been premature.

Avraham's phone rang in the middle of the night, waking him and Marianka. When she saw his expression, Marianka realized something had happened even before he told her, because the angst that had vanished from his face for a few days reappeared all at once.

'Listen, Avi,' Ilanit said on the phone, 'I'm sorry to call so late, but they found a body I think you need to see. Unidentified older man, sixty or sixty-five. Can you go to the morgue first thing tomorrow to look at it?'

Part Two

Murderers

6

THE POLICE LEFT LIORA alone for a few days, but she assumed they were working quietly, underground, like mice.

The girls went back to school, and she went back to work. She woke up at half past five every morning, had two cups of Turkish coffee and ate a slice of bread with cream cheese and tomato. On the days when Mordechai had slept on the balcony, she folded up his mattress and aired out the blanket and sheets on the railing because she didn't like it when his smell lingered. If he came back after morning prayers, he brought bourekas and warm pitas for Ofrit and Eden, stayed with them after Liora went to work and locked the door when they left for school. When he wasn't there, Liora packed the girls' lunches herself, put out clean clothes for them on the couch and was gone before they woke up. At quarter past seven the parents would start dropping their children off at preschool, at nine they'd have breakfast and she'd wash the dishes, then start preparing lunch, put the children down for naps and wash the dishes again. There were eight new children this year, and she had to learn their names and how they liked to fall asleep; and since not all of them were toilet trained, she still had to change the occasional nappy. Just like last year, there were two vegans and one boy whose mother claimed he had a gluten sensitivity, and Liora had to make special food for each of them because Alice was adamant that every child's unique needs must be respected. She rejected Liora's claim that if parents insisted on special diets for their children, they should bring their own food.

And she knew this was only the beginning. The rest would be harder.

She sent Danielle's teacher an email: *Dear Iris, how are you? Danielle is on a trip abroad and will be back after the holidays. We'll make sure she catches up on the work. Thank you for understanding and have a good year. Liora.* The teacher wrote back and tried to find out the reason for such a long trip, but Liora did not respond. Rumours were flying at school, after all, and there was no doubt that the teacher knew. The bat had spoken with Danielle's friends and teachers, she'd spread rumours, tried to get to her any way she could. Avi Edry confirmed her suspicions. Michal was called in for questioning, and when Liora asked how it went, Michal was evasive. She said they'd asked if she'd noticed that Danielle had a stomach ache and who might have got her pregnant. 'What else?' Liora pressed, and Michal begrudgingly told her that the policewoman had asked who Danielle might be staying with in Paris and what her relationship with Liora was like.

'So what did you say?'

She had no doubt that Michal had given them Marcelle's name, even though Michal denied it. At least she didn't have Marcelle and Ronny's address or phone number. She claimed all she'd told the cop was that she hadn't noticed Danielle was pregnant, that they weren't close because of the age difference, and that she hadn't lived at home for years and had no idea who the father was because Danielle hadn't told her she was dating. Michal's attempts to find out from Liora if Danielle really was with Marcelle and Ronny, and why she'd gone to Paris at all, were obvious and stood no chance of tripping her up.

Mordechai was also summoned by the bat, although Liora did not immediately grasp the connection between his questioning and Michal's. Mordechai wasn't worried, even though he'd never been questioned by the police before. When it was over, he told Liora everything. His interview had lasted an hour and a half, and they'd asked him more or less the same questions: do you know where Danielle Talyas is? Did you notice that she was pregnant? What is your relationship with her? How is her relationship with her mother? Liora didn't have to work hard to get the answers out of Mordechai.

She considered sending a letter to Danielle, but decided that would be careless. She just had to hope Danielle did not need to be reminded of the very clear agreement they'd made: there's no chance they'll send anyone to find you there, but if they do turn up and ask questions, you don't answer. Don't say a word. You have no idea what they want and you're not talking without your mother, who's in Israel, and without a lawyer. You're a minor. But there's no chance they'll fly a cop over there for a baby, and you can't be touched as long as you're far away. The problem was, she wanted to hear Danielle's voice; that was the only way she would know if Danielle was holding up and following the rules and that she hadn't contacted anyone in Israel. In the end she phoned Marcelle from the phone at preschool, after work when Alice wasn't there. Danielle was asleep, and when Marcelle asked if she should wake her, Liora said no.

'How does she feel?' Liora asked

'All right,' Marcelle replied. 'She's still weak, quiet. She doesn't want to eat. Spends half the day sleeping. Lots of mood swings. She reminds me of you. But Ronny gets along well with her. He watches TV with her and takes her out running in the park. Did you know she smokes? She asked him for a cigarette, but he wouldn't give her one.'

She hadn't known. And since she assumed Michal had given the bat Marcelle's name, she decided to warn her that they might get a call from the police.

'The police? But why, Liora? What did the girl do? Is there something you didn't tell me?'

She'd only told her part of the truth. She'd said Danielle hadn't done anything, but the abortion was illegal. 'We didn't want to go through all the bureaucracy, so we went to a private doctor. And they might come looking for us because of that. Anyway, if the police contact you, let me know and don't let her talk to them. Are you making sure she's not talking to anyone in Israel? Not using your phones? I don't want her to be in touch with the boy who did this to her.'

Marcelle said she thought Liora was probably overreacting and the Israeli police weren't going to waste their time investigating an abortion, even if it was done illegally. 'Besides, you're too protective of her. She's a big girl and you need to be more trusting. Don't keep controlling her like this, honey. When you were her age, you also had a baby. Remember how well we managed with that?'

This was the stage in the plan that Liora found most frightening, because it was out of her hands and it forced her to trust Danielle. All the things that had happened up to then – being recognized on the security camera, having her flat searched, the DNA test – Liora had known she would be able to handle. But there were stages that depended on Danielle, and contrary to what Marcelle said, Danielle did not have Liora's strength or even the strength Liora used to have back when she was her age and gave birth to Michal.

David had been thirty-five at the time. Divorced, which was her fault, but fortunately with no children. When they got married, she already had a little bump that she hid under her dress, but her fear of the wedding, of the marriage that she still wasn't sure she wanted, of the girl who would be born when she didn't even know how to give birth – all that, she had not been able to hide.

So David helped, and his mother did, too, teaching Liora how to bathe and change and feed the baby and soothe her at nights, because her own mother was opposed to the marriage and refused to help. Marcelle had known nothing about children because she had no siblings and she was afraid to even hold Michal. Perhaps everything that happened then was the reason Marcelle chose not to have children.

But with you it was all different. That's what she could have told Danielle if she'd asked Marcelle to wake her.

And that's why Michal is angry at me, and why she is angry at you, has been ever since you were both little girls. By the time I had you I was twenty-four, and I was working, and I was certain that your father was my joy and my rock in life. I wanted you so that we'd have another child, and also so that you would be the correction. And that's what I felt you were, from the moment you were born: my correction. That's how I thought of you from the second we met, even though at the time it hadn't occurred to me that, in Hebrew, 'baby' is an anagram of 'correction'.

It's not that Liora felt like a mother then.

Quite the opposite: most of the time she felt like a big sister, or a friend. But she did enjoy going shopping with Marcelle to buy clothes for Danielle – soft little dresses, wool hats with pom-poms, tiny trainers – and she enjoyed playing with her, and going for walks with her on the promenade in the mornings, when Michal was at school, or in the evenings, when she was with David after he came home from work. *That's how it was between us: Michal was Daddy's girl, the child he'd waited for for thirty-some years, and you were my girl. You probably don't remember any of that. But that is why I won't let you fall, until you get strong again and you don't need me.*

The phone call with Marcelle was over, but Liora kept talking to Danielle in her mind. She saw her writhing in pain when she couldn't get the baby out of her body. The doctor standing between her legs, sweating from the effort and the stress. Danielle's squirming body was thin and boyish – an undeveloped boy's body, not a girl's – the way Liora's had looked at that age, except without the strength. She'd put her hand on Danielle's mouth and whispered, 'Be as quiet as you can, sweetie, so no one hears,' and when she saw that Danielle was too weak to stop shouting, she had said, 'Bite my hand, okay? Bite hard, instead of shouting.'

What frightens me about you is that from a girl who reminded me of myself, you turned into a woman without any strength.

That's what frightened me when you told me about the pregnancy — that you didn't care what happened. That you let me decide for you, as if this wasn't your life, or as if someone had sapped all the strength from you and passed it on to the baby, who should have died but insisted on living.

THE NEXT SUMMONS FOR questioning arrived a few days before Rosh Hashanah.

Liora asked Edry if she had to go, and he said yes and asked if she wanted him to be there. She didn't because without him she felt braver around the bat. She also rejected his offer to help her prepare for the interrogation in his office because she did not trust him to keep what she told him — or his hands — to himself.

Edry warned that some of their questions would probably surprise her. She didn't believe that. He also predicted that there would be investigators she hadn't met yet, but she found herself in the same room with the same Esty Vahaba. 'I thought we wouldn't meet again. And that made me sad because I didn't have time to wish you shana tova,' Liora said.

Right at the start it turned out that the bat had arrived at some absurd conclusions, which amazed Liora and proved to her how sick this cop was.

Vahaba noted the date and time of the interrogation, and Liora interrupted her. 'First of all, I'm glad you're continuing the investigation. That means the Israeli Police has nothing better to do. There are no crimes and no criminals. No thieves, no millionaires evading taxes. People aren't dying because of contractors who cut corners at the cost of their employees' lives. We're in good shape.'

Only when the detective looked up and said, 'Have you finished? Because I'd like to update you on some significant progress we've made in the case since we last met,' did Liora notice that her eyes weren't as red and were no longer covered with congealed ointment, which made it easier for the detective to look at her. 'I'd like to talk about Danielle,' said Vahaba.

'I'm not talking to you about my daughter.'

'Why not?'

'I don't have to. It's none of your business.'

'I want to help Danielle. Don't you?'

'Not with you. You're not here to help us. On the contrary. You're here to take her down, and me. To frame us. You're no psychologist. Besides, Danielle doesn't need help.'

'It's true, I'm not a psychologist, but I've spoken with people who know your daughter. And who do want to help her. I tried to understand who got Danielle pregnant and what happened in that pregnancy that made you try and get rid of the baby, and I have a few theories. And I'm really not talking to you as a police officer now, Liora, but as a woman trying to help your daughter. Are you willing to talk to me about it?'

'Do I have a choice? And I've already told you the baby's mine, not hers.'

'Can you tell me who Mordechai is?'

This was indeed a question Liora hadn't expected. Not because it was shrewd but because it had nothing to do with anything.

'What do you mean, who's Mordechai? You sat here and questioned him, didn't you?'

'I mean who is he to you? Are you a couple? Does he live with you and the girls in your flat?'

'Of course he doesn't live with us. He has his own place. But why am I even answering you? It's none of your business who Mordechai is.'

'I'll be very direct with you, Liora. I'm asking you if there is a chance that I'll find out that Mordechai is the baby's father, if I have him take a paternity test.'

All the bat's conversations with relatives and neighbours had amounted to this fantastical conclusion.

'Are you asking me if I'm sleeping with Mordechai?' Liora asked, even though she knew what the cop meant.

'I'm asking if Mordechai hurt your daughter,' replied Vahaba.

Liora lost her temper then and shouted, 'What are you, a pervert? Do you understand what sort of baseless accusation you just made?

What you said is slander, and I hope for your sake that you can afford what you'll have to pay him! Mordechai is a saint.'

Vahaba looked straight at her, as if not only her vision but her courage had grown stronger. 'I'm not slandering anyone. And don't make threats you don't understand. Please, Liora, it makes you sound ridiculous. You have no idea what a libel suit is and when it can be filed. All I'm saying is that I know who the baby's mother is. It's your daughter, Danielle. Despite your pointless denials, the purpose of which I do not understand. I now want to know who the father is and I'm positive you have the answer. So before I put Mordechai through an unpleasant paternity test, and maybe do the same to a few other men you know, I'm trying to get you to cooperate with me and tell me willingly who the father is and whether his identity has anything to do with your decision to move Danielle to France and your attempt to kill the baby. You're welcome to include all that in this imaginary slander suit you think you can file. I wish you the best of luck.'

This was a different Vahaba and, for a moment, she managed to weaken Liora, perhaps in part because she'd mentioned an attempt to kill the baby. So Liora reminded herself of David's face and imagined he was there with her, and said to the policewoman quietly, 'If you knew who Mordechai was, you wouldn't have dared say what you said.'

She had not killed the baby. In fact, that baby was alive thanks to her.

'Then please tell me who he is. He was a friend of your husband, David, if I understand correctly.'

A childhood friend whom David hadn't seen for more than thirty years. The only one of all his friends who hadn't forgottenen him.

Liora did not answer.

'Have you been close since your husband died?'

When Mordechai walked into their flat, three days after David was murdered, she didn't know him. He told her he'd gone to elementary school with David and that the last time they'd met was when they were twenty-two. When he had read the news story about the accident and had seen David's picture, he had felt he had to come to the *shiva*. Liora had told the people who visited over and over again how she'd had to identify David's broken body at the hospital, and before Mordechai left, he had promised to come back when there were fewer people and tell her a story that would give her strength. And unlike those who had promised her all sorts of things, Mordechai had kept his word. He had come to the cemetery for the gravestone unveiling, and afterwards he had gone home with the family, and that was when he told Liora the story of Rabbi Eleazar's wife: how when she saw her husband's arm exposed for the first time, she had both laughed and cried. She had laughed with joy at being able to live with such a body, and she had cried because one day that body would perish.

The story had horrified Liora.

Not only because it brought back the memory of David's shattered arm on the hospital bed and his body on the gurney in the cemetery before he was lowered into the ground, but because it had revealed to her how she herself had felt since realizing how much she had loved

David. She did not want to spend one day in this world without him, but she'd had a premonition that it would happen – that he would die before she did. He would go too soon and leave her on her own, not simply because he was eighteen years older than her, but because he would experience a tragedy that she could not prevent.

She had laughed because she said to herself: how happy my lot that I have been able to cleave to the body of so righteous a man! She had wept because she said: alas the body of so righteous a man is destined for the dust.

Those words, which Mordechai had read to Liora exactly thirty days after David's murder – she had said them to herself every day since she was twenty-two or twenty-three, without knowing them.

As always, when she thought of that story, she could feel the weeping inside herself, which never stopped. She hoped the bat hadn't noticed her weakness, and she fell silent in order to stifle the sobs.

'I can see you find it difficult to answer questions about Mordechai,' Vahaba said.

In the weeks after the *shiva*, as the house emptied of relatives, Liora had had the feeling that no one remembered David and his murder apart from Mordechai, who had kept visiting. They reread the story together often, and when Mordechai told her that Rabbi Eleazar's wife had left her husband's body in their attic for twenty years, Liora said that if she'd heard the story before David was buried, she would have had the courage to do the same thing. The words they read together in the Bible and in the other books that Mordechai brought were the only ones in which she found an expression of her internal, unstoppable weeping.

She kept quiet until her weakness was under control and she knew it wouldn't lead to crying. 'Mordechai is not the baby's father, and he's never hurt anyone in his life. You can do as many paternity tests as you want. God will count them against you on the Yom Kippur reckoning.'

'Very good. Thank you for authorizing me to test him, Liora. I appreciate that. And since you mentioned Yom Kippur, can you tell me if Mordechai is religious?'

She understood that question even less. 'What do you mean?'

'He goes to the synagogue, right? He wears a yarmulke. His older kids became Orthodox—'

'Are you going to arrest him for that?'

'God forbid. I just want to know how that influenced you and your family. And about his relationship with Danielle.'

'What relationship? There's no relationship.'

'But didn't it affect you? Your relationship with her? Didn't it make you stricter with her?'

Only now was Liora able to guess at something else from the bat's pathetic conversations with Danielle's teachers and friends. And the parts of her exchange with Michal that her daughter had hidden from her. 'Are you insinuating that I did something to Danielle and to the baby because Mordechai is religious? I'm trying to understand. First you claim he's touching Danielle, and now he—'

'I didn't claim he touched Danielle. What I'm trying to understand is why your daughter hid her relationships from you.'

Had the bat been able to find out more than Liora thought she would? For the next several moments, until it turned out that she didn't know anything about him, Liora was tensely bracing for her to mention the name Amir Souen.

'She hid what? My daughter didn't hide anything,' she replied.

'Then let me put a hypothetical question to you, okay? Not about Danielle. What would you do if you found out that a daughter of yours, an adolescent, was having sexual relations with boys? Is it acceptable to you that a girl her age would have sex?'

Danielle swore she hadn't talked to anyone about what had happened to her with Amir Souen, but she might have lied.

'The real question is what I would do if you told me *you* were having sex with boys. Because that would be the funniest thing I'd ever heard. It hasn't happened yet, has it?'

The bat turned red, but she recovered quickly and looked for Liora's eyes again. 'But it did happen to Danielle. She did sleep with boys.'

This time Liora did not smile. 'You should know by now that I'm not talking to you about my daughter.'

'You will in the end. You won't have a choice. And I know that Danielle didn't tell you she'd had sex because she was afraid of your response.'

Liora could have let it go on, but there was no point. And she wanted to find out what the bat was hiding. She said, 'Look, you're making all kinds of assumptions that are only getting you further away from the truth. Can I say that to you? Maybe it'll help clear your eyes. You're assuming that Danielle had the baby, when I'm telling you that I did. She came out of *my* belly. You want to check? Bring a doctor and check. Furthermore, you're slandering a man like Mordechai who has never hurt a fly. And then you slander my daughter with all kinds of accusations. There is no fear between me and Danielle. I love my daughter and I take care of her, and if you talked to her, you would know that.'

The detective looked at her for some time without saying a word. She neither denied nor confirmed that she'd spoken with Danielle, and now Liora was almost positive that she hadn't got to her yet.

'Then I'll tell you what I do know, okay, Liora? I know that Danielle had a relationship with a boy in her class. Ido Atar. He admitted to having sex with Danielle, but he claims it was three months ago, in June, and that he couldn't be the baby's father. We've petitioned the court to give him a paternity test to make sure he's telling the truth.'

'But why are you telling me this?' She didn't know Ido Atar and had never heard the name.

'I'm telling you this because one of the possibilities I'm looking into is that he's lying or mistaken. That Danielle did get pregnant by him. And that you were opposed to the pregnancy when you found out about it and forced her to get rid of the baby. And, based on the medical report we received, I can also tell you exactly how it happened. And I promise you that I'll find the doctor who helped you very soon.'

For a moment, Liora saw the baby on the morning she'd placed her in the black bag on some old towels and nappies. When Liora fed her, before leaving, the baby had wrapped her finger around the bottle's nipple.

'I've told you a thousand times I don't know what you're talking about. That baby is mine. If you want, you can press charges against me.' Vahaba sighed while she gathered her papers and stood up. 'But what exactly would you charge me with?' Liora continued, her strength now back. 'What is it that you're actually persecuting us for? Explain that to me. Let's say I did try to get an abortion, but I couldn't – so what? Are abortions illegal in Israel? I thought it was the right of any woman who doesn't want to give birth, isn't it?'

7

RAFAEL CHOUCHANI'S BODY WAS found in the almost completely dark sea, a couple of miles from the beach along which Avraham and Marianka had walked several days earlier. Elisha Getenio, a thirty-eight-year-old ultra-Orthodox man from Rishon Le'Zion, a drummer and a father of four, came across it while he was having a night swim. When he realized what he'd found, he hurried out of the water and called the police. A team from the marine-police unit located the body in the water, and it was transferred to Wolfson Hospital for the night. At half past six in the morning it was taken in a burial society van to the Institute of Forensic Medicine, where Superintendent Avraham Avraham, Investigations and Intelligence Branch Commander, was waiting to identify the body and confirm that it was under his jurisdiction.

The institute employee who walked Avraham to the morgue explained that the deceased had been in the water for a few days.

There were no gunfire wounds on his body, and regarding other marks and the cause of death, 'I can't tell you anything until the autopsy, but don't even dream of that happening today. Only after the holiday. We're swamped today and tomorrow we're closed.' The body was bloated, but Avraham was almost positive the grey face was that of the man he'd seen on the security footage from the hotel and the airport. The man who said he'd come to Israel to meet an old friend and look for another friend who'd disappeared. The man who'd tried to make sure he was remembered by the border-control agent at the airport and the front-desk clerk at the hotel, as if he had known something might happen to him during his visit. The man who Avraham had mistakenly concluded did not need to be searched for with any urgency. This was the first time Avraham had seen him up close, and even though he'd been dead for a few days, there still appeared to be fear on his face.

He thought about what he would say to Annette Mallot when he phoned her.

Your father's body was found at sea, but I don't know how it got there. Or how he died. And he probably was not the man you thought he was.

When the employee slammed the morgue's metal door shut, Avraham asked if there was really no chance of getting an autopsy report that day, but the employee was adamant: 'We do things in order here, and your old man is not first in line.'

Other than official responsibility for the deceased man, Avraham was given a box containing underwear, a white T-shirt, two rings – one gold and one silver – and Rafael Chouchani's brown suit, which he recognized from the video footage. 'All this was on the body when it was pulled out of the water,' explained the man. 'Other than this, there's nothing. And I recommend that you send it to the lab ASAP because they're probably closed from tomorrow, too.'

HE WAS HOPING TO get to the station after the branch commanders' meeting was over, but when he walked into the meeting room on the third floor, Saban called out, 'Ah, he finally joins us! The man who came in from the morgue.' There were remnants of chocolate cake with sprinkles on the table, and Avraham remembered the message about celebrating the precinct commander's fiftieth birthday at the weekly meeting. Next to the cake were bottles of the blueberry juice that Saban liked, and little plastic dishes with pretzels, which Saban asked someone to move away from him and then pulled back towards him.

The young woman Avraham had seen in Saban's office and hadn't recognized sat next to the commander, in uniform this time. When Avraham walked in, she was reading and writing messages on her phone, but trying to hide it under the table.

Avraham wished Saban a happy birthday, apologized for being late, and said he had nothing further: as far as he was concerned, they could wrap up the meeting.

But Saban didn't want his party to end. 'Why should we wrap up?' he said. 'Give us an update first. I understand you have a new body.'

Avraham nodded to confirm, then explained that the tourist who'd disappeared from the hotel in Bat Yam had been found overnight.

'Wait, this is the same guy you thought was . . .' Saban stopped himself just in time to avoid embarrassing Avraham.

Avraham gave him a grateful look and said, 'That's correct. It turns out he isn't. I checked with a reliable source.'

Saban smiled at him, as if he'd never entertained the idea to begin with. 'So do you have any theories about what happened to him?'

Other than the theories he'd considered when he'd talked to Keren – before the body was found – Avraham didn't have a single lead. 'Until we know the cause of death, it's hard to say. At the moment, he seems to have died by drowning, but that doesn't give us much. The fact that he used two passports and two names might indicate that he was a smuggler, but it's unclear. I have a feeling this is not going to be an easy case because we have very little information about the man and we'll have to get help from the French.'

On the way to the station, he'd phoned Jules, at the French Police, to tell him about the body and ask for details about Rafael Chouchani's work, his financial situation, his criminal record, if there was one, and a list of phone calls he'd made in the weeks before his trip to Israel. Avraham had put off the call to Annette Mallot, but he would have to make it later that day – not just to inform her that her father was dead, but to try and understand who he was and whether he might have been working as a courier for drugs or counterfeit goods.

Saban used his thick fingers to pick up some cake crumbs from his plate, which was a sign that the meeting was almost over. 'I'll try and prod the institute to get you an autopsy before the holiday,' he promised, 'and if this is drug smuggling, we might have to search the hotel room.' When Avraham said he'd been in Chouchani's room at the Palace on the first day of the investigation, Saban said, 'But maybe at the time you didn't know what you were looking for. We'll need to ask Forensics to go over the room with a fine-toothed comb.'

Avraham promised to do another search and hoped that would be the end of the meeting, but Saban asked, 'And what about Esty's case? Would you like to say a word about that?'

So Avraham tried to explain the situation with the baby investigation, as he understood it from Vahaba: the baby was still in the NICU at Wolfson, where the doctors were fighting for her life. Overnight, Chouchani's body had spent several hours in the same hospital, and that was the second time the two cases had converged. 'We're still searching for the girl who is the mother. Her name is Danielle Talyas, sixteen years old. She went to France but we're looking into the possibility that she's now in Brussels or Geneva. Esty considered contacting Interpol and asking them to issue a blue or yellow notice, so that Talyas could be stopped at border crossings, but since we don't have clear grounds for an arrest, for now the decision is to make do with the information Vahaba is getting here. We did find the doctor who delivered the baby and questioned him, and he gave us his version of events.'

'And why are they hiding her? Do we understand that?' asked Saban.

'It's unclear for now, but we're—'

The young woman who'd been texting under the table looked up from her phone and interrupted. 'What crime is this girl suspected of anyway? I'm sorry, I don't get it.'

Perhaps because of the surprised look on his face, Saban asked Avraham if he'd been introduced, and then said, 'You really haven't? Then I apologize. Avi, this is Ilana.' She was the new precinct spokeswoman, he explained, whom he'd 'plucked straight from the army spokesperson unit'. Then he added, in a whisper, 'You have no idea how great her English is, Avi. It's incredible.'

'Nice to meet you, I'm Avi,' Avraham said, and he thought he saw something cold and distant in her eyes when she replied, 'Pleased to meet you, too. Ilana Assayag. But I really don't get it – what exactly do you suspect that this girl has done?'

OVER THE NEXT FEW hours, contrary to everything Avraham had thought would happen, the fog over the Chouchani investigation cleared with surprising speed. He'd never before had a case in which the picture sharpened and filled out with details so quickly, and in retrospect, it might have been that swiftness which aroused his suspicion.

It began with a phone call from the Israel Police representative in Paris, Chief Superintendent Idit Gerti.

When she called him in the late morning, she already knew that the French tourist's body had been found at sea, even though Avraham had not informed her. Had Jules had time to do it? Or someone else at the Paris Police? And before Avraham could ask for her help gathering information on Chouchani, she said she'd conducted some background checks and she thought she was beginning to understand the story. Avraham asked, 'Really? What is it you understand?'

According to Gerti's sources at the Paris Police, Chouchani had no criminal record, but he owed large sums of money on the grey market and might have been facing bankruptcy. He was divorced, had one daughter, and his main business areas were residential real-estate investments, holiday flats in various countries in Asia and a men's shoe brand named Honoré, which he'd bought about five years ago. The shoes were manufactured in India and distributed in the Middle East and Africa as high-end French fashion, but it turned out Chouchani had paid too much for the company and taken out too many loans he could not pay back, especially when manufacturing costs soared and sales dropped. In the past two years he'd had to sell most of his real estate, but had still apparently been unable to repay his loans.

'So where does this lead us?' Avraham asked, putting his pen down while Gerti continued to confidently expound on her assumptions.

The crime organizations that control the French grey market, she explained, offer borrowers an alternative way to settle their debts: by acting as couriers, usually for drugs but sometimes diamonds or counterfeit goods. And it's hard to say no to the lenders. Sometimes the offer comes from a third party who promises to cover the debt or have it erased. The ideal couriers are white men and women, middle-aged or even elderly, since they arouse fewer suspicions.

There are cases in which it's not the borrower who is asked to do the job but their parents, who are told this is the only way to save their child's life. The couriers usually know nothing about the contents of the package or whom it's going to, so that if they are caught, they can say very little about who is behind it – and even that, they're too afraid to say. 'I'm willing to bet this is what happened to your man Chouchani,' she summed up. 'Or at least that's the direction you should look at.'

At half past two, his hunger having intensified, Avraham went downstairs to the cafeteria.

Most of the hot food was finished, so he bought a Tunisian sandwich and a Twix. The smell of the tuna and hard-boiled eggs that had been languishing in the roll since morning was pungent, and he hoped that Ilana, who was sitting a few tables away talking on the phone, would not come over and initiate a conversation. He wolfed down the sandwich in large, crude bites, which he regretted. But Ilana had her back to him anyway, and hadn't seen him come in.

How strange it would be to say the name 'Ilana' again at meetings, he thought.

Before leaving the meeting room, he'd tried to catch Ilana's eyes, but she had gotten a phone call and left first, so he couldn't congratulate her on the new job or do anything to sweeten the sour taste left in his mouth by their first meeting – and probably in hers, too.

He phoned Marianka to tell her he'd be home late, and when she asked how he was, he said he didn't know because at the time he hadn't yet put his finger on what was making him feel uneasy. In his mind's eye, he saw Rafael Chouchani packing his bags for the trip when there was a knock at his door. When he opened the door, he found a large package and a man hurrying away. Or perhaps it happened when Chouchani was on the train to the airport? A man or a woman was waiting for him at the station, he stepped off the train, they recognized him based on a pre-arranged marker—perhaps his brown suit—and handed him the package, and he got back on the train before the horn blew and the doors slid closed.

Is that what you went through?

Long hours of apprehension because you were about to smuggle a package against your will. If you got caught, it would be on you. You wouldn't be able to say who demanded that you take it, even if you knew, because that would be even more dangerous.

In Avraham's imagination, Chouchani went through security at the Paris airport. He was asked to walk through the metal detector, and then he waited for his suitcase to come through the X-ray machine. 'Who does this blue suitcase belong to?' asked a security agent, and Chouchani's heart skipped a beat. It wasn't his.

But what happened to you after that?

You landed in Israel, took a room at the Palace, didn't go to bed because you knew you wouldn't be able to fall asleep, and at sunrise you went out to deliver the package, but something went wrong. Something you'd feared might happen.

Was the package not the one the buyers were expecting?

*

ESTY VAHABA SENT HIM a WhatsApp message: *The boy we tested isn't the baby's father. That means it might be that Mordechai guy after all. And it looks like I've tracked down an address for the couple hiding Danielle Talyas in France. I tried to get hold of you loads of times but you were in a meeting and then I got call waiting. I know you're busy but can you let me know when you're free?*

He was going to call her from his office, but when he got there, he learned they'd done the autopsy on Chouchani, after all, perhaps thanks to Saban's intervention. The report from the Institute of Forensic Medicine was waiting on his desk.

The cause of death was drowning, but according to the report, Chouchani had been *beaten on all parts of his body, and suffered fractured ribs and limbs, bruised internal organs and internal bleeding, all inflicted before his death. The likely scenario is that the deceased was put in the sea while unconscious and drowned, although we cannot rule out the possibility that he entered the water himself. His body was in the water for well over 72 hours, perhaps even a week.*

Avraham didn't write a thing in his black notebook because it all happened too fast and because writing would have given his hypothesis a validity he was not yet ready to commit to.

He was supposed to write that the emerging investigation direction was that Chouchani was a smuggler, perhaps forced into it, and that for some reason, after delivering the package, he was eliminated by the criminal organization or smuggling network for which he worked. The question was: why? He hadn't been caught at the airport in Paris, or in Tel Aviv, so why would anyone kill him off?

The two men who had collected Chouchani's luggage from the hotel probably belonged to the criminal organization, and they were the clue that would lead to him, although it might be possible to track down who was behind the delivery using intelligence. Eliyahu Ma'alul had already dug up some information about smuggling networks active on the France–Israel route.

When Avraham finally talked to Annette Mallot in the early evening, he did not want to tell her any of this. She didn't pick up immediately, and Avraham became hopeful that he could postpone the conversation until the next day, but then he heard her voice. 'Is everything okay? Did you find him?' she asked in English.

Avraham said, 'Annette, I'm sorry to inform you that we found your father's body.'

She was quiet, and then apparently repeated what he'd told her in German to the man who was with her. 'Do you know how he died?' she asked.

'We're not sure yet,' replied Avraham. 'He drowned. We found his body in the sea.'

'But that can't be,' said Annette. 'He didn't even know how to swim.'

Avraham waited quietly for her to take in the news, then promised to do everything he could to find out the circumstances of her father's death. He said he would need her help obtaining more information, and that some detectives might visit and interview her.

She was clearly upset: 'He knew this would happen to him. He was afraid he'd get hurt. I wrote that to you in my email and you didn't answer me.'

Avraham hoped she wouldn't repeat her claim that her father had worked for the Mossad so that he would not have to correct her and explain that her father had lied to her.

'Can you tell me what he was afraid of? Does it have anything to do with his debts? Was he being threatened?' he asked.

Annette did not answer immediately. Only after the man whispered something in German did she say softly, 'I don't want to tell you on the phone. I'll explain it to the police when they come. And what debts? I don't think he had any debts.' After a moment she added, 'He was afraid they'd hurt him because of Sara. I told you that already. Did you find her?'

According to the records at the Ministry of the Interior, no one named Sara Nuweima had entered Israel, unless she had also used a fake passport and a fictitious name.

'Because she's also disappeared, and I'm sure something's happened to her. I've been trying to get hold of her since you told me Dad went to Israel, and she's not answering.'

He asked for Nuweima's phone number and promised to update Annette if there were any developments. Then he reiterated that he was sorry and would make every effort to find out what had happened.

'What will you do with his body?' she asked.

He wasn't sure what to say, as he hadn't thought of that. 'I assume it will remain here for the time being. Perhaps until we know more. Would you like him to be buried in France?' he asked.

She said she would.

THE LAST DETAIL TO be added to the picture that day explained the *why*, and once that was identified, Avraham no longer had any reason to doubt what had happened to Chouchani.

Oleg was sitting behind the front desk and handed Avraham the key to room 203. While Avraham and a young forensic technician walked upstairs, the technician asked what he was supposed to be looking for, and Avraham replied, 'Whatever you think. The tourist who was here for a few hours was probably smuggling something, so there might be traces left in the room. Apart from that, there were two men here who belong to the criminal organization that commissioned the smuggling. They were looking for something in the room for a quarter of an hour, and they might not have found it. They might have left fingerprints, though.'

Avraham walked in first, pulling on a pair of gloves, and switched on the light.

As soon as he set foot in the room, he had the feeling someone had been there since his last visit, although he wasn't sure what made him think so. The coffee mug was in the exact same place next to the bathroom sink – but had someone come into the room, wiped the fingerprints off the mug and put it back? He examined the double bed and the minibar carefully, but he couldn't say what exactly had changed.

The forensic technician had to bend over when he walked into the bathroom because he was so tall, and when he came out he stood at the window facing the dilapidated building across the way, drew the curtain open and said, 'I've never seen a hotel room with a view like this before.'

Avraham wished he'd taken pictures on his last visit because then he could have known if something had changed without having to rely on his memory. But when he looked at the window where the forensic tech was standing, he realized he wasn't wrong: someone really had been in the room.

The curtain hadn't been washed, but the writing in the dust on the windowpane was gone. The window had been cleaned.

Someone had written *Yaakov Ben-Hayat* on the glass, and Avraham had seen it when he'd first been there. But now those letters were gone.

'We may not find anything because it looks like someone has cleaned up here,' Avraham said.

Just then, the forensic tech opened the window, turned around and said, 'Are you kidding me? You didn't see this when you were here?'

At first Avraham couldn't tell what the man was holding.

8

Two days before Rosh Hashanah, Liora has a meeting with Avi Edry. He works in Jaffa, near the old flea market, but the building has been refurbished, as has his office, and it looks like Edry himself: too sleek, perspiring with the effort to demonstrate success, but nevertheless small and unimpressive. The old office furniture has been replaced with a blond-wood desk that takes up almost the whole room and beige armchairs, in one of which Edry invites Liora to sit. Where there used to be a narrow window facing the street, with blinds drawn, there is now a tiny balcony.

He still has no secretary.

He offers Liora something to drink from the café on the ground floor, and she declines. 'Start explaining to me what's going on because I have to be home in an hour,' she says.

Edry puts on a show of being hurt. 'That's all you can spare me,

Liora? And you haven't said a word about what we've done here. You haven't been to the office since the renovation, have you?'

All this furniture, the beige armchairs, the built-in shelves, the gold-framed painting next to the window – it was all bought with money that had belonged to her. Or, more precisely, to David.

And she can detect the scorn in Edry's smile. His office has changed, and he doesn't see that she's also changed.

Most of what Edry tells her she already knows, and his attempt to scare her is futile this time. At first, she thinks he's recording the meeting because his phone is sitting on the table, closer to her than to him. On the other hand, he's the one talking, and she says almost nothing until the last few minutes. When he notices her look, he tries to reassure her: 'I'm not recording you, Liora. Trust me, when I do record you, I'll let you know, okay?'

She has no intention of trusting him, of course.

Partly because she is certain that the settlement he forced her to accept four years ago was a mistake. He'd negotiated a compensation with the construction company's legal counsel and agreed to withdraw the lawsuit, but she'd sensed his real goal was to ingratiate himself with the company directors so they'd offer him a job. According to the settlement, Liora got less than a quarter of the sum she'd asked for, and Edry took a third of the final payout. She'd only come to him this time because he was close to David's family, and because she wouldn't have trusted any other lawyer anyway. As her father used to say: better a thief you know who let you live, than one you haven't met yet. In any case, this time Edry wouldn't be able to bend her to his will, no matter what he thought. Back then, Liora had believed him when he said they wouldn't get a better deal if the case went to trial. 'They've got the upper hand because they have money and lawyers on retainer, and they'll hire private investigators who will prove that David was sick or an alcoholic or mentally ill and suicidal and that the accident was his fault. Then, not only will you end up without a penny, you'll have debts you'll never be able to pay off,' he'd threatened.

At the time she hadn't had the strength to argue, so she'd given in. She'd signed a compromise deal with the murderers, even though what she really wanted was a trial that would drag on for as long as possible, preferably years, so that she could keep talking about David. She wanted to be called in to testify over and over again, so that she could say what he was and everyone would have to listen, including people who hadn't known him and hadn't wanted to.

This is how Edry's performance begins: 'Look, Liora, the news I have for you today is not so good. I'll be honest with you. I don't know what happened at your interrogation, who you pissed off, but at the moment they're planning to come down hard on you. They got to the doctor who performed the operation on Danielle. That botched abortion. We'll only get his complete version if they press charges, but from his perspective, what matters is that he got there before you did so, for now, his version is the only one they have, and they can also come down hard on you because you're not cooperating. This is not good for us. They won't do anything to Danielle at the end of the day. She's sixteen. But they could really screw you, and we'll have no way out of it. Do you understand what I'm saying?'

She waits for him to finish. His plan is clear to her: he's trying to scare her so that she'll make everyone's lives easy. And he seems to be positive that he's going to pull it off once again. After David was murdered, he'd even tried to hit on her. Put his paws on her in his office, supposedly out of friendship and a desire to comfort her, asked her out for lunch, wondered if she was 'seeing men'. He'd told her he was recently divorced and was buying a penthouse in a new building, all the while persuading her to give up the money she and David deserved. She had been disgusted by his short arm around her shoulder and his little hand that dropped as if by accident onto her chest, but the truth was that the presence of any man who was not David had been intolerable at the time.

That is not going to happen again.

It's true that she hadn't known that the blind cop had got to the doctor, and she couldn't imagine who might have given her his name, but she says impatiently, 'They're not going to do anything to me,' and she can tell that Edry is surprised.

'Don't be so sure of yourself, all right? Let's not let our guard down,' he says, while opening a cardboard folder and taking out some handwritten pages fastened with a paper clip. 'I want us to go over the version the doctor gave the police, okay? I was given it off-off-off the record from a friend who's on our side. And he told me explicitly that they're going to come down on you hard if we don't get our act together. This isn't his whole testimony, but it's the main points. And they got to Danielle, as I'm sure you know. She'll be questioned in France, and you might need to consult with a lawyer there, too.

I have someone who can help you and he'll give you a good price. But let's figure out what the doctor said that could work against us and discuss how to solve the problem with minimal damage. Are you sure you can't give me more than forty-five minutes?'

She looks at Edry and isn't sure whether he recognizes the wrist-watch.

It's the one they took off David's shattered arm, don't you remember? she asks him silently.

Liora isn't alarmed by the fact that Vahaba found out where Danielle was, or by her being asked in for questioning in France. She'd assumed that would happen when she realized the cop wasn't letting up, and she'd taken it into account in her plan, which, after this meeting, would move on to the next stage.

She listens to the doctor's account.

Dr Avraham Rubinstein, resident of Jerusalem, sixty-nine years old . . .

The version suits his needs, but it's not very far from reality. He testified that at the end of July he received a phone call from Liora Talyas, resident of Bat Yam, regarding her daughter Danielle. Rubinstein had worked in the gynaecology department at Misgav Ladach Hospital in Jerusalem, but had been fired due to rumours of inappropriate conduct with married patients. Since then, he'd run a clinic on Ha'Neviim Street, downtown. Talyas and Danielle had come to his clinic on Tuesday, twenty-ninth July, at 22.30.

'Is everything so far correct? And do you remember who gave you his phone number?' Edry asks. Liora says yes, and motions for him to go on.

She'd almost regretted everything at the beginning of that night.

The clinic was on the ground floor of a dilapidated residential building, and they had to walk through an unlit yard. An old lady with a head covering, who later turned out to be Rubinstein's wife, showed them into a room where the ceiling was covered with mildew. The sheets on the rusty bed had been laundered too many times. Liora explained to the doctor that Danielle was probably in her fourth month, as the girl had reported, but after the ultrasound Rubinstein informed them that she was in her twenty-seventh or twenty-eighth week, and that he could not perform an abortion at the price they'd agreed on. She thought he was lying to try and milk her for more money because Danielle was barely showing. But he insisted, and said that as far as he was concerned, they could go to a different doctor. According to his testimony, Rubinstein had explained to the two women that a medical procedure at this stage would be complicated, even if not necessarily dangerous, and had suggested they seek treatment from the public-health system. They would have to inject the girl's uterus with a substance that would cause cardiac arrest in the foetus, and only then induce labour to cause her to eject the pregnancy, he explained.

They could have gone home.

They could have left the clinic and gone to their health fund or to the school counsellor. And it's likely that a few years ago that's what Liora would have done, naively. Everyone would have advised Danielle to have the baby and keep it, or give it up for adoption, and Liora would have obeyed them out of fear and deference. She remembered the moment when Rubinstein said 'cardiac arrest in the foetus'.

Up until that moment, they'd called her the baby. And she hadn't had a heart, either, until the doctor had explained that they would need to stop it.

'There are some parts here that are working against us,' Edry continues while Liora recalls the moments when she considered getting in the car and driving home. 'I want you to think about how we're going to respond, okay? This is exactly the reason why we must cooperate and give them our own version. According to the doctor, "The girl did not say a word the whole visit. Only the mother." He thought the girl looked apathetic, mentally unwell, perhaps even suicidal, and that was also why he gave in to Liora Talyas' pressure. '*When the doctor told them the pregnancy was in its advanced stages,*' Edry reads, '*Talyas turned to her daughter and asked if this was true. When the daughter said she didn't remember, the mother yelled at her and demanded that she remember when her last period was, and the daughter started to cry because she couldn't remember. At some point the mother threatened Rubinstein that if he didn't perform the medical procedure, she would do it herself, and the doctor feared she was serious and that it would cause irreparable harm to the girl.*'

All that, of course, is untrue.

And so Liora does not get frightened, much to Edry's astonishment.

Danielle had indeed hardly opened her mouth that night, but she hadn't spoken for months, maybe years, and not because she was afraid of Liora. She hardly spoke at home, or, apparently, at school.

And Liora never yelled at her. And never threatened to hurt her. She was the only person who wanted what was good for Danielle and the only person Danielle felt safe around. She insisted that Liora not leave the room, despite the doctor's request, and that she keep holding her hands while Rubinstein injected her with the substance.

'Do you mean the digoxin that he mentioned?'

'I don't know what it's called, that stuff he gave her. To stop the foetus's heart.'

She remembers Rubinstein's thick arms. Pink, and covered with big, dark age spots all the way from his doughy elbows to his wrists. His coat gave off a sharp smell of isopropyl alcohol.

Rubinstein's wife came in, took the envelope containing the money and hurried out of the room, locking the door behind her.

Liora expected Danielle to squeeze her hand hard while he administered the injection, but she didn't even do that. Her hand was limp and cold, as if it were her heart the doctor had stopped, not the foetus's.

That night, they'd slept together in Liora's bedroom. Danielle on Liora's side, and Liora on David's side, where no one had lain since he was murdered. The air-conditioning was noisy and made the room freezing cold. Danielle had woken up in the middle of the night and asked Liora to turn it off, which is why they had both been sweating by morning, since it was so hot and humid that night. Liora had woken up first, brushed away the sweaty tufts of dark hair clinging to Danielle's forehead and cheeks, and Danielle had smiled, perhaps dreaming something pleasant that erased the night's events from her memory and pushed away thoughts of what awaited her that day.

Liora does not tell Avi Edry all this, even though these might be details he wants to hear, because it's not part of the plan and it's not any of his business.

Danielle had gone back to sleep, and Liora had stayed next to her in bed. She had kept looking at her and imagining how the doctor would come to induce labour and would expel not only the foetus but the weakness that was eating her up from inside, and perhaps even the sadness, although Liora knew that would not be easily achieved. Perhaps she would wake up and be a different girl, with an inner strength that could not be crushed. That had been her hope.

They'd been home alone all day because the younger girls had stayed with Michal. Mordechai had asked if he could come by and bring them something to eat, but Liora had told him not to. They'd watched Danielle's TV shows in the living room, ordered a giant platter from Japonica and Danielle had eaten the sushi rolls even more ravenously than Liora. After taking a shower, Danielle had put on her favourite red tracksuit, which was another encouraging sign.

They had not said a word about the pregnancy. Nor about what they'd done the previous night or about what was going to happen later that day or about the dead foetus in Danielle's belly, which Liora resisted touching. Nor about what Danielle had done a few months earlier which had caused all this. Rubinstein had made it clear that

Liora would be responsible for getting rid of the foetus, and although she wasn't sure what she was going to do with the dead foetus, it was clear she would find a way. She would be able to carry the body, wrapped in sheets or thin blankets, and bury it somewhere it would not be found. She had been able to bury David, and so there was nothing in the world she could not bury.

At three o'clock in the afternoon, Danielle had fallen asleep, and Liora had started to get the room ready.

The blinds were drawn, and she'd tried to soundproof the windows with pillows, even though Rubinstein had said there would be no need. Shortly before six, she'd made two cups of tea with lemon and honey, and they'd talked about the trip to France, going over the parts of the plan that Danielle needed to know. She was going to see family friends because she had to get away after a bad break-up. She would disconnect from all social media for a few weeks: no texting with friends, no mobile-phone calls, until Liora told her it was all right. If anyone asked, in France or in Israel, she would deny that she'd been pregnant. Liora would tell Marcelle, and no one else, that there'd been an unwanted pregnancy and they'd got rid of it.

The tea had made Danielle happy and she'd asked Liora for another cup, telling her she felt better, perhaps because she'd slept. But that was before they found out the baby had survived the injection.

The apartment was dark. Someone knocked at the door.

Rubinstein arrived at Liora Talyas' apartment, at 2 Ha'giborim Street in Bat Yam, at 19.00. That was how his account of the second day began.

The television was on loud and they'd hardly heard him knocking. He had not turned the light on in the stairwell, and when Liora opened the door, thinking she'd heard something, she had seen a shadowy, bear-like figure standing in the dark, with a tall young woman in a skirt next to him. She turned out to be his daughter, Leah.

According to Dr Rubinstein's testimony, he had discovered that the foetus was still alive, but Liora had still insisted that he induce labour. Despite his yarmulke and religious garb, Rubinstein was a liar, like everyone else, because, in actual fact, it was the opposite: he had given Danielle the Pitocin as soon as he arrived because it takes time for it to dilate the cervix and he hadn't wanted to spend all night there. He had taken the envelope with the second payment, counted the bills before handing them to his daughter, then had a cup of tea. And only when he'd checked Danielle's dilation for the first time and used his portable ultrasound, had he realized that the foetus had not died from the injection he'd given her the day before in order to stop her heart.

Danielle had panicked, and the sedatives Rubinstein injected did not help. Liora had given her a sheet to bite on, and later she'd simply held her and let Danielle bite her hand and scratch her. She'd turned up the volume on the TV news to drown out the sobbing and shouting. The doctor's daughter had also tried to calm Danielle: he'd told her she'd given birth five times and it would be over quickly if she let go, and she'd stroked her forehead. For a moment, Liora had been unsure as to what they should do, but that moment had been brief. Rubinstein had told the police that he'd continued to deliver the baby because Liora had promised to take her to the hospital, and that it hadn't occurred to him that she wouldn't. When asked why he hadn't taken the baby to the hospital himself, he had confessed that he'd feared another legal imbroglio. He had added that if he'd suspected Liora would withhold medical treatment from the baby, he would have taken her, despite the risk, or at least informed the emergency services that there was a baby in need of urgent care at the address.

It was useless to point out his lies because it didn't matter.

Rubinstein hadn't told them even once that the baby was 'alive'. What he said was: 'the heart's activity was not stopped'.

Liora remembers that sentence very clearly, as well as the panicked look on his daughter's face. He'd hoped the heart would stop beating at birth, without him having to do anything, but that did not happen either. The baby was unwilling to die. Danielle had been paralysed with fear and had no strength to push, but the baby was so tiny that she came out without any trouble, using her own strength, as if she'd birthed herself out of the fragile body.

The doctor's daughter had handed her to Liora. Her eyes were shut and her breaths were barely audible.

Rubinstein had removed the placenta and helped Danielle fall asleep, then left without so much as glancing at the baby, contrary to what he'd told the police. It was his daughter, not him, who had made sure the baby was swaddled and told Liora she would need to eat soon and that she'd have to be incubated. Before they left, she'd urged Liora to take her to a hospital.

When the door had shut behind them, Liora had removed the swaddle and seen the baby's near-translucent skin and dark tuft of hair. If she had covered the baby's face with the sheet, it would have ended right then and she wouldn't be sitting in Edry's office now.

Over the next few days, she'd waited for that to happen. Just as the doctor had waited during labour for the heart to stop beating.

She'd taken care of Danielle, and bought tickets to France, and waited for the tiny heart to stop. She'd gone to a chemist's in north Tel Aviv, where she wasn't afraid of being recognized, and bought formula, with cash, but that had not been to keep the baby alive — rather it had been to stop her from crying while she was still breathing. When she'd got home, the flat had been dark and quiet because Danielle barely left the room and spent most of her time asleep. Liora had thought someone had taken the baby she'd left in the bedroom and thrown her out, and when she'd turned on the light and seen that the body was still in bed, swaddled in a sheet, she'd gone closer, sensing that the baby was dead. This had happened several more times in the days that followed. The sense that the baby was not breathing. That her heart had stopped working. Getting closer to the tiny body to feel her breath. The motion of her chest, and the smell. Mordechai had also examined the baby and said he didn't believe she would survive. But the baby's heart had worked, and she'd insisted on breathing, and Liora had decided there was no point waiting any longer. She had realized she would have to leave the baby at the hospital, alive. Mordechai had agreed that it was a good idea.

And when she could no longer hide him, she took for him an ark of

bulrushes, and daubed it with slime and with pitch; and she put the child
therein and laid it in the flags by the river's brink.

After that, she'd also understood what she would have to do if
she got caught.

WHEN SHE LOOKS AT David's wristwatch, it shows four o'clock.
And although Edry has finished going over the doctor's testimony,
Liora does not get up because she has one more thing to say.

Edry looks at the clock hanging over the doorway, a gift from
an insurance company, and says, 'If the facts are correct, what we
need is a different version. Do you understand what that means,
Liora?' He explains that they need a version that will work in their
favour and include as few facts as possible that the other side can
refute. 'Maybe we should say you took Danielle to that doctor just
for an exam, let's say. He was negligent when he examined her, and
his negligence was what led to the miscarriage, and that was how
the baby was born. We need something that, in the end, will come
down to your word or Danielle's word against his. Do you understand what I'm saying?'

Does he really not recognize that she is a different woman from
the one he met back then? There is no other explanation for why
he continues to talk to her as if she's stupid, when in fact, she's two
steps ahead of him.

'We could also claim that as soon as you found out the foetus
survived because of the doctor's negligence, you did everything

128

you could to keep her alive,' he continues. 'You watched over her and took care of her, as evidenced by the fact that in the end you were the one who took her to the hospital. Not him. Everything you did up to then was done to protect Danielle. You thought you were doing the right thing when you sent her to France. You know what? Maybe we really can work with that version. I have to think about it a little more, but it's important that we give them our version immediately after the holiday, so they don't file charges based on the doctor's testimony.'

That is not a version — it's the truth. But Liora does not say that either.

In the end, the baby's life was saved thanks to her.

'What are they going to charge me with?' she asks.

Edry smiles condescendingly. 'What do you mean? Are you serious? There are a million things. Illegal abortion. Harming a minor. Abandoning a minor. Any number of things.'

'What harm? What am I supposed to do when my daughter gets pregnant and asks me to help her?'

But Edry keeps talking as if she's the Liora Talyas of four years ago, frightened just by being in a lawyer's office. 'Don't play the innocent,' he says. 'You could have done a million things. Taken her to the clinic, for example. They would have done everything you did yourself for her, but in an orderly and legal way.'

His phone is still on the table, but she doesn't care if he records what she's about to say. This is the moment of transition to the next stage, and before speaking she looks at the watch on her wrist.

'You're talking as if I'm a dumb woman who doesn't know what she's doing with herself and with her daughter, but let me explain to you why they're not going to press any charges – against me or against her. Do you know why we did it that way? Why Danielle wanted everything to be secret and not go to the health clinic? Because she was raped. Because the baby was born from a rape, and my daughter was ashamed and she didn't want anyone to know what happened to her. She hid it from me, too, at first.'

She sees in his eyes and in his expression that he's in awe of her. And she knows that everyone who hears this will respond the same way. He murmurs, 'I'm very sorry to hear that, Liora. That's terrible. But perhaps if Danielle was raped, that is precisely one more reason to go to someone, to get a proper abortion. They would have done everything legally, no matter how far along the pregnancy was. And they'd have given Danielle the treatment that she—'

She interrupts him: 'Danielle didn't want to face those people and tell them what happened to her. You think she wanted to talk about it? You can't understand it, but I understood and I had to help her because I'm the only one who is her mother.'

His next question is one she predicted, and she knew before she walked into his office how she was going to answer it.

'Can you tell me who raped her?'

She says she can't.

Not yet.

Not even when he tries to scare her again.

'He must be punished, and Danielle needs to get help,' Edry says.

'I don't want to talk about it, and I don't trust you or the police. Only myself. I'll only talk if I have to do it in order to prevent my daughter from suffering because she explicitly asks me to. But for now, I don't have to.'

'You do have to. Someone hurt your daughter and you know who did it and you are required by law to give that information,' Edry insists.

Liora raises her voice. And this outburst is also planned, even though for a moment she fears she might really lose control.

He no longer looks at her derisively when she speaks. Nor does he smile. This time, he's the one who is frightened, and he cannot hide it from her.

'No one's asked me so far, so I don't have to. And anyway, I don't owe anyone anything. How many people knew David was murdered and didn't hand over the information they had? How many people knew that crane was broken before the fall, and yet they didn't say what they knew in court because it paid off for them afterwards? And now you're telling me I'm supposed to say everything I know? Let's see someone try to force me. I promise you I'll talk about what happened to Danielle at the right time in the right place. And only I know when and where that is.'

SHE'D LIED WHEN SHE told Edry she had to get home.

Mordechai was there for the girls after school and helped them with their homework, so that she could go to the cemetery, as she always did before Rosh Hashanah.

Only when she sat beside David's grave did the fear spread inside her, for the first time that day.

She allowed herself to weaken because here she could do it, and because she would need her strength for the next few days.

Before she'd left, Edry had asked, 'So I shouldn't give the police what you told me?'

She'd said not yet, but took into account that the minute she left his office he would call his friend or the bat directly.

That was fine, as far as she was concerned.

She did not talk with David at the cemetery because she knew he could not hear, and because this was not what she lacked. She talked to him all the time. Everywhere. Besides, David would not tell her what he thought about the decisions she'd made, although she felt he would have liked the way she talked with Edry and Vahaba now. He himself had never argued, just taken everything with a smile, even when someone spat on him as if he had no feelings – but that was exactly why he'd been murdered. Because of the smile, which she'd told him countless times to save for home, for the girls and for her. Because outside, in the world, it was better to walk around with a different expression. But no matter how much they screwed him over pay or how the shift managers treated him, he would ignore it and say to her, 'What's important is that we can give our girls what we want, and we can be together. What more do we need in life, I ask you? Me, from the minute I saw you, I haven't needed anything else.'

*

132

THE NEXT DAY, ROSH Hashanah Eve, she had David's parents and his sister Adina with her older daughter, the slow one, over for dinner.

In the afternoon, before the holiday traffic started, she drove Mordechai to his oldest son's home near Jerusalem, then went to pick up David's parents in Kiryat Moshe. David's father resembled David so strongly it was as if David had survived the crane accident and gone on to live to the age of eighty. He sat next to her in the car both there and back. The rasping sound he made when he dozed off reminded her of David's cigarette breaths, and then of the baby's stubborn breathing. At dinner, everyone asked her about Danielle and how she was doing and why they couldn't talk to her and when she was finally coming home, and Liora believed that she was not lying when she said Danielle would be back soon.

She sent the first email to the news reporter the next morning, on the first day of the new year, perhaps in part because she hoped it would bring them good luck. *My name is Liora Talyas and I would like to share with you some information about the baby who was left outside Wolfson Hospital, if you recall that story. I watch your coverage of criminal cases and your exposés of criminals and swindlers that the police don't get to, and I think you'll be very interested in the information we have. I know the truth about what happened with the baby and who raped the girl who was pregnant with her, and about the failures in the police investigation. Please contact me urgently.*

9

THE COCAINE THAT SUPERINTENDENT Avraham Avraham found in the hotel was taken to Ayalon Precinct Station that same evening, where it was photographed and recorded, then driven to the forensic lab at the National Headquarters in Jerusalem. In the report that Avraham wrote the next day, after less than four hours of sleep, he described how he'd entered room 203 with the forensic technician, without a search warrant but having received consent from and in the company of the front-desk clerk, Oleg Jacobowitz. The search had lasted approximately thirty minutes, during which time the drugs were found hidden in a recess in the exterior wall, underneath the windowsill. The drugs weighed just under 600 grams and were packaged in two plastic bags wrapped in aluminium foil. According to laboratory tests conducted early in the morning of Rosh Hashanah Eve, the only fingerprints on the package belonged to Rafael Chouchani, the French citizen whose body had been found at sea. Apart from the package, nothing belonging to the tourist was found in the room.

AVRAHAM AND MARIANKA'S PLANS for the day were cancelled. They were supposed to go to Tel Aviv to buy Rosh Hashanah gifts for Avraham's parents and for each other. Avraham wanted to surprise Marianka with a huge television to replace his old one, just in time for the detective movies they were planning to binge on over the holiday. Instead, Marianka phoned him from the Zara store in the Holon mall to ask what size trousers he wore and whether he preferred lilac or khaki, while he sat at the station begrudgingly writing words he did not believe for a report on an investigation that seemed to be solving itself.

The circumstances of Rafael Chouchani's death and his autopsy report, along with the evidence and information uncovered by the investigation before his death, reinforce the conjecture that Chouchani was involved in smuggling drugs from France to Israel.

Given the 600 grams of cocaine found in his hotel room, valued at hundreds of thousands of shekels; the fact that his fingerprints were on the packages; and in light of intelligence information received from France, whereby Chouchani owed money on the grey market, it is likely that he was working as a courier, possibly against his will. He landed in Israel with the smuggled substance, which was not detected at Ben Gurion Airport, arrived at the Palace Hotel, and the next morning went out to deliver the smuggled goods to the buyers, at an unknown location.

He debated whether to add that the security-camera footage showed Chouchani leaving the Palace without a bag, but decided not to. After all, he could have been carrying the drugs on his body. And perhaps that is what happened?

It is reasonable to assume that the cocaine found in the hotel is evidence Chouchani tried to steal some of the smuggled drugs from the buyers, in order to sell them himself. The buyers suspected that Chouchani was trying to cheat them (did he try to convince them that what he delivered was the entirety of the package he'd received?) and held him for a number of days. The two men who posed as his relatives at the hotel work for the criminal organization responsible for the smuggling, and they came to the Palace to search for the drugs that Chouchani allegedly stole. They did not find them. At this point, it is likely that they tried to extort information about the stolen drugs' whereabouts by means of threats and physical harm, since, according to the autopsy, Chouchani was severely beaten and suffered from internal bleeding and fractures to his fingers, toes and ribs. Chouchani apparently continued to deny the theft, perhaps because he assumed that if he confessed and disclosed the hiding place, he would be murdered. Eventually, he was drowned, or thrown into the sea while still alive but unconscious and subsequently drowned. When we find the buyers, who probably belong to one of the criminal organizations active in the drug business in the Tel Aviv area, we will be able to reach those who held Chouchani and understand the circumstances of his death.

The letters in that last sentence appeared slowly, one after the other, on the old computer monitor, as if refusing to cohere into words. They seemed to offer a reasonable explanation, but they did not provide answers to so many of the questions that still troubled Avraham, which, unlike the official report, he wrote in his black notebook.

The phone call Chouchani had made before coming to Israel, for example.

In the morning, Jules at the French Police had sent Avraham the list of Rafael Chouchani's phone calls from the weeks before his trip.

He'd talked with his daughter, Annette Mallot, twice, as she'd testified. The first call lasted approximately ten minutes and the second fewer than five, and, according to Mallot, her father had not mentioned a trip to Tel Aviv in either of them. He'd phoned the French gas company, a bookstore named Compagnie, and a number registered to a lawyer named François-Marie Aubert.

'How do you know he's a lawyer?' Avraham had asked.

Jules said he'd called him to find out, and Avraham thanked him because that was not a given.

'I can also tell you that his main area of business is inheritance and wills,' Jules had added excitedly, 'but they didn't talk because Aubert was on holiday in the Costa del Sol. And Chouchani did not leave a message. There is no record of a call from him at the office.'

The number Chouchani had dialled most often was Sara Nuwe-ima's mobile phone, but she had not answered him even once.

Three days before the flight to Tel Aviv, he'd phoned the book-store Compagnie again, and had also called a few international numbers. 'One to a number in Lebanon, one to a German number in the city of Bremen and one to a number in Israel that I can give you,' Jules summed up. When Avraham asked if he knew who the Israeli number belonged to, the French detective was surprised: 'No, but surely you can find out. Are you writing this down?'

Avraham wrote the numbers on a new page in his black notebook. Underneath the Israeli number, which had a Tel Aviv area code, he copied the precise order of Rafael Chouchani's calls that day:

14.42 – German number (Bremen, call lasted two minutes).

14.51 – Lebanese cellular number (apparently not belonging to Sara Nuweima. Call lasted six minutes).

14.59 – call to the Israeli number (eight minutes), and shortly after, at 15.14 – call to Air France flight reservation number. Immediately after that, at 15.22 – another call to the same number in Israel.

What Avraham should have done, after thanking Jules, was phone the Tel Aviv Central Unit's Narcotics Division and give one of the investigators there the Israeli number, which must be that of whoever had ordered the drugs. Once the drugs had been found, Saban had made it clear to Avraham that the investigation was to be continued there. What he wanted to do was call the number himself, and he began doing just that, but stopped after dialling the first four digits. Instead, he phoned Ilanit, who was surprised to hear his voice on the eve of Rosh Hashanah. Avraham apologized for disturbing her while she was preparing for the holiday, and asked her to find out who the number belonged to. When she got back to him it turned out that this time he'd made the right decision.

'I don't understand. What do you mean the number doesn't exist?' he asked.

'It doesn't exist, Avi. As in, no such thing. That number isn't in the phone company's records. But something's not right because when I tried dialling it there was no message saying I'd reached an invalid number. It just sounded like an ordinary line, but no one answered. Which is very weird, don't you think? Do you want me to keep trying it? If it's an office or something, it makes sense that they wouldn't pick up on the holiday eve.'

Was this the first moment he thought Annette Mallot might not have been wrong when she said her father worked for the Mossad? Too many details written in his notebook could have supported her claim: the two passports, the two names, the Lebanese phone number, Sara Nuweima, who might also have disappeared, and now a phone number in Israel that was not in any records but did exist. Keren had told him expressly that Chouchani was not a Mossad agent and that the organization took a dim view of anyone posing as such, and Avraham had no reason not to believe her, but more and more details made it hard for him to accept the story he himself had composed in his report.

The silence in the almost-empty station was welcome, as it allowed him to be alone with his thoughts – at first, in his office, at the open window, and then sitting on the wide steps leading up to the station, as he used to when he smoked. The only police officers who walked past him were traffic controllers and volunteers setting off for an evening shift on roads filling up with families on their way to holiday dinners.

When he phoned Annette Mallot, he did not tell her anything about the drugs found in her father's hotel room.

He asked how she was, and she said she was still in shock.

He could hear it in her voice.

'I don't understand what happened to him. Because he didn't willingly go into the water and drown. That simply isn't possible. Someone drowned him. And he was afraid that was going to happen. And I think I know who did it. If it had happened here, I would know who to go to, but there . . . I'm afraid I'll never know.'

Avraham assured her that he'd called precisely so that that wouldn't happen. And he warned her ahead of time that he had an unusual request.

'Can you go into his home?' he asked. And he felt that his peculiar request was, in fact, what made her trust him.

It was three hours by train from Strasbourg to Paris.

Annette Mallot did not have a key to her father's flat, and to the best of her knowledge he hadn't left one with the concierge or a neighbour. Avraham suggested she call a locksmith. 'Tell him your father isn't answering and you're worried, so you have to break in.' There was a silence on the other end of the line, until the man whispered in German, and then Mallot asked, 'What would you like me to look for?'

Anything that will help me know if your father was a smuggler, as all the evidence attests, or a Mossad man, as you think.

'Letters, diaries, notebooks,' he said. 'If you can get into his computer and look for emails, that would also be excellent. And maybe old mobile phones?'

*

141

IN THE WINDOWS OF the tall blocks of flats that had sprung up in recent years opposite the Ayalon Precinct Station, lights began to go on, and sounds of the first holiday prayers came from the balconies.

Avraham had to leave.

To silence the internal voice that urged him to delete everything he'd written since that morning in the official report. To go home.

Had he lived in France, he would have left the station, gone to 89 Boulevard de Picpus and found a way to get into Chouchani's flat himself.

He sent the report to Benny Saban, to the Tel Aviv Central Unit's Narcotics Division director, and to the district commander's secretary, as Saban had asked him to, then drove straight to his parents'. He was amazed to discover that although the white cloth was still on the table, the dishes had been cleared. His mother was showing Marianka photographs from her days at boarding school, for the umpteenth time. In the kitchen, a plate of food sat waiting for him: delicious meatballs in lukewarm red sauce, rice and a wilting salad.

'You seriously didn't wait for me to eat?' Avraham asked.

'Well, what did you expect?' his mother said. 'Dad was hungry. And your wife hadn't eaten since this morning. We saved you some food, and we'll have the honey cake together with our coffee.'

His father was dozing in the armchair, with the TV on. When he fell asleep, Avraham carried him to bed.

All this was very far removed from how he'd imagined this day, apart from the way it ended, with him and Marianka sipping white wine on their balcony at home, listening to the sounds coming from lingering holiday dinners in nearby buildings. Marianka asked why he wasn't going to the synagogue, and Avraham said he never did.

'You know, I've never heard the shofar being blown,' Marianka said. 'Why don't we go together tomorrow?'

Avraham replied, 'I don't think they let Catholics into synagogues.'

She said simply, 'Then I'll go in disguise.'

'So what did you do on the High Holy Days when you were growing up?' she asked.

'Nothing much. We sat in traffic. That's what I remember. On the holiday eve and the next day. We took trips no one wanted to take.'

In truth, that was not all he remembered. Later, when they were in bed, he told her more. His memories of the Holy Days were of his father being home for a long time. Especially over Rosh Hashanah. Before the holiday dinner they would go for a walk in Holon, just him and his father, past the synagogues filling up with people, although they never went in. They would slow down to listen to the sounds, and his father would ask, 'So, how do you sum up the year we've had, Avi?' Avraham never knew what to say. 'Has your year been good, or not great?' his father would press.

Most of them had not been very good, back then.

He didn't say this to his father, nor did he ask him how his year was, and now it was too late because his father couldn't answer, and his thoughts, if he had any, were trapped in silence and reflected in his desperate looks.

'And what do you wish yourself for the new year?' his father would ask.

Avraham would answer, 'Sweets.'

Once or twice, he remembered, his father had tried to be witty: 'I wish for myself, and for you, that the coming year will be longer than all the years that came before it. Do you think there's a chance of that happening?'

The next day, Avraham and Marianka stayed in bed late. They watched *The Long Goodbye* and *Chinatown* and *The Lady Vanishes* on the old television, and Avraham tried to read the Leonardo Sciascia detective novel that Marianka had given him, but he couldn't concentrate because he kept thinking about Chouchani and expecting a phone call from Annette Mallot to tell him what she'd found in her father's flat. On the second day of the holiday, they cooked together all morning because Marianka had invited Esty for lunch. It was the first time Avraham had met Vahaba outside of work, and it was strange. She wore a green dress and had make-up on, and Avraham, who opened the door wearing tracksuit bottoms and the vest he'd slept in, apologized and hurried to his room to change into the khaki trousers and an orange shirt he'd received as gifts.

The closeness between Marianka and Esty surprised him, although he knew they'd become friendly. Vahaba's openness with Marianka; the light on her face – perhaps it was her make-up, but still, it was a light he'd never noticed before. With him things were completely different: Vahaba barely looked at him when she spoke to him at the station because of what he interpreted as extreme awkwardness or shyness.

Salads, a cheese platter and two quiches were set out on the kitchen table, but they ate on the balcony and tried not to talk shop. Vahaba said she was considering moving out of her parents' flat, hiring a Filipino carer to live with them and renting a place nearby, so she could see them every day. Marianka said her parents were thinking of leaving Brussels and moving back to Slovenia.

'Why don't they come and live here with you? You're an only child, aren't you?' Vahaba asked.

Avraham pictured himself opening the bathroom door in the morning and finding Bojan Milanich in there. There was no chance of that happening because Bojan and Anika had informed Marianka that they weren't even willing to visit Israel.

'I'm sure they'll come when there are grandchildren,' Vahaba said, and Marianka looked at Avraham and smiled because that was something they hadn't discussed.

Perhaps because of the silence, which Avraham found hard to tolerate, he asked Vahaba if there was anything new on the Liora Talyas case. Her smile vanished as she told him that Talyas' lawyer had informed Benny Saban that the pregnancy was the result of rape. Talyas was unwilling to tell the police who the rapist was, and Vahaba was supposed to ask her in for further questioning after the holiday to find out why and force her to give them the information. It wasn't the boy Danielle had briefly dated, whose paternity test had come back negative, and Vahaba thought it might be the man who was in a relationship with Liora and sometimes stayed over with her. He would be called in for another interview after the holiday, and they would run a paternity test. If it was him, that might explain why the girl was sent to France and why they'd tried to hide the pregnancy.

'Can't we talk to the daughter?' Avraham asked, and was surprised when Vahaba told him Danielle Talyas had been questioned the day before, in France, by the Israel Police's attaché in Paris, and had also refused to testify to the rape. This was the third time the two investigations that had begun on the same day had intersected, but Avraham still had no inkling of where their convergence would eventually lead him.

'You mean Idit Gerti?' he asked.

'I think you should interrogate her, Esty,' Marianka said, though she looked at Avraham. 'It's your case. You met her mother, you visit the baby almost every day. She might talk to you. Can't you send Esty to Paris, Avi? I could go along to interpret if necessary. What do you say?'

Was it because he was so immersed in the Chouchani disappearance that he hadn't been aware that Vahaba was visiting the baby every day? He hadn't even gone to see her once. 'How is the baby?' he asked.

Vahaba said she was improving. She was gaining weight and responding to stimuli but still not breathing on her own, and they didn't know how much damage had been caused by the digoxin, the premature birth and the delayed care. 'There's a young nurse there named Shira, a religious girl, who takes care of that baby as if she were her daughter or her little sister. She sits with her after her shifts are over, prays and watches her for hours, like she believes her eyes have the power to heal the baby.'

And this was not the final revelation because Marianka added,

'And you wouldn't believe how beautiful she is, Avi. She has such a tiny, delicate face.'

Avi hadn't known anything about that either.

Marianka told Avraham she'd gone to the hospital with Vahaba to see the baby, but he still did not grasp how touched she was by the story until later that night, before they fell asleep. 'Did you know that no one's named her?' she said.

Avraham asked whom she was talking about because his thoughts had gone back to Rafael Chouchani and the report he'd written, which he would have to present the next morning at the branch commanders' meeting.

'The baby. She doesn't have a name. If Esty goes to France, she can ask the girl what she wants to name her.'

Vahaba had clearly said she wouldn't go to question Danielle Talyas because she couldn't leave her parents, but Marianka wouldn't let it go. When Avraham asked why she'd gone to see the baby, she said, 'Not for the reasons you think, Avi.' He pressed her to explain, and she replied, 'Maybe for the same reason you can't stop thinking about the tourist who drowned? Because that baby is a person who was left alone in the world.'

Was that the reason Avraham kept imagining what must have been the final hours of Chouchani's life? The last hours of his freedom, before he left for a place he thought he may not return from. He'd boiled water in the kettle and made himself a cup of coffee, opened the window and looked at the few rooms where lights were still on in the building across the way. And he had not—Avraham was convinced—hidden any cocaine in any recess under any window.

In fact, the main reason Avraham couldn't stop thinking about Chouchani was one Marianka knew nothing about: his sense that behind everything that had been uncovered about the man with dizzying speed, there was a truth that not only had yet to be revealed, but was covered with layers of falsehoods.

At the branch commanders' meeting the next morning, Benny Saban gave an update on the drugs Avraham had found, complimented his work and reported that the Narcotics Division had no clear direction yet as to which crime organization was responsible for smuggling the cocaine and murdering the French courier, as if these were incontrovertible facts. To further clarify to Avraham that the case was closed, and certainly no longer under his jurisdiction, Saban added that the district commander had given authorization for the body to be flown to France.

Avraham considered voicing his doubts, but this was not the right time because he had no proof. He was the only person in the room who had looked at Chouchani's grey face up close and recognized the fear he believed it still showed, yet everyone was convinced they completely understood who the man was and what had happened to him, and they were all in a hurry to get rid of the body – to bury it, along with the investigation, and move on to the next case.

Towards the end of the meeting, Ilana, who'd ignored Avraham again when he'd walked into the room, asked him if there was any news on the baby. When he relayed the suspicion that the baby had been the result of a rape that had not been reported to the police, and that Vahaba would be questioning Liora Talyas again later that day, Ilana said she'd been contacted by a crime reporter and would be glad to receive updates from him. 'Keep me in the loop,' she said, as if she'd been appointed his direct supervisor rather than the precinct spokesperson.

During the meeting, Avraham received two unexpected messages. The first was a complete surprise because he'd forgotten all about the letter:

Hi Avi, this is Gary Lis. I wanted you to know that we're still looking for the letter Ilana left you. The problem is that we found the envelope, but it was empty. We don't know what happened — maybe Ilana took the letter out to add something. Anyway, I hope we can still find it because there are some papers we haven't gone through yet. When we do, we'll let you know. Other than that, I hope everything is well with you and your wife. Shana tova.

Then there was a voicemail from Keren at the Prime Minister's office, who seemed to already know everything about Chouchani:

'I heard you found the body of the French citizen who was posing as our employee,' she said in her soft voice, 'and that you found out he was a drug smuggler. If you have any information about the circumstances of him posing as a Mossad agent, or where he introduced himself as one, I'd appreciate an update. And congratulations on the speedy resolution, of course. Great work. When you uncover more details about the smuggling network he belonged to, please let us know, so we can find out if they're continually pretending to be our agents and if there are other impersonation cases. That's it. Oh, and a belated happy new year!'

But Avraham had no information about the circumstances under which Chouchani had posed as a Mossad agent, nor about the places where he'd claimed to be one. On the contrary. Chouchani had not told anyone that was his job. In fact, Avraham was increasingly sceptical that Chouchani had smuggled the drugs, even though Keren, just like Benny Saban, was treating this as a firm fact. A few hours later, when he heard Annette Mallot's startled voice, Avraham was convinced he was right.

When she phoned, he was in his office, wondering whether to dial the non-existent number Chouchani had called before flying to Tel Aviv.

'Inspector Avraham,' Mallot said, 'do you have a moment to talk?'

He hoped she would tell him she'd found a goodbye letter from her father which would explain everything. Or an email Chouchani had sent or received that would shed some light on why he'd really gone to Tel Aviv.

But Mallot did not tell him either of these things, and her tone of voice gave away her fear.

'Someone broke into his flat. It's been turned completely upside down. Nothing is in its place.'

Wasn't that exactly what had happened in room 203 at the Palace? Someone had beaten Avraham to it.

'Did they take anything? Could you tell?' Avraham asked.

'I don't know,' Annette said. 'I haven't been there for ages. Besides, I don't know exactly what he owns. Is there any way to tell if someone took something?'

Avraham said that the only way was to find someone familiar with the contents of Chouchani's flat. Sara Nuweima, for example. 'Can you take photographs and send them to me?' he asked, then added, a moment later, 'Did you report the burglary to the police?'

Annette Mallot said she hadn't yet. She'd left the flat as soon as she realized it had been burgled, and was afraid to go back to take photographs, even though there was no one there now. Of that she was sure.

'Then can you hold off letting them know for the time being?' he asked. 'It would really help us, Annette. So we can find out if what happened to him really is connected to his former job. You understand me, don't you?'

ILANIT TOLD HIM VAHABA was in an interrogation room with Liora Talyas, but he asked her to tell Esty to come to his office urgently.

Vahaba looked upset, but he did not ask why; he only said that he wanted to question Danielle Talyas. At first, she couldn't understand exactly what he was asking.

Avraham explained that they would tell Saban it was an urgent investigation requirement that had come up because of the rape allegation and the possibility that the rapist was the mother's boyfriend, who she was protecting. He would go to Paris and question Danielle Talyas, while Vahaba stayed here to interrogate the mother, Liora, and they might even be able to conduct a video confrontation between the two.

Vahaba still couldn't understand what was going on, and he couldn't explain it to her. 'That's fine, Avi,' she said. 'I can't go anyway, and I wanted us to work on this investigation together from the start. Also, it looks like the case is even more complicated now. Liora is denying that this Mordechai guy touched her daughter, and she says the rapist is a young Arab from Jaffa. Will Marianka go with you?'

He hadn't thought about that, but it was an excellent idea.

He wasn't yet sure the trip would be authorized when he phoned Annette Mallot, who was on her way back to Strasbourg, and told her he was planning to come to Paris as soon as possible. In his mind, he was already in the flat on Boulevard de Picpus, but first there was something he had to do. He drove his white Hyundai towards Tel Aviv, left it in the car park by the beach, then crossed the street and went into a convenience store on Herbert Samuel Road, which ran parallel to the promenade. He explained to the startled shopkeeper that he wasn't there to search the shop: he'd lost his mobile phone somewhere nearby and wanted to call it in case anyone had found it. The shopkeeper gave Avraham his phone and said, 'No problem, pal. Use it as much as you want.'

The first time he dialled, there was no answer, nor the second time. But when he tried a third time, someone picked up. He walked outside with the shopkeeper's phone and stood some distance away, on a heavily trafficked street, and hoped the person on the other end of the line couldn't hear the cars or the roar of the sea. The voice that answered the supposedly non-existent number that Chouchani had phoned before flying to Israel was a deep female one, and she spoke to Avraham in Hebrew with a foreign accent.

'Good afternoon, I'm the DHL delivery guy,' Avraham said. 'I'm here on your street but I don't know the house number. Are you home?'

'Which last name are you looking for? We're not expecting any packages.'

'What do you mean? I have a package here for you. Something you ordered from overseas, or a gift someone sent you. I don't know. What name have I reached, ma'am?'

The woman hesitated before answering. 'This is the Ben-Hayats. Who do you need?'

He hung up immediately.

He handed the phone back to the shopkeeper, who asked, 'Did you find it, pal?'

'I think so,' Avraham replied.

10

JUST AS LIORA HAD expected, Edry did the job.

Once again it was unclear which side he was on, but this time she was using him instead of the other way round. He'd reported the rape the second Liora left his office, that was obvious, and the phone calls she received over the holiday confirmed it.

The calls were also a sign that it was time to enter the final stage. And that everything was still under her control.

In the empty hours of the holiday, she searched for the right words to use when she met with the news reporter: my goal was to keep my daughter safe. Everything I did was to protect her. Maybe I should have taken the baby to the hospital earlier, that's possible, but I'm the one who took care of her after the abortion and I saved her life. The Israel Police is persecuting the victim, and not for the first time. Instead of protecting Danielle and punishing the person who hurt her, they're interrogating us, inflicting more trauma on our family after the injustice they committed against my husband.

It was wrong to conflate the two cases, but David was clearly going to be mentioned in the news. His name, his life story and his death would be brought up again, and they might even show his picture, the one with Danielle at the dolphin reef in Eilat, which Liora had given the reporters back then.

She spends the second day of Rosh Hashanah with Eden and Ofrit, and they have the holiday lunch at Michal and Maxim's.

There is no talk about the investigation. The atmosphere is tense, mainly because Maxim keeps giving Liora hostile looks, even though he is more familiar with interrogation rooms than anyone. He spends most of the time on the balcony with his brother, smoking. Eden and Ofrit play with Michal's baby and then make a TikTok video with him. When the phone rings in her bag, Liora has a hunch that it's Danielle, even though the number is unidentified. She goes into the bedroom, where the bed is covered with piles of bras and men's underwear, and when she says 'Hello' and no one answers, she is positive it's her daughter. 'Danielle? Is that you?' she asks.

After a pause, Danielle answers, 'Yes.'

Since Liora hasn't heard her voice for a long time, she has to get used to it, to recognize it as Danielle's.

But then again, that's how Danielle always is on the phone, as well as in the few conversations they have at home. Most of the time she keeps quiet. Answers with a word or two. Hides her face with her hair, or with her hands, which are covered in scratches from the cat that never leaves her room.

'What's wrong? Why are you calling?' Another long silence. She asks if Danielle is using the cheap phone she bought her, as they agreed.

Danielle says she is. Then she tells Liora that two days ago a policeman came to Marcelle and Ronny's home with a summons. He said she would be questioned at the request of the Israel Police, and that an Israeli policewoman would be present. Danielle was not a suspect in anything but was being asked to testify regarding a crime committed by someone in Israel, and that he couldn't say anything more about it. If she wanted, she was entitled to ask Marcelle or Ronny or a lawyer appointed by them to be present at the questioning.

Liora is surprised: 'Two days ago? And you're only calling me now? So has the questioning happened yet?'

Danielle replies, 'Yes. Today.'

Although there is no chance of her saying much, Liora tries to get some more information out of Danielle, but she only hears most of the details later, from Marcelle, who sounds a little stressed. Danielle does say that she was asked about the rape and that the policewoman explicitly mentioned Mordechai and asked if he'd touched her. She also tried to find out if Danielle was being threatened – if Mordechai was threatening her, or someone from her family or his. They didn't ask her about Amir Souen, and this was the only thing she wanted to tell Liora. After that, it becomes even harder to get anything out of her, and she obviously wants the conversation to end.

'And you didn't say anything about him, right?'

Again, no reply.

It was the Israeli policewoman who actually questioned Danielle. The French one wasn't even in the room. For a moment, Liora suspects they sent the bat to France, but Marcelle later describes a woman in her fifties, with light hair and blue eyes.

'I asked them to talk to you,' Danielle says.

'So she didn't pressure you?' asks Liora.

Danielle says no, and adds, 'But she left a phone number for Marcelle. Marcelle and Ronny don't know, do they?'

Not yet. For the time being, Marcelle knows exactly what she needs to know in order to agree to host Danielle: that Danielle got pregnant and had an abortion, and that she needs time and a quiet place to recover. Later that day, when Marcelle asks Liora what rape the police are talking about, Liora says she doesn't want to discuss it on the phone and she'll explain soon.

'Did you go to the doctor? Did he check and make sure everything's okay?' Liora asks. Liora can't hear the answer, so she asks again. Danielle says yes, louder this time. And what Liora finds discouraging about the call is that Danielle doesn't ask anything. She doesn't want to know how her sisters are or how the holiday's going, she doesn't even ask when she can talk to her friends or when she can come home. She is not getting stronger. And it's not clear whether she's not asking about the baby because she's forgotten about her, or precisely because she remembers and is afraid to ask.

'A few more days, my girl. Just a few days and it'll all be over,'

Liora says, and she can feel Danielle's powerlessness weakening her, too. She needs the call to be over. 'I know it's hard for you, but I'll bring you home soon, okay? Stay strong for me and for Dad, all right?'

When Liora goes back to the living room, Michal is clearing dishes from the table. Perhaps because she's gained weight since giving birth and must weigh over seventy kilos, Liora thinks about how this woman, with her thick arms and heavy thighs, was once the size of the baby. That she gave birth to this woman when she herself was Danielle's age, perhaps a few months older, and that she'd managed to raise her, even though things weren't easy.

What a difference there is between Liora at seventeen and the voiceless girl she just talked to on the phone. The girl who barely managed to push a tiny baby out of her body because she did not have the strength to fight for what she wanted.

Liora also wasn't as strong at that age as she is now, but she did know what she wanted and she was determined enough to insist on what was important to her, even when it was difficult. That is the story she retold countless times to Danielle, and before that to Michal, especially after David's death. She'd also tried to write it down so that she could read it in the cemetery at the funeral, or at the memorial service, but she hadn't been able to.

I will never forget the way your father looked at me the first time. That look he had in his eyes.

How hard it is to believe that she's no longer the same age. That she is over forty, and that her girls are the age she once was. That she will not relive those years. They are so tangible to her that it doesn't make sense that she will never be able to experience them again.

They'd gone to a relative's wedding. She with her parents, he with his wife. And from the moment he saw her, it was clear that he wanted her – wanted to talk to her, to get to know her, to touch her. That was what was special about his look: people had looked at her before – because she had the slender body of a dancer, even though she didn't dance – but she'd never been looked at with such hunger.

David was thirty-four years old. He had no children. Liora knew his wife, Sima, because she was a distant relative, the daughter of her father's cousin. He did not talk to her at the wedding, perhaps because Sima was there or because of Liora's parents, but three days later he was waiting for her after school. He drove past in his pick-up truck as she walked out, honked his horn and stopped, and when he saw her walking with Marcelle, he beckoned her over. He said he was working in the area and had spotted her, and he asked if she'd like a ride home or to get something to eat. Ali sat next to him in the truck, which was full of sacks of cement and paint cans and heavy work tools, and the two of them smoked the whole way. On the seat that Ali cleared for her were packets of cheap cigarettes, half-empty bottles of Sprite and CDs. The upholstery was ripped and faded and covered with dog hair and cigarette burns. And although David wasn't all that old, there were silver hairs in his stubble, which even her father didn't have yet.

Liora didn't want anything to eat, and David stopped to let her off at the corner of her street. He said he hadn't just happened to see her, and asked if she understood that, and she laughed and said of course she did, even though up to that moment she'd been convinced it was a coincidence.

'*I came because I couldn't stop thinking about you since the wedding and I had to see you,*' he told me. '*And if you don't believe me, ask Ali. He'll tell you I haven't been able to talk about anything else since the wedding.*' And do you know what I told him? I said, '*Well, now you've seen me.*' And he clammed up and didn't know how to go on because your father is not good with words — more with acts, with his hands and the paints he mixes and the things he builds us. Each of you has something in your room that he built with his hands, especially for you. And because he didn't say anything, I said things instead — and just think how old I was then, only a little over sixteen. I said to him, '*I bet you're going to ask if you can come and see me again, aren't you?*' And your father lit a cigarette and smiled his smile and said, '*How did you know? That's exactly what I wanted to ask.*'

Could Danielle conceivably talk to a man with such confidence? Not today, and probably not in a few years either. Maybe not even Michal, who leans over the table to slice a cake, her new rolls of belly fat visible.

Two days later they slept together for the first time, in a guest house not far from Tel Aviv, and a week later David told her he wanted to leave his wife and be with her, despite her not having said a word about that. When she told him she was pregnant, he said he would ask Sima for a divorce and that he was going to marry her and they would have the child, even though it would obviously cause tension in the family. And since David wasn't good with words like she was, Liora told him what to say to her father and how to tell Sima he didn't want to live with her. She fearlessly absorbed the phone calls from Sima and her sisters, who cursed and threatened her, and warned they would hurt her and the baby, and predicted that David would do the same thing to her one day. And the most amazing thing was that she had all that power, even though she wasn't sure she wanted to get married and have a child.

David left home and moved into a friend's apartment, and then he went back to his parents' house. She left school and moved in with him, even before he got divorced, so that his mother could help with the pregnancy and the birth. There was one truth that Liora did not tell anyone, and she wasn't even sure David knew: she did not love him then the way she loved him later. Even standing under the *chuppah* at the wedding hall, she was not happy. She envied Marcelle, who had nothing in her belly and whose worries amounted to exams and money for new clothes. That was a period when Liora got depressed, too, and sometimes even wanted to empty herself of everything, just like Danielle did. But unlike Danielle, Liora had a strength that prevented her from cracking, and on the outside she was always fine. It was only around Danielle's birth, seven years after she and David met, that everything changed and she understood that David was the man she must stay with. Along with the love that burst out of her came the fear that David would die before she did, and the knowledge that she would not be able to prevent his early death. The cigarettes he refused to stop smoking would take him from her, or his job, or his driving late at night after a long day of work. When he was on a job far away, she left the window open so that she could hear his pick-up truck when he came home late at night. And she was so relieved when he told her, at the age of fifty, that he wasn't going to freelance any more and had taken a regular job with a construction company in the Tel Aviv area because he was sick of worrying about his income from month to month, and so that he could spend more time with her and the girls.

Less than two years later, she caressed his shattered hand.

THEY GOT HOME AFTER five, and Liora tidied up and washed the floors, in case the reporter wanted to come over the next day after their meeting. The calls from Mordechai and the bat came as soon as Rosh Hashanah was over, one after the other. Mordechai phoned after nine and said they'd asked him in for another interview, and when Liora said there was nothing to worry about because she was going to tell them everything tomorrow, he said he wasn't worried.

'They'll ask you if you raped her, so don't get scared. Do you understand how sick she is, that police detective?'

Mordechai said he had no problem because you could not sully a man whose hands were clean. He'd spent the whole holiday at the synagogue, and you could hear it in his voice, which was quiet and tender, and she wished she'd gone with the girls to prayers because it might have calmed her, too.

'So they didn't ask you to come in?' he asked. Liora said she was sure the bat would call later that evening, and Mordechai said,

'Maybe they'll interview us together. And tomorrow you're seeing the woman from TV, right?'

She was. The next afternoon, at Caffe Caffe in the Bat Yam mall. And if the reporter wanted to move quickly, she might come over to their apartment afterwards. That would be the time and place when she told everything, in the hope that it would be enough to save Danielle and herself.

The reporter had answered her email message three hours after it was sent, even though it was a holiday: *Liora, I'd be happy to listen to your story and help you, if I can. Thank you for writing. Would you like to talk on the phone first? Or meet straight away? Tell me what works for you. Sigal.* Liora had written back to say they could meet the next day, preferably in the afternoon or evening because she worked at a kindergarten in the morning.

Everything I did was to protect my daughter; no mother I know would have acted any differently. But instead of protecting the girl and punishing the person who raped her, they're interrogating her and me and other relatives and humiliating us all.

As if the plan was more perfect than she herself had realized, or as if someone up there was helping her to implement it, the phone call from Vahaba came a moment or two after she hung up with Mordechai. She told the policewoman, 'I've been expecting you, Esty. I know what you want but I'm not going to say any more than the lawyer did. I won't confirm or deny. I'm just repeating that it's not us you should be investigating. Definitely not Mordechai. We're not the criminals in this story, we're the victims.'

Vahaba was surprised by how prepared Liora was. It was the same the next day, in the interrogation room. When she said, 'We have obtained information that Danielle was the victim of a rape and that's how she got pregnant,' Liora stopped her: 'I wonder how you obtained it, Esty? In my opinion, you should be paying my lawyer a salary. He's working for you, after all.' She smiled, and then went on, 'What about Mordechai? Has he already been here today or are you torturing him after you finish with me?'

Vahaba was obliged to show Liora empathy because of the rape, and so instead of responding, she said quietly, 'The thing is that in order to investigate, we have to understand what really happened, and Danielle is not cooperating. I assume you know she was questioned in Paris? I'm sure you've spoken with her.'

Liora smiled again because the bat finally understood that she was running the show.

'Danielle refused to testify that she was raped. And since you are also unwilling to give me any details, I'm doing what I can. But for now, I have no evidence of a rape or of the rapist's identity. I'm giving Mordechai a paternity test today, and perhaps Maxim, too, Michal's husband, unless you help me and confirm that there was a rape and give me the rapist's name. Beyond that, I can't do much without you and without Danielle.'

'What's your problem with Mordechai? Can you explain that? Go and look for the rapist somewhere else,' she said, and she knew this was her first admission, even if indirectly, that there had been a rape. The bat gazed up at her with her moist eyes, which made her look as if she'd been crying or was about to, and delivered another speech meant to convince Liora that they were on the same side.

'Liora, I want to help Danielle. I really do. And rape is a crime that the police take extremely seriously. I certainly do. But I need you to share information with me so that I'll have something to work with.'

From the minute the speech began, Liora felt she could use it to pretend she was breaking down and give her the name.

Can you see with your eyes that I'm softening?

One more minute and I'll give in and tell you everything.

You can go on.

'Because I'll tell you what I know so far, okay? I'll share everything I have with you, even though I'm not supposed to do that, just to show you that I'm on your side and I want to help. You can ask your lawyer if I'm supposed to tell you what I'm saying now, and you'll see that what I'm doing is not above board. My assumption is that Danielle was raped, and that the two of you, perhaps because you're afraid to talk about the rape, perhaps because you were threatened, tried to hide both the pregnancy and the rape. That's why you had the abortion and hid the baby, and why you sent Danielle to your friend Marcelle. So that she would not get hurt. I believe you did it to protect your daughter. I really do. But my belief is not enough. I have to provide evidence that will prove everything in court, and for that I need the name of whoever hurt Danielle so that I can gather incriminating evidence against him and prove that he hurt your daughter. Are you willing to help me with that?'

This was the moment. Liora shook her head, and the bat sighed.

'Well, I don't understand you, but it's your decision. Wait here while I do the test on Mordechai,' she said, and stood up.

And then Liora shouted, 'Why don't you leave Mordechai alone? I suggest you run a test on a boy called Amir Souen, okay? Find out if he's the father, not Mordechai.'

'Amir Souen? That's the father's name?'

'Do the test. Let's see what you find out. It's not my job.'

'Can you give me his address? Or a phone number?'

'Do you want me to go to Jaffa for you and handcuff him, too?'

IN THE AFTERNOON, AT the café, the mood was completely different. The reporter was late because she couldn't find the mall, and Waze sent her all over Bat Yam. Liora ordered a strong latté and an egg-and-aubergine sandwich while she waited. She assumed the police were already at Amir Souen's home and might even have arrested him, partly based on the fact that they'd released Mordechai without giving him a paternity test or asking any more questions. When the reporter walked into the café, Liora stood up and signalled to her that she was the person she was meeting, and Sigal held out a tiny, damp, very cold hand, and apologized for being late.

What surprised Liora was not the fact that she looked older in real life than on screen, but that she was only a centimetre or two taller than Liora. When they sat facing each other, Sigal did not strike Liora as any more self-confident or strong than her, only more put together. A few of the people in the café recognized her and looked at them, but Sigal paid little attention, as if their gazes came nowhere near her. She ordered tea with ginger, mint and lemon, then said to Liora, 'You wrote to me about the baby. You said you know some details about the investigation, and it's important for me to tell you that I've made my own enquiries and I know you were questioned under caution several times at Ayalon Precinct. By the way, do you remember who interviewed you? Could it have been the Investigations and Intelligence Branch Commander, Avi Avraham?'

'I was the one who left the baby there,' she said straight away, ignoring Sigal's question. 'I didn't admit it at first, but in the end I did tell them. And I'm willing to confess to it again, even on camera, and explain to everyone why I did it.'

'Okay. Explain it to me first.'

'The baby isn't mine, as they suspected at first. She's my daughter Danielle's, who is sixteen. I told them that, too. She got raped that she hid from me and from everyone, and she only told me when she was six months pregnant. Maybe even seven. She wasn't showing until then, or only slightly, so she hid it and no one noticed, including me. When we tried to get her an abortion, everything went wrong and the abortion was not successful. Perhaps I should have taken the baby to the hospital a few days earlier, but we didn't want to hurt her. I took care of the baby the whole time, at home. I saved her life. We just couldn't keep her and raise her.'

The reporter touched Liora's hand, and just then the waitress came over with her tea.

'I'm very sorry to hear about what happened to your daughter,

Liora,' she said. 'I'm sorry for you, and mostly for Danielle. It's tragic that women – girls – are ashamed to say that they were raped, as if it's their fault, and they hide it even from their parents. Where is Danielle now?'

'She's in France. Recovering. But she'll be back. And she'd be happy to talk to you and tell you what happened. She'll tell you everything.'

'Have you already told the police everything you just told me?'

'Of course. I also told them who the boy who hurt her is. But I want to tell you something else. The rapist will probably deny everything. He'll say they were in a relationship.'

'That's what they always say.'

'Exactly. So I just want you to know that you can't believe him. Maybe he didn't do anything to my daughter by force, but he raped her. Rape is not just using force, I'm sure you know that.'

'Of course. Anything Danielle didn't want, that's rape. Even if there's no use of force. Can you tell me how old he is? Because if he's an adult and she was a minor, then it might be a crime even if she did consent.'

'But she didn't. She didn't want him. I can tell you that for sure.'

'What do the police say about his version of events? Do you know?' the reporter asked.

Liora said she didn't: 'I'm not sure they're even questioning him.'

'Why not?'

'I don't know. Ask them. They keep questioning me, questioning my relatives. We were burned by the police once before, about something that happened to my husband. I don't know if anyone updated you on that story. If you'd like, I can tell you about it. And we feel that once again they're persecuting us instead of punishing the person who hurt Danielle.'

The waitress was far away and no one was staring at them any more. The reporter's pink mobile phone was on the table. And since Liora's words were ready, from the moment Sigal turned on the recording app they came out naturally and without any confusion, and Liora could see that Sigal identified with what she was saying. She thought about the bat, about how Sigal would ask her to respond, perhaps even on camera, and she could imagine her stammering, trying to hide her rheumy eyes.

Sigal said, 'Then let's start. I'm just letting you know that the recording is only for my own use and I promise not to share it or any part of it with anyone, unless you give me your explicit permission to do so. All right? Let's go, the phone is recording.'

The prayer Liora said in her heart was the same one she'd whispered to herself in the interrogation room when it all started.

Because the Lord was with him; and that which he did, the Lord made it to prosper.

And as she'd planned to, she started with the day when Danielle came to her in tears and said she hadn't had her period for three months.

Part Three

Paris, by the River

EL AL FLIGHT 323 landed in Paris at 6 a.m., and four hours later Avraham was sitting with Annette Mallot in a café near her father's flat. As far as he was concerned, this meeting was the purpose of his trip, but no one knew it was occurring. Not Benny Saban, who had authorized the trip; not Chief Superintendent Idit Gerti, who'd sent a driver to meet Avraham and Marianka at the airport and take them to their hotel; not even Marianka. After leaving their suitcases in their room and having breakfast, Avraham told Marianka he was going to meet Gerti at the embassy, when in fact he descended into the depths of the Métro at Vavin Station, got on line 4, and switched to line 1 towards Château de Vincennes, following the directions he'd written down in his black notebook before leaving.

Nor did he tell anyone what Annette Mallot shared with him at the café. Or what he saw in the flat on Boulevard de Picpus. But after talking with Chouchani's daughter and searching his flat, Avraham knew he'd been right to come to Paris. And that if he did not act carefully and wisely, he might pay a high price for his decision.

THE TRIP HAD BEEN authorized promptly, as soon as Benny Saban found out that the abandoned-baby case had turned into a rape case, which might reach the media because of the parties' ages and the suspect's identity. Ilana Assayag warned him that she'd already had a call from a crime reporter and it was only a matter of time before the story blew up, and she advised him to do everything he could 'to make sure the Precinct looks good in the coverage'. So Saban was happy for Avraham to take on the task of questioning the girl. He authorized his Investigations and Intelligence Branch Commander to be absent for two days and instructed HR to buy his tickets. Avraham bought Marianka's ticket himself, with the excuse that a trip to Paris would be an opportunity to spend time together – 'we hardly see each other in Israel,' he told Saban – and said that Marianka's parents would come from Brussels to see her in Paris. He could tell neither Saban nor Marianka herself the real reason for wanting her to go with him: he assumed he would need her help in the other investigation, which neither of them yet knew he was conducting.

Marianka fell asleep before they even took off. Her head drooped onto his shoulder, while Avraham, who usually slept well on planes, barely managed to shut his eyes. He tried to watch a movie on the miniature screen, but the earphones hurt his ears. And the tall man sitting to his left was victorious in their battle over the armrest. It was the first time he'd travelled for a case, and it was not the only thing in this investigation that was happening for the first time. He'd never before avoided reporting a planned course of action or its results, but now he wasn't telling anyone about his phone call to an unregistered number, thanks to which he'd learned that Ben-Hayat was apparently a Mossad man whom Chouchani had gone to meet. Or about the fact that the purpose of his trip to Paris was to continue investigating why Chouchani had come to Israel and why he had been murdered.

As he always did when he thought about his investigations and how he conducted them, watching himself as if from the outside, Avraham could feel Ilana with him. Could the things she'd written to him in the lost letter have helped him? And what had happened in the last few days of her life that had made her open the sealed envelope and revise what she'd written? If Ilana had been there, Avraham would have told her the real reason for his trip, despite the distance that had opened up between them in recent years. They would have met in her office, which was now Benny Saban's. Avraham would have lit them each a cigarette, and Ilana would have got up to open the window and asked Avraham to explain why he was pursuing a secret investigation and not reporting to anyone that he was going to meet Annette Mallot and search Chouchani's flat.

Who and what exactly are you afraid of? she asks him in his imagination, and he replies that he's not sure if 'afraid' is the right word. I just don't know if I'm supposed to be doing this investigation, Ilana. And more and more, I get the feeling no one should be conducting it, don't you think?

175

Once, when Avraham had had trouble accepting the district attorney's decision to close a case against a businessman with ties to the mayor, Ilana had put it to him a different way: 'From the ground floor, you can't see what's happening on the roof, Avi. Or understand the whole picture. You and I live and work on the ground floor. That's our place. So what's the point of you craning your neck to see? You'll only end up with a sore neck. Or worse – vertigo.'

Outside the aeroplane it was utterly, monotonously dark.

The flight attendant came down the aisle serving dinner, and Avraham took a meal for himself and one for Marianka. About an hour before landing, he finished off her cold blintzes.

In order to calm himself and get a little sleep, he had to stop imagining that he was standing on the edge of a roof with his feet touching the void, and that the people who had beaten him to room 203 and to the flat on Boulevard de Picpus were closing in on him from behind. He tried to fall asleep by reading the brief Esty Vahaba had written for him, and then the Leonardo Sciascia novel he'd brought, but after the first few lines his thoughts wandered.

The last time he'd been to Paris, he remembered, he'd gone with a girlfriend he was supposed to marry a few months later. But he'd already been having second thoughts, and the trip had accelerated their break-up. When they got back to Israel they had postponed the wedding, but it took another year before they had separated, mostly because they had both been attached to Sherlock, the mutt they'd adopted. When Sherlock had been hit by a car and died, they had finally been able to start new lives, separately.

The memory of the huge black dog lying crushed on the road, his tongue wetting the asphalt, returned Avraham's thoughts to Chouchani's body.

Chouchani had been flown back to Paris in a coffin by then, perhaps even on the same plane Avraham was in now, he thought. He made a mental note to ask Annette Mallot where her father was going to be buried, and with that thought his eyes drooped shut. Four minutes later he was startled awake by the captain announcing they were landing soon.

ANNETTE MALLOT WAS WAITING for him at the café. He recognized her because she resembled her father.

She was shorter than Chouchani but still quite tall, thin and lanky like him. She looked older than Avraham had expected – in her early or even mid-forties – wearing jeans and a thin black blazer, and when she held her hand out, he noticed her long fingers but no wedding ring. His first thought when their hands touched was that he did not know what she did for a living. Her husband, who was introduced as Frederick Glauser, was shorter than Annette. He was bald and wore glasses. Avraham assumed this was the German-speaking man who was with her every time they spoke on the phone.

Before their meeting, Avraham had debated whether or not to tell Mallot that their conversation was not part of an official investigation. But as soon as he sat down, even before ordering coffee, Mallot asked if he could explain what had happened to her father, and his dilemma was resolved. He replied that although the investigation was still ongoing, the police suspected that her father had been murdered by the drug smugglers on whose behalf he had apparently gone to Israel. 'We don't have any names yet, but that is our main line of inquiry at the moment. I'm here partly to make sure we're not missing any other leads,' he added, without saying that no one had sent him there for this purpose but using 'we', to indicate that he was in Paris representing someone other than himself.

Mallot was clearly upset. Her father had not been involved in criminal activities, and she refused to accept this explanation for his death.

'But it must be said that we hadn't seen him for a long time, and we don't know much about his life, yes?' Glauser interjected. 'When was the last time we saw him? More than six months ago?'

Avraham looked at Annette and saw her father's ashen face after he was pulled out of the water.

Glauser's scepticism irritated her, but she nodded, and Avraham wondered if her body language and facial expressions also resembled her father's. He had no way of knowing, since he'd never met Chouchani when he was alive, but he suspected that yes, the similarity between father and daughter did not end with height or skin tone, even though Chouchani had left Annette when she was six and she'd rarely seen him since. The way to make Mallot reveal to him what she thought had happened to her father was to share his own doubts with her, without giving away too many details. 'The reason I'm here,' he said, while Glauser looked over his shoulder at the square as if expecting someone, 'is that we are also not convinced the murder is connected with the drug smuggling. There is evidence pointing to that, but there is also evidence pointing in other directions. I would like to ask you some questions about your father and his life, and to see his flat, if that's all right with you. I want to stress that I have no authority to question you in France, and that you are not obligated to answer me, and also that I have no authority to search the apartment. But I believe that if you cooperate with us, it will help us to make progress in the case.'

'Of course. That's why we came to Paris and still haven't notified the police about the burglary,' Mallot said.

Avraham could not resist asking her the question he most wanted to ask: 'You told me that in the past few weeks your father had the feeling his life was in danger. That someone was threatening him. Can you tell me what he said that gave you that impression?'

Glauser shifted in his seat as if Avraham's question was making him uncomfortable.

Annette hesitated for a moment, as though she had to decide whether or not to trust Avraham, and then she said, 'Yes. And he wasn't only concerned for himself but for Sara. Perhaps mostly for Sara. I know he felt that they were both in danger. And that it was connected to his work for the Mossad. You don't work with them, do you?'

THE CAFÉ WAS ALMOST completely empty. At one distant table, which Avraham walked past on his way to the bathroom, sat a toothless man who looked to be in his nineties, wearing a maroon suit. Next to him, on a red velvet sofa, were two fair-haired women, probably in their forties, one of whom was fondling the old man's hand, perhaps doing his nails.

Avraham did not record his conversation with Annette Mallot, and he did not take notes until he was in the Métro heading back to the hotel. He drank three espressos with sugar to overcome his weariness from the night flight, and only on his way to the hotel, as he wrote down the salient points of Annette's account, did he realize there was more conjecture than actual fact. Still, he now knew a lot more, thanks to her.

Rafael Chouchani was born in the city of Tunis. He came to France with his family as a boy, in the late sixties, after the family suffered harassment in the businesses they owned, which included importing fabric, clothing and shoes from France.

According to Mallot, one of Chouchani's brothers and a few distant relatives had stayed in Tunis and continued to run the family business. Chouchani visited Tunis and Djerba regularly, including one or two trips she vaguely remembered from her childhood, but she was not in touch with any of the relatives — if, indeed, they were still alive — because her parents had separated when she was six.

'That's why I don't speak Hebrew,' she told Avraham apologetically. 'My mother is not Jewish. She was an atheist, like me, but she came from a Catholic background and she didn't have much sympathy for Dad's family, or for Jews, or for Israel. She knew my father's family disliked her because she wasn't Jewish. And I think

I sensed it, too. My father's parents, for example, whom I used to meet in Paris sometimes, treated me differently because of Mom, and even as a child that seemed wrong to me. After all, my last name was Chouchani at the time, and my father was their son. To this day, I've never visited Israel, perhaps because of that. Anyway, that wasn't the main reason their marriage was not a good one, probably from the beginning. My mother mostly attributed it to my father's travels. He would say he was going away for two weeks but the trips would stretch out for no clear reason, and he seemed to have had relationships with women in some of the places, which my mother found out about.'

Rafael Chouchani and Helene Mallot divorced in 1985. Two years later, the mother remarried an engineer who worked for Kodak, and she and Annette left Paris and moved to Metz.

After the divorce, Chouchani kept in touch with his daughter sporadically, mostly through phone calls and postcards he sent from his travels. On his rare visits to Metz, he met Annette at a bistro, since her stepfather refused to let him into their home. 'I think we had four or five of those meetings at most. He promised to take me on one of his trips, but it never happened.'

It was around that time, Mallot estimated, that her father began going to Israel. 'Perhaps to meet distant relatives – although I'm not sure of that since most of his family had come to France – and also because of his ties with the Mossad. That's what my mother said at the time. She also thought he hoped to find a woman to marry in Israel, but the main thing was his Mossad ties and his work for them.'

'How did she know he was working for the Mossad? Why would he have told her something like that after they divorced?' Avraham asked.

'I have no idea. Maybe he told her before the divorce, but they stayed in touch, even when she remarried. She still loved him, and I think he still loved her, too. I know she hid their relationship from Hervé, her husband, and she met my father without him knowing. The thing about his work was just something we knew. I knew, too, at some point. That his trips were not ordinary business trips. It was something we knew but we didn't discuss it because he never mentioned it either.'

Avraham wondered if he should tell Mallot about his phone call from Keren, who had denied that Chouchani worked for the Mossad, but he decided not to for now. He would let her keep telling her story and hope it contained facts and not just family lore. 'So you didn't hear him say anything about his Mossad work himself?' he asked. 'Don't you think it might have been his way to hide the fact that he was seeing other women on his travels?'

Annette Mallot said she had heard him talk about his work for the Mossad. At least twice.

In 2001, she moved to Paris to study history and philosophy at university, and her relationship with her father improved. 'We didn't have Friday-night dinners together, but we met every few weeks. He used to visit me at my flat in the 18th arrondissement, and every time he came, he brought something he thought I needed. A television, a fan. He lived in the 14th arrondissement at the time, in a small but pleasant flat on Rue de la Gaîté, and I was there a couple of times, although I never stayed over. For some time he lived there with a woman who used to dress like a nineteenth-century madam. I think her name was Pascal, and I have no idea how he met her or how long they were together. He was proud of me going to university and of what I'd chosen to study, and that's mostly what we talked about. Sometimes I asked what exactly his job was, and he would say he invested in real estate, exported shoes and clothes and brokered export deals. 'I trade in France's reputation,' I remember him saying once. I also remember being surprised that this was what he'd chosen to do because even though he had no schooling he read a lot; you'd never find him without a magazine or a book. He spoke French, Arabic and English, and I think he had pretty good Hebrew, too, from childhood. I once asked him if he found his work satisfying, and he said yes, that what he did was important, even if it didn't appear to be. I think that was the first hint he gave me. Or the first time he tried to hint that he wasn't just a businessman.'

'Do you know if he could write in Hebrew?'

'I think so. When I was little, he taught me how to write *Annette* in Hebrew letters. I can't remember how any more.'

This was not the explicit reference to working for the Mossad that Avraham had hoped to hear, nor were these the facts he wanted to bring back from Paris, but at least he'd found out that Chouchani could have written the name *Yaakov Ben-Hayat* on the hotel room window.

'And that's it?' he asked.

183

Annette hesitated. 'No. There was one time when he really talked about it.'

She sipped her coffee, which she hadn't touched until then, and her eyes briefly searched for Glauser's.

Avraham said, 'You can trust me, Annette. I want to find out the truth about what happened to your father.'

On his way back to the hotel, later, Avraham wrote: *Explicit reference to working for the Mossad? From June 2016, maybe July. Can we conclude role and type of work?*

Chouchani was sixty by then.

His Mossad work had ended, or was about to, or at least that's what Annette Mallot assumed, and so he was freer in what he told her. He was travelling less, too. He phoned more often, and she had the impression that he needed her help, so she went to Paris to see him. For some reason he didn't want her to come to his flat — he was living on Boulevard de Picpus by this time — and they met at a little Portuguese restaurant he liked, in the 14th arrondissement. And what she saw at that dinner worried her.

Her father had never been much of a drinker, but that evening he got drunk. And he struck her as mentally unstable. He said business was down, he didn't have the energy for long trips, he wanted to retire but he wasn't sure he had enough money. He was completely alone and seemed miserable. Annette asked him to stop drinking, but he didn't. And she thought he was about to cry. He said he missed Helene, Annette's mother, who had died of cancer. He said she was the love of his life and he had been wrong to let her leave him. That if he could live his life over again, he would have chosen to stay with her and Annette, and that his greatest regret was how little they knew each other, how little he knew about his daughter and her life, even though she was the only thing he would leave behind when he died.

'What don't you know?' she had asked.

And he'd said, 'I don't know anything. I don't know why you chose to be a teacher and if you like your job, and what you think about your husband and why you don't have children. I wasn't even at your wedding. I would like to sit in your class and listen to you teach history. And for us to travel together like I promised when you were a little girl. Remember? What memories do you have from the years when I still lived at home?'

Avraham tried to picture the daughter and father sitting opposite each other in the restaurant. Chouchani drunk, on the verge of tears, dressed in the brown suit he had been wearing when he arrived in Israel. The things he said to his daughter reminded Avraham of what he'd told the taxi driver and the border-crossing agent at the airport.

Mallot had said to her father, 'It's true, you don't know those things. I don't know anything about you, either. That was your choice.'

And then, to her surprise, Chouchani had said, 'You have no idea how scared I've been my whole life.'

His unexpected frankness had alarmed her. When she'd asked why he was scared, he'd replied, 'It doesn't matter. Life is scary, don't you think?' before drinking more wine and saying – and she remembered this word for word, and Avraham did, too, recording the words later in his notebook – 'You have no idea how frightening it is to be heading into a meeting in Beirut, not remembering if you're supposed to be a shoe salesman from Tunis or a Swiss businessman looking for real-estate investment opportunities. You have total blackout. You don't remember which name you gave the secretary who set up the meeting and showed you in, and you know that a mistake could cost you your life.'

'So what do you do?' she'd asked.

Chouchani had laughed: 'You practically wet your pants. From fear. And then you apologize, ask the secretary where the toilet is, go in there and lock the door to the stall and flush. And as you do all that, you take your passport out of your jacket and discover that today you are Jacques. Only then does the fear subside slightly and you can wash your face in cold water and leave the toilet and smile at the secretary. And you just hope you didn't make a mistake that morning and grab the wrong passport, and that Jacques is really who you're supposed to be.'

Avraham had tried to conceal his excitement when he asked Annette: 'Are you sure he said Jacques? "Jacques is really who you're supposed to be"?'

Mallot had nodded. 'I remember every word he said that evening. He said, "Why am I even telling you all this? So you'll pity me?" And it made me so sad that he'd been through things like that in life and that no one knew anything about it. But why are you asking about the name Jacques?'

Avraham had not answered.

That's who you wanted – or were supposed – to be on the night you checked in to the Palace. Jacques Bertoldi. And, it now turns out, not for the first time.

'Didn't that strike you as odd? Why would a shoe salesman or a real-estate investor have to do things like that?'

'I told you. I never thought he was a salesman.'

From that moment on, Avraham was certain his trip to Paris had not been in vain.

In his black notebook, alongside the things Chouchani had told his daughter, he noted some ambiguities: *Could indicate working for the Mossad, but also could be business scams, impersonation to commit fraud, any number of delivery jobs.* Nevertheless, he had the feeling that Annette, like her mother, Helene, had not been wrong about what Chouchani was hiding from them. The fear that Chouchani had described was now inside him, and it increased as their meeting drew on, but he had continued. 'There's something I don't understand,' he had said to Annette. 'When I called to tell you that your father was missing, you said you thought his trip to Israel had something to do with his work for the Mossad. Now you say you think he retired a few years ago. So I'm trying to understand how the trip was connected to the Mossad or why you think it was.'

'Because of Sara,' Annette had replied immediately.

'Can you explain? I don't know anything about Sara.'

'She's the reason he felt threatened. He told me that explicitly the last time we talked.'

Rafael Chouchani met Sara Nuweima a little over a year ago, in

Paris. After many years of being alone, in a state of acute loneliness and emotional distress.

'She's twenty years younger than him, maybe more. Around my age. I only met her once, and she made an impression on me. She's beautiful, with real light in her face and a glint in her eyes and in her smile, and she's very sharp. She has perfect French, even though she came to Paris less than a decade ago. Here, this is a picture he sent me from a trip they took together, to Djerba, I think.' In the picture she had showed Avraham on her phone, which he had asked her to send him, Chouchani looked completely different than in the security-camera footage. He and Sara were sitting at a table in a beachfront restaurant, with a deep blue sky above them, and Chouchani looked vivacious and happy. His arm was around Sara and her head rested on his shoulder. 'Sara was a journalist in Beirut,' Annette had continued, 'married, with a son who's grown now, I think. She met a French radio producer, left her husband and son, married him and came to Paris. But then she divorced the producer and split her time between Paris and Beirut. I don't know what she did here, I think she wrote for Lebanese magazines. Dad said she was writing a book. I think he fell in love with her in a way he hadn't with anyone for many years. Maybe ever. I'm sure it was her age and beauty and vitality, her independence, and the fact that he met her after some very lonely years, but maybe also because she took him back to his roots, at his advanced age: to the Arabic language, to reading in Arabic, to a world he'd been cut off from since leaving Tunis. She let him read her work, and when I met them, in his flat, they spoke Arabic part of the time. And judging by what he told me, the Mossad wasn't happy. They suspected Sara or thought she might pose a risk for him.'

'Why do you say that?'

Annette Mallot had looked at her husband before speaking again, as if seeking his approval. Glauser was looking tenser by the minute. In fact, Annette had no way of being sure that Avraham himself wasn't working for the Mossad and trying to extract information from her. 'He felt they objected to his relationship with Sara. He was concerned mostly for her, not for himself. That they would hurt her because of their relationship. They didn't live together and almost never went out together, I don't think. When I visited him and met her, I suggested we go out for dinner, but he said they preferred eating at home.'

'Maybe they were afraid of the producer she'd divorced? Or the husband she'd left in Lebanon?'

Mallot had shaken her head. 'I don't think so. This is what I didn't want to tell you over the phone, and one of the reasons I'm convinced his trip was connected to Sara. The last time we talked, about a month ago, he phoned me late, after ten p.m., to ask if Sara could stay with us for a few days. I said yes because it was obvious that something had happened, but the next day he phoned again and said she wouldn't be coming, they'd made a different arrangement. When I asked if anything was wrong, he said, "There are people who don't like our relationship, but we'll be all right. We've found a way to make sure Sara doesn't get hurt." When I tried to find out which people, he said, "People from my previous job who have trouble accepting that they no longer control everything and that I don't work for them any more."'

The two conversations Annette mentioned were on the log Avraham had received from Jules, and this was further proof that she was not lying.

'Do you know when Sara went missing?'

'I don't know for sure that she is missing. I can't get hold of her. Not on the phone number I have and not on another one I was given. Her ex-husband doesn't know where she is either, and hasn't been in touch with her for weeks. I tracked him down and phoned him after you told me my father was dead. I asked him for Sara's family's phone number in Lebanon, but he doesn't have it and I don't know how to get it.'

On the log from Jules there were countless attempts to phone Sara Nuweima. Did the Lebanese number on the log belong to her family in Beirut? Avraham suddenly thought the log was hiding a story he hadn't yet been able to decipher, and that he must go back and reread it with fresh eyes. 'You said they didn't live together, right?'

'Yes. She was back and forth between Paris and Beirut, as I said, and I don't know where she lived when she was here.'

'When was the last time they talked on the phone? Do you happen to know?'

Annette Mallot hadn't known.

Then Avraham asked her a question he hadn't thought he would — because he'd promised himself he would be cautious and not mention the man Chouchani had called before his trip and whose name he'd written on the hotel window before leaving the room in the morning, never to return. 'Does the name Yaakov Ben-Hayat mean anything to you? Did you ever hear your father mention that name?'

Annette Mallot had tried to remember, but she hadn't been able to.

AVRAHAM HAD GONE TO Chouchani's flat with Annette's husband because she did not want to go back there. Frederick Glauser had waited at the doorway as if he, too, was afraid of what he might see inside.

The flat had been turned upside down. The bedroom wardrobe had been emptied, the clothes thrown on the bed, the books from the small bookcase in the living room were on the floor, and every single drawer – from the kitchen to the bathroom – had been opened and emptied out. Avraham had walked among the rooms, not touching anything with his hands, instead moving objects with the tip of his shoe or with his blue pen. Some of the coats and blazers were ripped and turned inside out, the linings and pockets having been searched. And most of the books were open and face down, as if they'd been shaken out before being tossed aside. When Avraham asked Glauser if he and his wife had taken anything and if they'd locked the door when they'd left, he'd said, 'Of course. We didn't touch anything.'

There was not a single object in the flat that might have belonged to Sara Nuweima.

Not a nightgown or a bra or a hairbrush. As if she had never set foot there.

And there were no papers. Not even one. The rectangular living room faced an inner courtyard, at the edge of which was a small bedroom. Chouchani's desk was in the corner of the living room, next to a medium-sized window. The contents of the desk drawers were spilled on the floor in a heap that contained old keys, brochures, batteries, pens and a torch, but nowhere did Avraham see any papers or documents of the sort a sixty-two-year-old man accumulates during the course of his life. Financial records. Certificates in folders. Old notebooks. There wasn't a computer either, but the dust-free square on the desk indicated that Chouchani had owned one. As they walked down the dark staircase, Avraham had asked Annette's husband if Chouchani had owned a laptop.

Glauser had said he didn't know. 'I really had no contact with him, you must understand,' he insisted.

Annette, on the other hand, had confirmed that her father had owned a laptop, but she didn't know if he had a storage unit where he kept his papers, or why he had phoned François-Marie Aubert, the lawyer who specialized in wills, before he'd gone away. Nor could she say whether Chouchani had been in touch with a different lawyer, one who had given him legal advice on his businesses.

That was the first thing Avraham asked Jules when he phoned him from a payphone in the basement floor of the café where he had lunch. They would have to conduct a thorough search of Chouchani's flat, both for fingerprints – although Avraham assumed there would be none — and to make sure all of Chouchani's papers had really been stolen.

Jules recognized the Israeli detective's voice, and Avraham thought he sounded happy to hear from him.

Avraham said that Annette Mallot had just reported that her father's flat had been burgled, and he asked Jules if he could send him the forensic report when it was done.

Jules paused for a moment, then said, 'I'm not sure if I can get that. It's not . . . Are you looking for something in particular?'

I need to know if someone removed any documents confirming Chouchani's ties with the Mossad, Avraham thought. But he said, 'No. I'm looking for anything that might move our investigation forwards.' Then he asked Jules for any information he could get about Sara Nuweima, a Lebanese citizen who probably had a French passport. There was another silence, following which Jules asked if these were official requests from the Israel Police, in which case, shouldn't Avraham submit them through the proper channel?

Avraham surprised him by replying that he was in Paris.

'On an official visit? About the case?' Jules asked.

Avraham said yes, although the truth was more complicated, and added that he hadn't meant to mislead the young French policeman. Then he asked, 'Could we meet in a place where no one will see or hear us?'

THE SECOND DAY IN Paris began at the Luxembourg Gardens. Marianka ran four laps around the park, Avraham made do with one and then sat down on a bench. Hidden behind a bowed oak tree, he took out his phone and read Esty Vahaba's report on the baby investigation, in preparation for the interview he would be conducting later that morning. The sun rose late, and it was surprisingly cold for early autumn.

This was roughly the time of day when Rafael Chouchani had left his hotel room, the last time anyone had seen him. He'd walked along the promenade in Bat Yam, but now Avraham saw him strolling along a sandy path in the Luxembourg Gardens, wearing the brown suit, his eyes searching for Sara Nuweima among the joggers, parents walking their children to school, and people on their way to work.

If he had been able to, Avraham would have tracked Rafael Chouchani that day, too. He would have searched for Sara Nuweima himself so that he could ask her who Chouchani was afraid of and why he thought someone was going to hurt her. He would have kept interrogating Annette Mallot and her husband, tried to get to the lawyers or accountants who took care of Chouchani's business and asked Jules for information about Chouchani's bank accounts so that he could understand his sources of income. He might have even found, with the French policeman's help, a warehouse or an office where Chouchani kept his papers if they hadn't all been stolen in the burglary. He didn't know what he would find, but he assumed that if Chouchani had worked for the Mossad, there would be paperwork indicating that. The man who had written the name *Yaakov Ben-Hayat* on the window in the Palace Hotel to leave a trace of his reason for coming to Israel must have kept records documenting his work and life.

Except that Chouchani's case was not why Avraham had been sent to Paris, and it was not what he was supposed to be working on that day. So instead of thinking about it, he read the brief Vahaba had written to prepare him for questioning Danielle Talyas.

On Monday, 25 August, a message was received from Wolfson Hospital Emergency Room about a baby . . .

Avraham was very familiar with the initial information, so he scrolled down.

. . . In her next interviews, the suspect changed her version. At some point she admitted to abandoning the baby and claimed she was the mother. However, a DNA test proved that she is not the mother, but a second-degree relative, and after the doctor who delivered the baby was questioned

under warning, it was determined unequivocally that the baby's mother is the suspect's daughter, Danielle Talyas, aged sixteen. The father is Amir Souen, fifteen and a half years old, a resident of Jaffa, and this too has been confirmed by a DNA test. They met at a McDonald's on Yoseftal Street in Bat Yam, where Souen began working a month before Danielle Talyas did, and left two weeks after she started.

But here things get complicated, Vahaba had written, and her deviation from the official wording grabbed Avraham's attention. *Liora Talyas told her lawyer, who is in close contact with Saban, that Danielle was raped. But there was no complaint filed and the mother did not say anything about it in my interviews with her. My first presumption was that she hadn't complained because she feared Souen's family would hurt them and that's why the girl was removed to France. But the mother does not confirm this, and based on an initial check-up, the boy's family has no ties with criminal elements. The father is a pretty serious businessman, an infrastructure contractor, and the mother is a school headmistress. Apart from that, the boy says the relations were consensual and he showed me text messages the girl sent him which attest to them having had relations (look at the attachment: I'm sending portions of the testimony and messages from Danielle). I wasn't able to find any of the girl's friends or relatives whom she told about a rape, but on the other hand, nor did she tell any of them about consensual relations. In fact, none of Danielle's friends knew about her relationship with anyone called Amir. So at the moment it's her word against his, but since the girl isn't talking, it's actually his word against the mother's, and I don't believe the mother. That's why we have to talk to the girl.*

Esty concluded with her thoughts about the girl he was going to interrogate after breakfast:

At the questioning with Chief Superintendent Gerti, Danielle Talyas was not cooperative. And if she's anything like mother, you won't have an easy time because the mother is difficult and manipulative. Maybe the right way is to scare her, but you can make that decision on the spot, right? My estimations are: either she was raped and is scared of what will happen if she tells, or she was actually afraid of her mother's violent response and lied about the rape. I wouldn't discount that possibility, so if you can, try to go in that direction as well.

In the second attachment, apart from the main parts of all the testimonies, I'm sending pictures of the baby so you can show them to the girl. I don't know if it'll help, but it can't hurt to try.

IN THE SMALL BUT elegant hotel dining room there were two other couples, one older and one around their age, and a pair of young parents whispering with four blond children in a language that Avraham thought was Norwegian. The civilized quiet in the room was accentuated by the chiming of spoons against teacups. Avraham spread butter and strawberry jam on a baguette, but most of it remained on his plate.

Marianka looked joyous, not only because of the adrenaline from her morning run and the crisp air, but because her parents were due to arrive from Brussels. She piled her plate with warm pastries and thick slices of sourdough bread with poppyseeds and walnuts, and filled her bowl with the berries she hadn't seen since moving to Israel. When she asked Avraham why he wasn't eating, he said he wasn't hungry. And even though she could see he was preoccupied, she could not fathom why – because he still hadn't told her about his meeting with Mallot and her husband, his search of the burgled apartment or everything he thought he knew about what had really happened to Rafael Chouchani. She asked if he wanted her to accompany him to Danielle Talyas' questioning, but he said no, and when she asked if he felt prepared, he said he wasn't sure.

Esty Vahaba had sent Marianka a message that morning saying she'd been to the hospital again to visit the baby, who was improving. The doctors were hopeful that she'd be able to breathe on her own soon.

Marianka tried to encourage Avraham: 'All you have to do is show Danielle that you want to listen, Avi. You know how to do that,' she said. But what if this time he wasn't able to listen because his mind was elsewhere? 'Do you have any doubt that she wants to talk to someone who will try to understand what she's been through? She's a child herself, she's experienced a trauma, maybe even more than one, and she's in a foreign country without her family. Are you sure you don't want me to go with you? Bojan and Anika can walk around the city, and I'll join them later.'

Avraham said no.

He drank a second espresso and left the dining room before Marianka. When he went upstairs for his bag, he could see from the end of the hallway that the door to their room was open. He approached silently and frightened the young maid, who apologized and offered to leave. He said there was no need, and was relieved to see his bag where he'd left it, under the desk.

A black Audi was waiting outside the hotel, and a short driver with a moustache got out to open the door for Avraham. Idit Gerti was sitting on the spacious white leather seat in the back, and she welcomed him warmly. But he quickly realized what she was after, as they drove to the police station at Neuilly-sur-Seine. She asked if he'd been to Paris before. Avraham said he'd only been once, many years ago, and so Gerti lowered the tinted window so he could see the city. She was a few years older than Avraham, elegantly dressed and well groomed. 'So, do you already know everything about Danielle Talyas?' she asked. She mentioned that her interrogation of Danielle had lasted only half an hour, then abruptly changed the subject: 'What happened with that Frenchman they found in Israel? Are you still working on that case?' Avraham said he wasn't; the investigation was currently focused on tracking down whoever had bought the drugs. Gerti asked who was working on the case at the Tel Aviv Narcotics Division, and Avraham said he didn't know.

They crossed the sprawling Place de la Concorde, which Avraham couldn't remember if he'd visited the last time he was in Paris.

'But there's no longer any doubt that he was a courier, right? And you're the one who found the cocaine in his room, aren't you? You have no idea how many of these cases we get. Not just here. It's the same in Spain, Portugal, the Netherlands, sometimes Belgium. This is what I deal with most of the time – I visit Israelis who get caught carrying drugs through airports around Europe and ask our embassies for help.'

Avraham did not respond, but then Gerti asked, 'Did you know that someone broke into his flat?' and he could no longer hide his astonishment. According to her sources at the Paris Police, Gerti added, the burglary was unrelated to what had happened to the man in Israel. There'd been a wave of break-ins in his neighbourhood in the 12th arrondissement.

'Someone broke into Rafael Chouchani's flat? How do you know about this?' Avraham asked.

Gerti smiled and searched his eyes as she spoke. 'Good connections in the Paris police, don't you remember? Everything that happens here and has anything to do with us, I need to know about. That's why they sent me here.'

Avraham immediately understood that she was relaying a warning from someone. Officially, Gerti was the Israel Police representative in Paris, but her office was at the Israeli Embassy. Wouldn't it be reasonable to assume she also worked for the Mossad, or at least shared information with them? And if she had been asked to give Avraham a message, it was possible that 'everything that happens here and has anything to do with us' also referred to his conversation with Annette Mallot and her husband at the café, his search of Chouchani's flat, even his contact with Jules. Was that why Frederick Glauser had been so tense – because he'd seen someone watching them and eavesdropping?

The Audi stopped on a narrow street at the end of which the

Seine was visible. When the driver opened the door for Avraham, Gerti added, 'I won't come in, there'll be a French policewoman there anyway, that's their protocol. If you need anything, you can phone me. And most importantly, let Albert know when you're almost finished, so he can come and pick you up, okay? We can't have you wandering around the city on your own. We might lose you.'

As Avraham walked into the corporate-looking interrogation room at the suburban Paris police station and saw Danielle Talyas, Gerti's last words were still on his mind.

Danielle was wearing white Adidas joggers and a red sweatshirt with a hood that swallowed up her face and her gaze. If he'd had to guess her age, he would have said thirteen or fourteen. He could not imagine a baby in such a small, boyish body. How could it even be possible? A moment earlier, he'd phoned Vahaba to make sure she was taking testimony from the mother. They'd agreed that he would be tough on the girl, pressure her with warnings and threats, but upon seeing the child sitting before him he was not convinced that was the right approach. Nevertheless, his first words, which he spoke in a severe tone and without looking at her, were, 'We'll have a few minutes' delay before starting because I'm waiting for information from Israel. And you should know that the interrogation might be short and continue tomorrow or the next day at our station because we're filing an extradition request with the French police to move you to Israel.' Even before finishing, he felt inside him the anger and the shame, and he also missed Marianka and regretted not letting her join him.

This was the strategy he and Vahaba had come up with: Avraham would imply that Danielle's mother had been confronted that morning with Amir Souen's testimony, according to which he'd had consensual relations with Danielle and had not raped her. Avraham would further suggest that after Liora Talyas had been shown Danielle's messages to Souen, she had changed her testimony to say that Danielle might have lied to her about the rape, out of fear. Avraham would encourage the girl to talk to her mother on the phone so that she could hear for herself what she'd told the police that morning, but Liora Talyas' phone would be off because she would be in the interrogation room with Vahaba. This would serve to increase Danielle's anxiety. 'Maybe she doesn't want to talk to you,' Avraham would say. Meanwhile, at the mother's interrogation, which would be conducted concurrently, Esty would insinuate to Liora that Danielle had confirmed that her relationship with Souen was consensual, hoping that one of them would crack and start cooperating, providing details that they had both hidden up till now.

His longing for Marianka and his desire that she be there, with him or in place of him, were related to the fact that she, unlike him, did not want to scare Danielle Talyas or pressure her so that she'd crack. She wanted to understand what had happened to Danielle and why she'd given up her baby – the nameless baby that she had gone to visit with Vahaba at the hospital because she was 'a person who was left alone in the world'.

His anger and shame were related to the fact that when he sat facing Danielle Talyas, he behaved like a police detective, whereas in the investigation that was his true motivation for coming to Paris, he had not had the courage to do so. He was afraid to ask Yaakov Ben-Hayat, the man Chouchani had gone to Israel to meet, to come in for questioning, even though he'd had his phone number for several days. As for Chief Superintendent Idit Gerti, who'd hinted that she knew 'everything that happens here and has anything to do with us' and had warned him not to walk around Paris alone because he might get lost, he was afraid to tell her openly what he'd come to investigate.

But with this girl, who seemed lost and paralysed with fear – with her he was tough and determined, as befitting a police detective who wants to know the truth.

They sat facing each other silently. Avraham checked his phone every so often, and told her, 'We'll start in a few minutes.'

Ilana Lis had understood who he was when she warned him that his place was on the ground floor and that any attempt he made to understand what was happening on the upper floors would end in heartache or vertigo. Perhaps that was what she'd wanted to tell him in her farewell letter? 'You and I live and work on the ground floor. That's our place in the world.'

With Danielle Talyas, he was there again.

Avraham pretended to read a message on his phone. Then he said, 'Okay, it's arrived and we can start. We're at a police station in Paris. With us is a police officer from the Paris Police, according to the regulations between the two countries, and the conversation is being recorded and videotaped. My name is Superintendent Avraham.

I'm the Investigations and Intelligence Branch Commander at Ayalon Precinct, and I was sent to interview you regarding an alleged rape that led to a pregnancy and the birth of a baby. I have new information that I will share with you shortly, but first I want to know if, unlike at your previous interrogation, you are interested in volunteering any details about your relationship with Amir Souen, the pregnancy and the decision to withhold care from the baby you gave birth to.'

Danielle Talyas replied quietly but unhesitatingly, 'No.'

'Why not?' he asked.

She answered in a barely audible voice, 'My mother will tell you whatever you need to know.'

'Your mother was, in fact, questioned by us this morning. And she did tell us what we wanted to know. That was the information I was waiting for. I just want to confirm with you that what she said is correct.'

Danielle Talyas looked up at him. 'Whatever my mother said is right. I have nothing more to say, and I'd prefer to leave. Can I?'

Avraham thought he was beginning to understand something about Danielle Talyas.

The way she hid her eyes under a hoodie, her feeble voice, her terse answers – all that was not out of fear. He could not frighten her. Not even when he accused her of being responsible for abandoning the baby or hinting that her mother did not believe she was a rape victim. She was not keeping quiet because she was scared, or because she was manipulative or tough, but because she did not have the desire or the strength to speak. It was all born of apathy. When he asked her to remove the hood because he couldn't hear her, she did so without arguing, moving slowly, revealing long, black, straight hair.

'Before you leave, I would like to tell you what I gather from your mother's testimony this morning, which I just received. I understand that there might not have been a rape. We'll go into the details together soon. But first of all, Amir Souen denies that there was a rape. I'm sure you know that. He gave us text messages and voice messages that you sent him, and we've confirmed that they are genuine. That you sent them. So in that regard, he is not lying. When your mother was shown them, I understand she was in shock. Apparently, she did not know anything about those messages, did she? I understand this seemed to make her reconsider what you'd told her about the rape. Perhaps she even thinks you lied about it. Because you were afraid of her. Is that true, Danielle?'

He hoped the question would anger her, but it generated no response.

'Do you want to hear it from her? You're welcome to call.' He held out his phone, but Danielle whispered, 'Whatever she told you is okay.' And then she added the only thing she said on her own initiative, rather than in response to his questions: 'I'd be happy to go back to Israel with you,' she whispered. Only in retrospect did Avraham realize that it was a cry for help.

He took a sip of water from the bottle in front of him. 'I'm not sure you understand what you'll be facing in Israel. Honestly. You have committed a very serious crime. Do you even understand that? Your baby needed medical care, which you decided to withhold. And even though her condition got worse, you continued to prevent her from getting care for several days and you put her life at risk. There's no way of knowing if she'll pull through. If, God forbid, she doesn't, this case turns into an involuntary manslaughter charge. I don't even want to think about that. And I understand you did everything with your mother, but if she now feels that you cheated her, that she helped you because you told her you were raped but that wasn't true, then she may not keep protecting you. You have two little sisters, and if your mother goes to prison because of what you did, there will be no one to take care of them. Your mother must be thinking about that, too.'

None of this had any effect on Danielle Talyas.

He continued, but only because he couldn't end the interrogation he'd been sent to Paris for after just twenty minutes.

'It doesn't matter that you're sixteen, don't you understand that?' Avraham leaned closer, and for a moment he caught her eye. 'The responsibility is yours. You should have notified the hospital as soon as the baby was born. The circumstances of your pregnancy won't change the whole picture, but they might impact our opinion and the way we handle the case. If you weren't lying to your mother about the rape and Amir Souen hurt you – and if you can prove that – then obviously it will affect our approach. We'll make sure he's punished for what he did, and we'll protect you, if you're afraid of him. I promise you that. But if you lied to your mother, and the relations were consensual, then that's another offence: false accusation.'

It was as if he hadn't said a thing.

Silence, and the French policewoman's breaths.

The phone call from Esty Vahaba saved him because he had nothing more to ask or say.

'Avi, can you talk to me for a second?' she asked.

Avraham got up and indicated to the policewoman that he was stepping out. At the end of the hallway, he saw a glass door to a small balcony for smokers, and he stood out there to talk to Vahaba.

'I think it worked, Avi, although it's hard to know with this woman. Bottom line, she's turning her story upside down again, but now she's finally talking, and giving me a pretty detailed version. But she said something I don't completely understand, and I wanted to ask if the daughter is telling you the same thing.'

Danielle Talyas hadn't told him anything.

'The mum claims the relations were supposedly consensual, as Amir Souen says, and that's how she explains the messages her daughter sent him, but she says the boy didn't tell her he was an Arab.'

Avraham couldn't understand why that was important.

'She claims he concealed his identity. That he was impersonating. That if her daughter had known he wasn't Jewish, she wouldn't have agreed to sleep with him. *That* makes it rape. Not just that, but she claims he was motivated by nationalism, do you understand? That he wanted to sleep with her because she's Jewish. He wanted to get a Jewish girl pregnant, or something like that. The daughter only found out he was an Arab a few weeks after he left her, and she was ashamed, and that's why she didn't tell anyone she was pregnant. Not even her mum. Also – can you hear me, Avi? I think the line is bad – also, the mum went to a TV reporter and she says there's going to be a story about how Souen deceived Danielle and how we're hounding the two of them instead of investigating the impersonator. I should let Saban know, right? Or the new spokeswoman?'

Vahaba sounded confused and stressed, and Avraham tried to calm her. He said he would talk to Saban. Then he asked, 'Do you believe her?'

'I'm not sure,' she said. 'That's why I was hoping the girl had said something to you about it.'

'Not yet.'

'So what do you think?'

He told her to try and get as many details as possible out of Liora Talyas about what she was calling the impersonation. 'Ask her for proof that he was actively hiding his identity, or that he lied to her daughter. And get testimonies or proof of what she says about him having a nationalist motivation. How does she know? She has to tell us who he said that to, and how she even came up with this motivation. Then bring him in and confront him with her version and ask him to prove he wasn't impersonating. Get him to show us in their text messages that he told her he was an Arab. Okay? And we need to find out if we can put a gagging order on the case for now. I'll talk to Saban about that, too.'

Vahaba thanked him. Then she added, 'But Avi, I think we need to find out if it's really considered rape. I mean, assuming it's true. I remember there was a story about a guy who posed as an El Al pilot or something, to seduce women to go out with him, but I think we need the prosecutor or the DA to give us an opinion, don't we?

We should find out if it's illegal or not to do that. Is there someone at the DA you think I should ask?'

WHEN AVRAHAM WENT BACK into the room, Danielle Talyas looked somehow older. She gazed up at him out of the hoodie that was once again obscuring her face.

'I'm sorry,' said Avraham. 'Let's pick up where we left off.'

This time, when he sat down in front of her, he was able to imagine that the red-faced baby with the scrunched eyes whose pictures Vahaba wanted him to show her had grown inside this girl's body. He was supposed to confront her with her mother's new version, to understand whether there were contradictions between the version Liora Talyas had given Vahaba about what she called the impersonation, and the information the daughter would give. But he already knew Danielle wasn't going to say anything. He asked her a few questions about her relationship with Souen – how she met him, how often they'd seen each other, how it ended – but she merely repeated the same answer: 'My mother told you, didn't she? Ask her.' When he asked if she wanted him to show her a picture of the baby taken yesterday at the hospital, she said, 'If you want to.'

Shortly before the end of the interview, when he shared her mother's new version about how Amir Souen hadn't told her he was an Arab and that this was what she'd meant when she'd said it was rape, she said simply, 'That's right.'

13

W HEN AVRAHAM GOT TO the restaurant on Boulevard
Saint-Germain, Bojan and Anika Milanich were already
there with Marianka, drinking beer in tall glasses and eating mussels
and chips from a shared platter. Since they'd been together all day,
to Avraham they looked once again like the cohesive unit that had
formed years ago in a small town on the Black Sea – the unit that
had fallen apart because of him. Marianka stood up to hug him, but
her touch was limp, perhaps cautious, as it always was in her parents'
presence. Bojan's large hands, conversely, tried to crush his fingers.

There was no way around it: Avraham had abducted their only
daughter, and he would never be forgiven.

The first thing Anika said to him was, 'You look wonderful, Avi.
You've gained weight, haven't you? It suits you very well.' Avraham
thanked her warmly.

The waiter came over and Bojan said something to him in French.

He pointed at Avraham's empty plate, but no more food was brought to the table for the rest of the evening. Fortunately, there was still a greasy pile of lukewarm chips on the platter, and having eaten nothing since breakfast, Avraham picked at it. He didn't like beer, anyway.

Marianka told him they'd taken the Métro to Montmartre from the train station, climbed up to the Sacré-Cœur, and after lunch in the autumn sunshine had continued to the Musée d'Orsay, their favourite museum, where they'd argued at length – and not for the first time – over whether Gustave Courbet's The Origin of the World was a great work of art or pornography. Avraham didn't know the painting, but he smiled anyway.

He did not bring up Danielle Talyas, hoping it would not become a topic of conversation, but Marianka asked how the interview had gone. When he confessed it had been terrible, she wanted to know why: 'Couldn't you get her to talk?'

Avraham nodded, although there were other reasons. Mostly the shame and the anger. He was embarrassed when he realized how disparate his tough treatment of Danielle Talyas was from the cowardice that characterized his search for Rafael Chouchani's murderers. There was also recognition of the fact that he could not get the girl to talk because he was not taking the case seriously. He hadn't gone to the hospital to see the baby, hadn't sat in on most of Liora Talyas' interrogations, hadn't heard her talking about her daughter and hadn't really observed her. He'd merely skimmed Vahaba's brief, so how could he have hoped to understand Danielle's silence and persuade her to talk? He was busy with a different investigation and had left Vahaba alone with a case that would probably end up on the evening news.

On his way to the restaurant, Avraham had received a call from Saban: 'Avi, you're aware of the information Vahaba gave me, right? That we're about to get hit with a story about how we're harassing a grandma who saved a baby instead of investigating the racially motivated rape that led to her birth? You're on it, yes? I assume you've taken the girl's testimony?'

He'd promised Saban he was absolutely on it, even though Danielle Talyas had told him nothing. But he did tell Vahaba to bring in Amir Souen for questioning immediately, and to get help from Eliyahu Ma'alul in collecting testimony from Souen's parents and friends. They had to find out if there was any evidence of him posing as Jewish when he met other girls or on social media. From initial inquiries, it turned out there was a precedent for convicting an Arab of rape by deception if he really had presented himself as a Jew to a woman he'd had sexual relations with. Liora Talyas' accusations should, therefore, be seriously examined.

Marianka was upset when she learned about Talyas' accusations and Avraham's subsequent instructions. 'But how can the mother claim it was rape just because he didn't declare that he wasn't Jewish?' she asked. 'What are you going to do, check if every time he met someone he showed her his ID card?'

But it wasn't just that Souen hadn't told Danielle Talyas he wasn't Jewish, or hadn't shown her his ID. In Vahaba's investigation summary, she'd written: *Talyas alleges that Souen posed as Jewish by speaking English with her daughter part of the time, claiming he'd once lived in Scotland. He also avoided inviting her to his home and erased anything that could testify to his (Arab) background from his social media accounts. The two met when they worked at McDonald's, and there, too, Souen did not say that he was Arab. They started communicating on messaging apps, sometimes in Hebrew but mostly English. They met on the beach in Bat Yam and in the girl's apartment when her mother was not home. They had sexual intercourse twice, at the boy's request, the girl being unaware that he was not Jewish. He later informed her that he was no longer interested in seeing her.*

Marianka was not convinced. 'So what if he spoke English and didn't ask her over? If she slept with him because she wanted to, without him forcing anything on her, I don't understand how it could be considered rape. And I'm sure the girl understood who he was, even if he hid it.'

When Bojan weighed in, saying, 'You're wrong, Marianka, of course it's rape,' Avraham realized the conversation was going to drag out and turn into a bitter argument between Marianka and her father, in which the relationship between Amir Souen and Danielle Talyas was only ostensibly the topic.

If Anika and Avraham had got up and walked out of the restaurant, it's doubtful the father and daughter would even have noticed.

Bojan had a little beer left in his glass. Judging by the way he sipped it, he was clearly enjoying his verbal sparring with his daughter. Was Marianka enjoying it less? Avraham thought so, although he wasn't sure. Her glass was empty.

'Rape by deception is just as bad as violent rape,' Bojan said in a preachy tone, 'and morally speaking, you cannot talk of consent when there is no free will. If the girl did not know who he really was, she couldn't have wanted to be with him. Meaning, she could not have consented.'

'She met him and she talked to him. They worked together. I'm sure she understood who he was, and apparently, she liked him well enough. Why do you think the religion he was born into is who he really is? What if he's not religious? Or doesn't believe in God?'

Bojan smiled at Marianka as if she was a little girl who had yet to learn all the things he'd already forgotten, and Avraham knew that was going to cost him dearly. For a moment, he imagined something he'd never seen: Bojan, twenty years younger, thin, his beard short and only just beginning to grey, coaching Marianka in karate outside their house in Koper. Marianka tries to hit her father using the moves he has taught her, and Bojan easily repels them and knocks her to the ground with a rapid kick she doesn't see coming, but she gets up and keeps trying.

'I didn't say that was his whole truth. It's part of it. You'll probably think this sounds racist, but if the girl or her parents think his religion is important, and if he hid it from her because he knew that, then there was no genuine desire on her part and there was no consent, and it doesn't matter how well she thought she knew him because they'd flipped burgers together at McDonald's. It's very simple.'

'You think I asked Avi before I slept with him if he was Jewish or Muslim or Catholic? Or that he asked me?'

That was the revenge. Or the start of it.

Bojan sighed, and then said softly, 'Maybe you didn't ask, but it was obvious to you. Don't play the innocent. And it's a shame that you minimize the significance of the role that religion and faith play in identity, for some of us. For a person of faith, religious laws are part of one's identity and part of the truth. And if this boy – and I'd prefer to talk about him, not about you and whatever men you might have been with – knowingly made the girl violate her faith or her parents' faith, without her knowing that she was doing it, then of course he violated her consent and her volition. And of course that played a part in his motivation. In his desire to be with her. To hurt her the way he might have thought he was being hurt. And that is clear intent.'

'How do you know someone's motives for sleeping with someone else? Maybe that was one of Avi's motives in wanting to sleep with me? And maybe that was also what attracted me to him at first – precisely the fact that he's Jewish? How can you know that, and why the hell is it wrong?'

The direct allusion to his daughter having slept with the over-weight man sitting at the table with them made Bojan turn red. Anika put her hand on his and gave Marianka a pleading look.

'It's not the same thing because you did not mislead him. Nor did he, as far as I know, mislead you. And the two of you, or you know what, at least one of you, were grown adults when it happened, and if that's what gave you pleasure, then that's your right. As for the children you may one day have and the repercussions of your acts on them, I assume you haven't given that any thought,' Bojan said without looking at either of them.

Marianka replied, 'That's true, we weren't thinking about children the first time we were together. Do you really want to live in a world where we're all required by law to tell someone what our religion is before we touch them and get undressed?'

Bojan choked on a piece of food, got up and disappeared up the staircase to the Gents.

THAT NIGHT, AFTER WALKING her parents to the train station, Marianka was melancholy and taciturn, as she always was when they left. She and Avraham walked over the cobblestones by the Seine and sat down on a bench, with the Louvre glowing from across the river. Avraham tried to touch her hand, but she moved it away.

'Can I ask you something?' she said. 'This is going to sound critical, but please don't be hurt and shut me out.'

He said she could ask.

'Why don't you ever intervene in those arguments?'

It wasn't the first time a meeting with Bojan and Anika had created tension between them, but still, he was surprised. 'What do you mean? Intervene how?'

'Take my side. It's like you're neutral, even though the discussion is about us. About me and you. About our lives and the choices we've made together.'

He said he had felt she was getting along fine without him.

Marianka said, 'That's not the point. I don't need your help. But you never say what you think.' Then, after some hesitation, she added quietly, 'It's as if you're afraid of him.'

'Of Bojan?'

'Yes. You hide what you think or only tell me when we're alone. Don't be hurt, please. Just try to answer.'

Marianka's question surprised him – perhaps because just a few hours earlier, in the interrogation room, it was the very thought that had gone through his mind. That he was hiding what he believed had happened to Rafael Chouchani. That he didn't have the courage to call Yaakov Ben-Hayat and ask him flat out if he was the man Chouchani had gone to meet on the morning he'd disappeared because he was afraid of the response from this man, who was probably Chouchani's Mossad handler.

Are you also responsible for Sara Nuweima's disappearance?

Did Chouchani come to Israel because you threatened to hurt Sara, or was he trying to find out what had happened to her after you'd already hurt her?

He said to Marianka, 'You're right, I should have intervened. But I always think these are matters between the two of you and they're not really my business.' Then, since he felt his answer was evasive, he added, 'But I really am afraid.'

When she asked of what, he did not reply.

Was this the vertigo Ilana had spoken of? Perhaps he'd accidentally climbed up to the roof and was now standing on the edge, afraid to look down. Or perhaps his fear was warranted and someone really was sneaking around behind him because what he'd uncovered put him at risk.

'Can we talk on the way back to the hotel? It's very late,' he said.

But Marianka said, 'No, let's stay.'

A few hours later, when dawn set an orange flame alight in the clouds hovering over the river, Avraham realized what he had to do when they got back to Israel, and he knew he was capable of it. Marianka had been right to make him stay.

Two men sat embracing on the riverbank, perhaps tourists, and a loud group of boys and girls went by. A man of about fifty walked a dachshund along the pier for too long, chain-smoking. Avraham kept looking for the gleaming eyes of the Audi. Every so often he thought he saw them and the short man with the moustache whom Chief Superintendent Idit Gerti had called 'Albert, my driver'. Gerti, who had explicitly told him: 'Everything that happens here and has anything to do with us, I need to know about. That's why they sent me here.'

This was the first time he'd told anyone out loud what he thought had happened to Chouchani. He told Marianka the true reason for his trip to Paris, and about his secret meetings.

Marianka looked astonished as she listened to Avraham. 'But what does the Mossad have to do with Chouchani's murder and the disappearance of the Lebanese woman?'

'I'm not sure yet. What I have at the moment is conjecture. I only know that what I found out myself in the official investigation simply can't be true.'

'But you were in his hotel room when they found the drugs. You saw the package,' she said, and he thought he could see worry in her eyes.

'Yes, but it wasn't there the first time I searched the room. Someone planted it there in between my two visits. That's what's been happening since this investigation started. Someone is one step ahead of me, marking the path, leaving a trail of crumbs that I'm supposed to follow.'

She said nothing for a moment, then asked the question he knew she would.

He also knew exactly how he would answer it.

'Maybe you missed the package the first time you searched the room and you're not willing to admit it, Avi? After all, that's not your job. You're not a narcotics cop and you don't know the hiding places where people usually leave drugs. And you didn't know what you were looking for that first time. Maybe you just didn't see the package?'

The answer was the name that had vanished from the window. *Yaakov Ben-Hayat*. The name that had been written in the dust on his first visit and was gone on his second. The name that proved definitively that someone had been in the room between the two searches.

'So what are your conjectures? Can you explain how Chouchani is connected to the Mossad?'

The smoking man with the straggling dog was behind them now, and Avraham waited for him to get farther away.

Based on what Annette Mallot had told him and the information he'd received about Chouchani's export business and real-estate investments, he assumed Chouchani had been working for the Mossad in Lebanon, Tunisia and perhaps other countries, under the guise of a French businessman and, most likely, at least one other identity — that of a Swiss businessman.

'But what did he do?' Marianka asked.

Avraham said he didn't know for sure, but he'd moved closer to the truth when he'd heard about the dinner where Chouchani had too much red wine and told his daughter about the job he'd retired from. 'I assume he purchased assets – flats, mainly – in enemy states, rented them out and maintained them,' he said.

You have no idea how frightening it is to be heading into a meeting in Beirut, not remembering if you're supposed to be a shoe salesman from Tunis or a Swiss businessman looking for real-estate investment opportunities. You have total blackout. You don't remember which name you gave the secretary who set up the meeting and showed you in, and you know that a mistake could cost you your life.

'The flats were probably used by the Mossad as safe houses for their agents, or bases for their operations. I assume that was his main role, but he and his businesses were probably used for courier services, too, covert deliveries of whatever the Mossad needed to move between countries.'

Everything, in his view, was evidence that this was what Chouchani had done. Including the fact that within a short while he'd lost the assets he'd allegedly owned. In his notebook, Avraham had written: *He did not go bankrupt as Gerti said. Those assets were not his, they were not purchased with his money, and so when he retired and allegedly sold them, the profits did not go to him.*

'And Sara Nuweima?'

There, too, Avraham had more guesses than facts, but he was convinced he was right.

Chouchani's tragic death had something to do with the disappearance of the woman he was in love with.

'My assumption is that someone in the Mossad did not like their relationship. According to Mallot, her father had said so, more or less explicitly. That in his "previous job" they'd asked him to avoid contact with Nuweima. They must have suspected that she was working for someone. And perhaps she was. Or maybe they just thought it was risky for this person, who surely knew a great deal about Mossad sites all over the world, and therefore about their people and operations, to be in love with a former journalist from Lebanon.'

He waited briefly before going on because he thought the pair of men were calling something at them. Marianka explained that they were asking for a light.

Chouchani had gone to Israel to meet Yaakov Ben-Hayat, who must have been his handler, he continued. There was no other possible explanation for why the name of the man Chouchani had spoken with from Paris was written on the hotel room window, and why that number was unlisted.

The phone log Jules had sent him, in Avraham's view, told a clear story.

Chouchani had tried to phone Sara Nuweima several times. On

the twentieth of August, he'd called someone in Lebanon, perhaps her family, and they hadn't answered. On the twenty-first, at 10.44 a.m., he'd tried to talk to her and then phoned Yaakov Ben-Hayat in Israel. After that conversation, he'd phoned Sara again, and immediately after that he'd contacted the travel agency and booked his flight to Israel.

Avraham was less able to imagine the phone call between Chouchani and Ben-Hayat, but he could envision a few plausible scenarios. One was that Yaakov Ben-Hayat was not involved in Sara Nuweima's disappearance and knew nothing about her, but promised Chouchani that the Mossad would help find her and asked him to come to Israel. The second was that Ben-Hayat knew exactly where Sara was and threatened Chouchani that if he didn't come to Israel, she would get hurt. 'He got to Tel Aviv as fast as he could because he believed he would be able to rescue Sara – of that I have no doubt,' Avraham said. 'Perhaps he even thought she was being held there and that he was going to meet her.'

'And he didn't tell anyone about it? Not his daughter, not anyone else?'

'Of course not. Secrecy is a way of life for him and the organization he worked for. Besides, do you think he would have put her life at risk?'

'So what do you think happened? He was murdered, Avi. He didn't just drown.'

This, he could not answer.

And perhaps it was better not to know? To ask no more questions, to forget his conversation with Annette Mallot, to go back to Israel and investigate Liora Talyas and Amir Souen's impersonation.

In his notebook he wrote only questions, no answers. *Did something go wrong or was that Ben-Hayat's plan – to make Chouchani go to Israel and take care of him there? Did Chouchani assume that might happen and was that why he behaved like a man heading to his own death, even though he did still go to Israel, hoping to find out what had happened to Sara?* And the question that troubled him more than any other: *was it only the fact that the hotel reported Chouchani's disappearance, and that his name and presence in Israel wound up with the police, that led to him being beaten to death? Is it possible that if not for that report, he would have been held in a secret facility and no one would ever have known he was in Israel?*

Marianka thought it was impossible that Chouchani hadn't left any other clues to the reasons for his visit. Avraham said he might have left such clues in his flat, just as he had at the hotel, but the flat had been burgled before he could get there, with his laptop and all his papers stolen. 'Do you understand? The only evidence that does exist is what I uncovered in my investigation, by means of which someone is spinning – or actually, I'm spinning for him – a cover story, instead of exposing the truth. I'm the one who found the cocaine in his room, I'm writing the report about how Chouchani owed money on the grey market and so was probably working as a courier, I found the body and got a pathology report that showed he was beaten or tortured – whether in revenge for the sting operation or to get him to tell them where the coke was. I'm basically their monkey, just like in crime organizations, you see? I'm the one covering up the truth for them, without even knowing it, and I can't do anything about it.' He remembered the ape that had escaped from the zoo that summer but didn't get far before Avraham captured him.

I'm the ape, he thought. He recalled how silent the creature had been when they'd put him in the van, not protesting or struggling, even though just a short while earlier he'd been desperate enough to escape the zoo.

Marianka said, 'Of course there's something you can do about it, Avi. And you're not alone.'

That was true.

I have you, he thought, and I love you. I also have Eliyahu Ma'alul and Esty Vahaba and perhaps Jules. So it's me and a detective who's going blind, a sergeant major about to retire, a former traffic officer from Belgium who works as a private investigator on divorce cases and maybe a clerk from the information bureau of the French police whom I've never even met – against the national intelligence agency of Israel.

In which case, anything could happen.

'Who's Jules?' Marianka asked.

'A French policeman who's helping me with the case unofficially, and whom I hope to meet later today.'

Marianka gave him a look in which he thought he detected esteem rather than surprise.

'You have nothing to be afraid of, Avi, really. If what you found out is true, if someone from the Mossad hurt Chouchani or Sara Nuweima, they have to be exposed. And I'll help you do it. I'll come with you to meet Jules, and also to question this Ben-Hayat guy, if you want. You have to phone him. Tell Benny Saban you want to bring Ben-Hayat in for questioning. Nothing will happen to you. The Mossad is not above the law.'

He wasn't sure that was true, but he hugged her and said, 'We'll see what happens when we get back to Israel.'

'But I'll only help you with Chouchani on one condition,' Marianka said.

He thought she was going to ask him to kiss her because they hadn't kissed even once since coming to Paris. And the sun rising over the river in shades of pink and orange was the perfect setting. 'I want you to question Danielle Talyas again. Listen to her instead of letting her mother do the talking. Ask her to tell you if the boy lied to her. Promise me,' she said.

Although he didn't fully understand why it was so important to her, he promised, and when they got back to the hotel, he called Danielle Talyas in for another interview that afternoon at the station in Neuilly-sur-Seine.

Towards the end of the interrogation, Avraham received a phone call from Benny Saban making it very clear to him that he was going to lose his battle to find out the truth in the Chouchani case. This, despite the encouragement from Marianka, and despite his meeting with Jules on a bench outside the old Paris Police building on Quai des Orfèvres, at which the handsome French policeman had given him new information about the circumstances of Sara Nuweima's departure from France.

Saban had already called three times before Avraham finally left the room and took his call.

'Why aren't you answering my calls, Avi? Listen, they caught the guy who ordered the smuggled drugs you found, and the guy who beat up that courier of yours. You've heard of the Bassisis, yeah? Three brothers. The oldest is doing time for drug crimes but he runs the family business from inside. He confessed yesterday that he was involved in the drug deal and that one of his men beat up Chouchani. Can you hear me, Avi? You're still in Paris, right?'

He heard every word. And did not believe a single one.

'Anyway, Bassisi's men didn't kill Chouchani, he just bloodied him. That's the investigators' conclusion. Apparently, they also threatened Chouchani before letting him go, and that's why he committed suicide.'

Avraham stood on the balcony at the police station for a few moments longer, looking down at the street leading to the river where he'd sat early that morning with Marianka, still hoping they had a chance.

It was a while before he walked back to the room where Danielle Talyas was waiting for him because he was trying to picture Rafael Chouchani wading into the sea. Alone. The water covering his waist, then his shoulders, then finally his head, until he disappeared.

That's not how it happened, he thought.

If it had been up to Avraham, he wouldn't have resumed questioning Danielle Talyas, but he'd promised Marianka he would get her to tell him the truth, in her own voice, about what had happened with Amir Souen – and that evening, he finally succeeded.

Part Four

The Betrayal

14

WHEN TWO WEEKS HAD passed with no word from Esty Vahaba, Liora realized something might have gone wrong. The reporter had also vanished off the face of the earth. Liora tried calling her but she didn't answer, and when she sent her a WhatsApp message – *Sigal, what's going on? When are you moving ahead with our story? Hoping to hear from you, Liora Talyas* – she got no reply. Liora turned on the TV, although she knew there was almost no chance the story would air without her having been updated. Instead of a piece about her and Danielle, Sigal reported on a *rebbetzin* who had taken thousands of shekels to dispense blessings for children with cancer and hadn't given the money back when the children had died.

There was no explanation for these developments. One moment Liora had been giving a detailed account of what had happened to Danielle and the bat had seemed to believe her, and ever since then – radio silence. Was it because the policewoman really had been convinced? Had she closed the case against Liora and started focusing on the rapist?

Edry also thought it was strange that there'd been no update from the police since they'd taken Liora's testimony, and he promised to find out what was going on. When he asked when Danielle was coming home, Liora said it would be soon, even though she was no longer sure.

Danielle was supposed to come back to testify about the rape, and to be interviewed for the TV story, as Liora had promised the reporter, but Marcelle called and said Danielle wanted to stay with them a few days longer because she hadn't fully recovered yet. And since both the reporter and the police detective had vanished, there was no point in rushing her. Liora asked to talk to her, but Marcelle said, 'Give her some more time. She asked us to tell you she wants to stay; she's uncomfortable telling you herself. We don't mind. We like having her here.'

And Marcelle was the only person in the world whom Liora trusted blindly.

The next morning, Edry called to say he had a feeling something was brewing because no one would talk to him. Not even the police officers who always cooperated. He wasn't convinced the case was going to be closed – in fact, he suspected the opposite – and he asked Liora to be prepared for the worst and to let him know as soon as she heard anything. Later that day, the bat called. She tried to sound calm, almost bored, when she asked if Liora could come to the station the next day. When Liora asked why, Vahaba said, 'To tie up some loose ends. We're getting ready to submit our final recommendations in the case, and there are a few little details I want to verify with you.'

Edry didn't answer when Liora called, and in retrospect, she realized that was part of the betrayal, the deception he'd been pulling on her the whole time, just like before, when he'd collaborated with the murderers. He knew, or at least presumed, that Liora was walking into a trap, and he hadn't warned her, probably to keep his friends in the police happy.

She could have asked to postpone the interview so she'd have time to consult a lawyer, but he wouldn't have helped anyway, and the truth was that Liora did not believe this was going to be the end.

The last interrogation.

After all, Danielle was still in France, and they would have to give testimony together, and Liora assumed that at some point the police would confront them with the impersonator. So what did Vahaba mean by 'loose ends'? And how exactly was she getting ready to submit her final recommendations? Liora still had so much to say.

Alice made a face when Liora asked for the next day off because it was 'Giving Day', and she needed Liora to be there. The kids put a lot of effort into making gifts for each other, and it created a lot of mess that had to be scraped off the floor and walls. Liora tried calling Michal for more than an hour to ask if she could have Eden and Ofrit after school, but she didn't pick up. And when she finally answered she was evasive, saying she'd get back to her. Eventually, she said she couldn't do it because Maxim needed the car. Something in Michal's voice sounded strange — too serious or formal — and her answer was surprising. But then again, Maxim had been hostile towards Liora for some time, and perhaps he was beginning to sway Michal. Liora then called Mordechai and asked if he could be with the girls after school the next day, and when he suggested coming over that evening, she agreed. He asked her not to cook, and at seven he turned up with a pot of chicken sofrito and a home-made semolina cake. He ate dinner with her and the girls and then watched TV in the living room. At half past ten he asked if he could spend the night, and Liora realized he meant in her bed. She said yes this time, even though she knew she would not touch him. Edry was still screening her calls, and Marcelle and Ronny didn't pick up either, so she left Marcelle yet another message, asking Danielle to call her back.

In the morning, perhaps because he could tell she was anxious, Mordechai suggested they read some psalms together to prepare her for the ordeal she might be put through. After he went to the syn-agogue, Liora took a shower, then got dressed. She put on David's wristwatch and drank a second cup of coffee alone, on the balcony, before waking Eden and telling her that Mordechai would come in the afternoon to stay with her and Ofrit because she might not get home in time.

VAHABA DID NOT MAKE her wait in the hallway, as she had pre-viously. She quickly showed Liora into the interrogation room, and only a few hours later did Liora understand why. It was their fourth meeting in this room, or perhaps the fifth, and Liora already knew that she was stronger than Vahaba, but this time she was tense; she suspected there was a lot she was in the dark about, and as it turned out later, she was right. Still, even when Vahaba surprised her, Liora's confidence was not completely undone, and she remained in control of what was going on in the room until the moment she walked out, on her own two feet, at the time of her choosing.

'As I told you yesterday,' Vahaba began, 'we're submitting our case conclusions soon. Perhaps even this week. I wanted to go over some details and get your final version before we make our decisions.'

On the desk were a green cardboard folder and a few bottles of water. The policewoman did not look up from the piece of paper she removed from the folder, and for a moment Liora thought that if she'd met Vahaba somewhere else — say, if she was the mother of a child at the kindergarten — she wouldn't have been one of the parents Liora hated.

'In our first interview here, on Tuesday, twenty-sixth August, the day after the baby was found, you denied any connection with the events. Your statement is here, signed by you, and you can read it. A few days later, when we had DNA results connecting you with the baby but proving you were not the mother, you claimed you *were* the mother and that you were unable to keep the baby for financial reasons. Do you remember? You signed that statement, too. Then, when you realized we knew the mother was your daughter Danielle, and that we would question her in Paris, you gave yet another version. You said Danielle was the victim of rape by deception, and that the perpetrator was a young man named Amir Souen, who had hidden his real identity from Danielle, posing as a Jew in order to have sexual relations with her. As far as I'm concerned, all these versions were attempts to hinder and obstruct an investigation and to prevent the police from pursuing legal action against the only perpetrator in this story: you. You are the only person we're currently planning to file charges against. I see no other explanation for your conflicting testimonies, unless you can explain that now.'

As in the previous interviews, Liora was not planning to respond.

Mordechai had suggested that she might recite a psalm while she was being questioned, and she tried to recall the first few lines of the third psalm he'd read early that morning on the balcony, just as darkness had begun to dissolve.

'It's a shame you're keeping quiet again, Liora. I'm giving you a chance to explain yourself. One last chance.'

Vahaba was trying to sound threatening, and Liora said, 'You're the last person in the world I need to give me a chance. Who do you think you are? So if that's all you want, I'd be glad to leave and continue with my day.'

Liora did not understand every detail in the plan that had come to her mind during those first days, but she knew it was all for Danielle's sake.

The attempted abortion that no one was supposed to know about. Waiting for the baby to stop breathing after the abortion failed. The decision to leave the baby at the hospital only after Danielle went away, so that if they got to them, Liora would take responsibility and confess to having put the baby there and bear the punishment alone. She hadn't thought anyone would bother to find out who the mother was if she was arrested and said the baby was hers, and perhaps no one would have if the case hadn't ended up with the bat. But Vahaba just wouldn't let the baby be, almost as if it was her own child. Perhaps that was her role in the world: to take in this baby that someone up there wanted to live, and to care for her, just as Pharoah's daughter had done with Moses.

Vahaba smiled. 'I want to know if you're sticking with your latest version, the one where Danielle told you she was raped and so you decided to perform the illegal abortion and withhold medical care from the baby. I'll read you some parts of the last interrogation record and you tell me if there's anything you want to recant. Okay? This is what you told me:

At the end of July, after suffering stomach ache and exhaustion, my daughter Danielle told me she suspected she was pregnant because she hadn't had her period for three or four months. When I asked her why she hadn't told me before, my daughter admitted she was embarrassed to tell me or anyone else about the pregnancy because it was the result of rape, by a boy named Amir Souen whom she'd met at work. Danielle told me that the boy hadn't forced her to have sex by violence, but by misrepresenting himself as Jewish. After they had sex twice, on his initiative, he left her. We did a pregnancy test that came out positive, and we considered reporting the rape, but my daughter was emotionally distraught and did not want to do that. So we decided to keep everything a secret and have an abortion, so that the rape and the pregnancy wouldn't be discovered and affect her future.

'Later on, you told me that after the attempted abortion failed, you took care of the baby devotedly and then left her outside Wolfson, so that her life would be saved and so on, but that's less important right now. Do you confirm the statement I read? That your daughter claimed that she was raped through deceit by Souen, and that she asked you to hide the rape and do everything you did?'

'Why does everything have to be said twice with you, hey? Is it because you have double vision? I didn't say my daughter asked me to, but that I did those things for her. That's what she wanted. And I suggested that you investigate the impersonator instead of investigating us, didn't I? So did you? Did you find out if he did the same thing to other girls? Aren't you ashamed to call me a criminal when we're the real victims in this story? And don't forget: I warned you that harassing us would blow up in your face. You'll see, that's what's going to happen.'

Liora was less confident about these last words and hoped Vahaba couldn't detect that in her voice. The policewoman looked at her with the same hint of a smile that had been on her face since the beginning of the conversation, and it occurred to Liora that she might have been in touch with the news reporter. Was that the reason Sigal had disappeared on her?

'We'll wait and see what blows up in whose face,' said Vahaba, and turned the computer screen towards Liora.

At first Liora thought she was seeing herself on the screen, wearing different clothes.

She'd put on weight and her chest looked fuller, almost voluptuous, but the real reason it took Liora time to recognize Danielle was that they were so similar.

She was wearing a new pair of faded jeans, with her favourite white hoodie – the baggy one with the big pocket in front, which Liora had washed and dried dozens of times since she'd bought it for her.

'What you're going to see was recorded in Paris ten days ago. Since then, we've conducted further investigations, and everything Danielle says here has been confirmed. I've printed out a transcript for you because you can't always hear clearly, and we're going to watch the important parts together. All right? As you'll see, once Superintendent Avi Avraham – our Investigations and Intelligence Branch Commander, who flew to Paris especially – managed to convince Danielle to talk, she told a different story from the one you gave. According to her testimony, you alone are behind the decision to abandon the baby, to withhold medical care and to subsequently attempt to obstruct the investigation and pressure Danielle to commit perjury.'

The policeman sitting opposite Danielle was the one Liora had seen in one of her own interviews at the station. 'You can stop,' she said. 'I don't care what your film shows. I'm not buying any of your tricks.' In order to hide the tremor in her hands from the bat, she placed them on her lap, under the table. The thing she couldn't understand about the bat's ruse was what she'd said about pressuring Danielle to commit perjury.

The policeman was wearing a dark windbreaker over a white shirt.

And from what he said, this was not the first time he'd met Danielle. How had Marcelle not told her anything about these interviews? He began by telling Danielle, 'In the testimony you gave me yesterday, you confirmed that Amir Souen hid from you that he was an Arab and that that is what you meant when you said he raped you. That it was rape by deceit.' Danielle nodded. 'On the other hand,' he continued, 'you refused to give details about what happened between the two of you, and you said your mother would tell us. So I'd like to explain what my problem is and why I need your help. I met your mother, by the way, and she really does know how to talk, there's no doubt about that. She's actually a little scary, maybe, isn't she? But she wasn't with Amir and you in the room. Her testimony is hearsay. Do you know that term? Hearsay is the testimony of someone who heard about a crime but didn't experience it themselves or see it with their own eyes, and so it carries less weight in court. And it's because I believe you, Danielle, and I want to put Amir on trial for rape and find out if he did the same thing to other girls, too, that I have to get testimony from you. Not from your mother. I need to hear the details. How he hid it from you and how he pretended to be someone else. Your mother isn't enough at this point. I need you, and she isn't you, even if she thinks she is.'

Danielle hid her gaze in her hoodie, as she'd done at home, except when he mentioned Liora. It was only then – for example, when he said Liora was scary – that Danielle looked up at him. She seemed distraught, and only later did Liora realize that her distress was an act.

Vahaba fast-forwarded the film because it took the policeman time

240

to make Danielle say what he wanted. His strategy was obvious: as the interrogation proceeded, he leaned in and got closer to her. He pretended he believed them and promised the impersonator would go to prison, but at the same time he was trying to come between Liora and Danielle. He said, 'I understand that your mother promised she would tell us everything and that she was doing it to help you. But she is wrong. Your mother isn't a lawyer and she doesn't know the law, and instead of helping us punish the rapist, she's causing harm. To us, but mostly to you. And I'm sorry to say this, Danielle, but you're past the age where you just blindly do whatever your mum thinks you should. Even if you're afraid of her. I think you're old enough to make up your own mind.'

The weakness in Liora's fingers moved to her arm, and she rested it on the table. The policeman on the screen kept trying to drive a wedge between them. He asked Danielle, 'Is it possible that your mother is thinking about herself, not just about you?' Danielle tried to evade him and looked up at the camera, as if she knew Liora was going to be watching. When she didn't answer, the cop continued: 'Is it possible that your mother is using what happened to you so that we'll go easy on her? She's committed some serious crimes. She should not have prevented the baby from getting medical care, no matter the circumstances of her birth. Perhaps she thinks that if she says she did it at your request, or because of what happened to you, we won't lay down the law with her. Is that why she told you not to talk to us?'

'Why are you afraid of her?' the cop asked.

Danielle said quietly, 'I'm not.'

He pressed her. 'Yes, you are. You won't confront her. You let her decide that she's the one who speaks in your name, and you keep quiet. And you won't do anything she doesn't let you do.'

Danielle tugged on the strings of her white hoodie to tighten it around her face, as if she were trying to disappear.

'I understand your fear, Danielle. You don't want to come out against your mother. But sometimes you have to get over it and say what you have to say.'

What Danielle said next, Liora could not have foreseen.

Danielle said something the cop couldn't hear, and then she repeated it, louder: 'I'm not afraid of her. I feel sorry for her.'

When Liora looked at Vahaba, the bat's eyes did not contain the triumphant flash she'd expected, but something else, something she preferred not to see.

The policeman asked Danielle what she meant, and she said, 'I feel sorry for what she is and what she's been through in her life and what she's trying to do to me because of it. She doesn't control anything else, so she's trying to control me and what I do. But I don't only do what she lets me. Fact is, I was with Amir, even though I knew very well what she would think.'

Liora asked to stop the film, and to her surprise Vahaba turned the screen away. 'I understand this is difficult. But you need to know what comes next. Should I leave you here alone while you read it?' She put the pages on the table, took the folder and left the room.

Liora skimmed the transcript quickly because she already knew what she would find in it.

Investigator: What do you mean, you knew very well what she would think?

Talyas: (no response)

Investigator: Do you mean that you knew your mother would object to your relationship while it was going on?

Talyas: (nods to confirm)

Investigator: If you thought Amir Souen was Jewish, then why would your mother object?

Talyas: (no response)

Investigator: Explain it to me, Danielle. Why would she object to the relationship?

Talyas: Because I guess I did know.

Investigator: Meaning?

Talyas: Anyway, she would have been against any relationship. It has nothing to do with who he is. I had another relationship, and she didn't approve of that one either. She wants to control everything I do in my life.

Investigator: Wait, but I want to go back to what you said. This is important. You said, 'I guess I did know.' What am I supposed to conclude from that? Did he hide who he really was or didn't he?

Talyas: I think he did try to hide it, but I knew. And I saw his WhatsApp messages.

Investigator: Let's slow down and get the details. You say he tried to hide it. How exactly?

Talyas: (answer incomprehensible; needs to be filled in. Three or four words.)

Investigator: How did it work practically? Give me an example of what you call 'hiding'.

Talyas: He wanted to meet at my place and didn't ask me over to his, and he didn't talk about his friends at all or about his family. At work they didn't know either, I'm pretty sure. He spoke Hebrew without an accent, and he said he was more comfortable speaking English because his family was in Ireland or Australia and he'd grown up there until he was ten, and he wanted to move there after school and get a job. He didn't have anything in Arabic on his phone, except some WhatsApp threads I saw, like I told you. That's it.

Investigator: So how did you pick up on it? Based on what? Just the WhatsApps?

Talyas: Based on my feeling that he was hiding something. The way I do with some things. You can sense it when someone's trying to hide something.

Investigator: Yes. How did you sense it?

Talyas: I don't know.

Investigator: And it didn't bother you? When you were having sex, did you know?

Talyas: It bothered me afterwards.

Investigator: But while you were having sexual intercourse. Twice, wasn't it? Did it bother you then?

Talyas: Did what?

Investigator: That he was hiding something.

Talyas: It bothered me afterwards, like I said. And I didn't tell anyone that we were together because of that.

Investigator: Because of what?

Talyas: Because I knew. And because I wasn't sure if he was serious.

(. . .)

Investigator: So when did it bother you that he was pretending to be Jewish and not telling you?

Talyas: I saw him with his family in Jaffa, too, after he ended things.

Investigator: Was that when it bothered you?

Talyas: When what bothered me?

Investigator: That he hid it from you.

Talyas: It bothered me that he broke up with me without saying anything.

Investigator: Why did he break up with you?

Talyas: (shakes her head)

Investigator: So I'm trying to understand when it bothered you.

Taliya: When I thought I was pregnant, I didn't know what to do. I was stressed out and I didn't want to tell my friends because I was scared they'd say something at school and I'd get kicked out. It was almost the end of the year. Also, recently, some of my friends haven't been so great. I didn't want to go to my mother because I knew how she'd react, so I thought of going to him. To Amir. I sent him loads of messages. I even called him. He didn't answer. And then he blocked me on WhatsApp.

Investigator: Why didn't he answer?

Talyas: Maybe he was afraid I'd find out. He'd already left the McDonald's and we weren't in touch.

Investigator: And then you told your mother?

Talyas: Not right away. That's why too much time had gone by. I couldn't hide it any more because I was showing. Before that I was embarrassed.

Investigator: How did she respond when you did tell her?

Talyas: (no response)

Investigator: Is this difficult for you to talk about?

Talyas: She took it hard.

Investigator: What?

Talyas: Everything. Even harder than I thought she would.

Investigator: Did she ask who the father was? How you got pregnant?

Talyas: (nods)

Investigator: And what did you say? Did you tell her about your relationship with Amir?

Talyas: I told her who the father was.

Investigator: Did you tell her that Amir hadn't told you he was an Arab?

Talyas: I told her that at first I wasn't sure. Because I really wasn't at first, like I told you. She thought of talking to his family, but then she changed her mind.

Investigator: And you never asked him? I don't understand — if you weren't sure, why didn't you ask him?

Talyas: You can't ask something like that. I thought he would tell me when our relationship continued, and anyway it didn't matter all that much to me until he cut things off.

Investigator: Okay. So what happened then?

Talyas: After a few days, Mum said we could get an abortion, and she took me to the doctor.

Investigator: Did you object? Or did you want an abortion?

Talyas: I wanted it. I didn't want to be pregnant. (She pauses. The investigator gives her some water.)

Investigator: Are you all right? Do you want to take a break?

Talyas: No.

Investigator: So your mother took you to the doctor.

Talyas: Yes.

Investigator: And then what?

Talyas: The baby didn't die. I don't know why.

Investigator: How did you feel about that?

Talyas: What do you mean?

Investigator: What did you want to do with the baby when she didn't die?

Talyas: I didn't know. Mum said she would take care of it. I trusted her.

Investigator: You mean your mother decided on her own what to do with the baby?

Talyas: Yes.

Investigator: She decided to keep her at home and then leave her in a bag outside the hospital?

Talyas: (nods)

Investigator: All those decisions were your mother's and not yours?

Talyas: Yes.

Investigator: What did you want?

Talyas: I wanted the baby to die.

WHEN THE BAT CAME back into the room, the weakness in Liora's arm had disappeared because all the cards were on the table, and she didn't think she had anything left to fear. The only part she didn't understand was why Danielle had said that she'd sensed Souen had been lying and it hadn't bothered her. Was she trying to placate the detective because she was frightened? Only later did she realize: it wasn't fear, but rather a sophistication she had not believed Danielle possessed.

It was as though, along with the baby, the girl's body had birthed a vicious strength that was trying to destroy Liora.

That line from the psalms she'd read that morning with Mordechai was, in fact, a warning sign, which, she now thought, she'd failed to notice.

A psalm of David, when he fled from Absalom his son.

She suddenly felt exhausted, and tried to hide it when she told Vahaba, 'I read it. So now what? Are you going to give me a pop quiz?'

'What do you have to say about what you've read?' Vahaba asked.

'Nothing. My daughter walked into the trap and told your hotshot detective what he wanted to hear. That's all. Now can I ask you something, after all the questions you've been asking me?'

The bat gave her a surprised look.

'Why are you so fixated on the baby? Is it because you don't have one? You don't, do you?'

Vahaba tried to look her in the eye, but she had to look away again, perhaps because Liora's eyes were too powerful for her, despite her weariness and weakness.

'I'm fixated on her because it's my job. And also because I'm concerned for her and about your daughter. I'm even concerned about you, Liora, although I understand you don't see that.'

That was transparent.

She was trying to break Liora with tenderness instead of threats, and it was precisely this that hardened Liora again. 'You have no reason to be concerned about me. Who do you think you are to be concerned about me?'

'I'm no one. But it hurts me to think of everything you've done to yourself. You could have saved yourself and your daughter so much suffering if—'

'No suffering at all,' she interrupted because she didn't want to hear any more. 'Believe me, my daughter didn't know Souen was lying and he sure as heck did deceive her. That's what she said when she told me about the pregnancy and asked me to get her an abortion and keep it secret. And that's exactly what she'll say in court when she comes back to Israel and isn't under your illegal pressure. If you think Detective Avi has managed to break us, think again. No judge is going to punish us after Danielle gives her testimony.'

Vahaba said, almost in a whisper, 'But she already is back in Israel, Liora. She came back and gave testimony to me, and also to the therapists who are treating her.'

Liora smiled because this trick was transparent, too.

Danielle wouldn't have come back without telling her, and Marcelle would also have let her know. Even if someone from the police had demanded that she kept quiet.

'Go on then, bring her into the room. What are you waiting for?'

'I'm not going to bring her in because she doesn't want to see you. I've received an assessment advising that the two of you should only meet while supervised by welfare services, and only if Danielle wants to. You won't be able to hurt her any more, Liora.'

This was not possible.

'You think I hurt her? Are you mentally ill, too?'

If Danielle had really come back without Liora's knowledge and testified that she knew Souen wasn't lying and that she didn't care, had she done so in the knowledge that Liora would be held liable for everything, or out of stupidity?

'I'm informing you that Danielle has been in Israel since Friday afternoon. Ronny and Marcelle Nizri drove her to the airport, the Israel Police representative in Paris accompanied her on the flight to Tel Aviv and I met her at Ben Gurion Airport, together with Superintendent Avi Avraham and your oldest daughter, Michal. She is staying with Michal, as per court orders, and you will not be able to meet her any time soon. You're welcome to file an appeal.'

Only when the bat said that Marcelle and Ronny had taken Danielle to the airport did she begin to understand how alone she was now.

And that she was going to be their scapegoat.

Marcelle had known for three days that Danielle was in Israel and that Liora was looking for her and had avoided talking to her. And Michal had talked to her on the phone yesterday and not said a word.

'You think you're going to take her away from me? Whether she's here or not, you won't take her from me.'

She'd known Marcelle since they were six. Her betrayal was even more painful than Michal's – from her, Liora had never expected much. And Danielle, who had come to her sobbing and begged her to save her life, and if it hadn't been for Liora? she'd be taking care of a baby now – a baby she'd wanted to die, as she herself had admitted.

I'm going to be their scapegoat, David.

They're going to tell their lies at my expense, so they get off scot-free.

Everyone knew what the police wanted to do to me, and no one even thought to help.

There was a line in one of the psalms she'd read: *How many are mine adversaries become! Many are they that rise up against me.*

As if Mordechai had also known.

'We have no desire to take her from you. But I do intend to protect her, and I will. That, I promise you.'

'Protect her from me? Sure, because you really care about her, right? All you wanted to do was get her to lie about Souen. Make her tell you he didn't pretend or that she did know he was an Arab. That's all you wanted out of her.'

'We wanted to know the truth, Liora. And now we do. She told you that she realized who he was, but that you pressured her to say he'd lied in case you got caught. She was supposed to say that she didn't know, and that would make it rape. In order to justify what you did, I assume. I don't know why you thought that was a justification, but then I don't understand how your mind works. Either way, we're talking about the life of a baby, and it doesn't matter who her parents are, Arab or Jewish. She almost died because of you. And we're talking about your daughter, who was traumatized and needed someone to care for her. And yes, I, unlike you, care very much. About the baby, and about Danielle. And I'm warning you that I won't let you hurt her. The charges we file against you will be the harshest possible, and Danielle will be the prosecution's chief witness.'

But thou, O Lord, art a shield about me; my glory, and the lifter up of my head. As she recited it to herself silently, Liora felt that her strength had not vanished completely. That she could get it back. And she did.

Liora stood up. 'You file whatever you want. You think you're better than me?'

'I don't know if I'm better than you. And please sit down, Liora, I haven't let you go yet. Sit in that chair. What's for sure is that *I* did not commit the crimes you committed. I met your daughter, and I can tell you that she needed help. Not to be sent to France alone. She needed someone to reassure her and talk to her and help her. Now she will finally get help.'

'You think you're a better person than me?'

Vahaba did not answer.

If Danielle had been there, Liora would have yelled at her: 'But you didn't tell me you thought he was lying! You didn't tell me that. So why did you tell the cop that?'

When Liora kept talking, she could see that the bat was startled by what she said. And that she knew Liora's words were not only for her, even though she was the only one sitting there.

'Is that what you think? That I cared if she got pregnant by an Arab? Then let me tell you that you're a thousand times more racist than me. No less. I didn't care who the father was. I, unlike you people, lived my whole life in a place where there was contact. Do you know who was murdered along with David? Look into it and you'll see who the other construction worker was who was murdered on the site. Ask Danielle to tell you. Ten years they worked together, like brothers. And me? Unlike you guys, I read the stories about Moses every morning and I know who raised him.'

'I don't understand what this has to do with Moses. And if you don't care, then why did you do it?'

'Do what?'

'All of it.'

'Why did I get her an abortion?'

'Yes. Why did you take her for a secret abortion and why didn't you bring the baby in for medical care and why did you then force Danielle to testify that she didn't know the father's real identity?'

She could have said that she'd never done that, but the bat wouldn't have believed her, and it wouldn't help Danielle anyway.

'You think I did that because I'm a racist? Is that really what you think? The only reason I did it was because of all of you. Not me. Because I know what you people would think about a sixteen-year-old girl from Bat Yam who gets pregnant by an Arab kid from Jaffa. I know very well how you'd look at her. It's not me who'd look at her that way. For me she was the same girl who lost her father and that's also why she went to him, to that boy who took advantage of her. You don't like hearing that? Well, it's true. It's all you people who would look at her that way. She's got a lot of shit ahead of her in life anyway, and with that baby you'd all have made it even worse for her.'

'I don't know why you keep referring to "all you people". Who exactly do you think I am? Besides, maybe if you'd helped Danielle, there wouldn't be so much shit ahead of her in life.'

Liora ignored this. 'Do you even know who that girl is, while you sit here talking about her like you're her messiah? So you met her twice. You think that means you know who she is?'

Vahaba remained quiet and the weakness that had come over Liora earlier almost completely disappeared now. 'She's a girl who has suffered since she was little, regardless of anything I did or didn't do to her. I know because I was just like her at first. Exactly the same. She wasn't liked. The other kids, her girlfriends, they didn't want to be with her, and she picked up on that because she has brains. And she wasn't happy back then. Childhood is something you all overestimate. There's nothing good about childhood. Danielle, at the age of ten, understood that being a woman is also not easy, but it's less bad. And even back then she was angry, both at not being allowed to be a woman and at the kind of woman you would force her to be. But at least a woman has moments of power, and if you get as lucky as I did, she can also have love. So do you understand what I wanted? I didn't want to kill the baby. Believe me, I asked God for forgiveness when we decided to have the abortion. But I wanted my daughter to have the opportunity to start her life as a woman without the stigma you all would have attached to her. And anyway, he really did hide it from her, didn't he? Did he hide it or didn't he? I'm asking about him now, not about what Danielle says she knew. Did he try to hide it or didn't he? But now, all of a sudden, you don't care about the truth. You're committed to the truth when it's convenient for you, but that's nothing new. When my husband was murdered, you people weren't committed to the truth. You had no trouble turning a blind eye and cutting a deal with the murderers.'

The bat had no answer. The only thing she could say, again, was, 'I don't understand why you keep saying "you all" and who these "all" are. I did not investigate your husband's death and I would not stigmatize Danielle at all.'

'I'm talking about all you people. The beautiful ones. Everyone who judges me and thinks they're better than me while they trample all over my life and on my husband's body and take the money out of our pockets, as if money is what you lack.'

It was only because she'd already started talking and had said more than she'd intended to that she ended up mentioning David. And she talked to the bat not as if they were sitting in an interrogation room, but as if the whole world could hear her. As if she were on the evening news.

Listen to me talking to them, David. This might be my last chance to say these things so that everyone will hear.

Vahaba simply sat there silently as Liora went on.

'There was another reason why I wanted her to get an abortion, but there's no chance you'll understand it.'

And what Liora said next was the greatest truth she'd spoken in that room since the first time the bat had brought her there.

'I wanted Danielle's first child to be born from great love, like the love I had with David. Not this way, from someone she barely knew and who dumped her afterwards. I don't know if she'll ever have that kind of love. I hope you never have that kind of love in your life, and I also know that's what will happen – that you'll spend your whole life alone, like a leper. And without children. Because you don't deserve children. Danielle may also not have love because not everyone is lucky enough to get it, and not everyone has the power to love that way. To love the way I loved David you need strength, and my daughter doesn't have that kind of strength, and maybe that's why that kid Amir left her. But I wanted her to at least have the chance.'

Vahaba sighed, picked up the transcript pages, put them in the folder and said, 'Whatever you say, Liora. Your lawyer will let you know about the charges. I'm also informing you that we will request an injunction to prevent you from leaving the country, and that you are under a restraining order to stay away from Danielle. Avi Edry will explain everything.'

Liora smiled again. 'You think you're going to get Danielle away from me? Or that she told you the truth? Then you understand her about as much as you understand me.' Then, before leaving the room for the last time, she said to the bat, 'And your injunction is pointless because I'm not going anywhere. Thanks to you, I can't afford to. Besides, I'm not a person who runs away.'

15

AVRAHAM FINALLY DID CALL Yaakov Ben-Hayat, as he'd promised himself he would. The reason he'd delayed it was not fear – not any longer. After getting back from Paris, he had thrown himself into helping Vahaba wrap up the Talyas case: bringing Danielle back to Israel and taking care of her, and preparing for the final interview with her mother. No, the main reason for the delay was that he wanted to be ready for his meeting with Ben-Hayat. More ready than he'd been for any other interrogation.

'If you're right and he's a Mossad handler, he's probably smarter than any criminal you've dealt with,' said Ma'alul when Avraham told him he was planning to confront Ben-Hayat with the information he'd obtained. 'And in my opinion, if that's the case, your chances of getting anything out of him are zero. And you know you're not going to get more than one chance, right? The minute you put your cards on the table, he'll shuffle them. And a few will go missing.'

Benny Saban was no less pessimistic. 'I don't understand what good this will do,' he told Avraham. 'The case was solved, wasn't it? The people who got fleeced by Chouchani confessed to what they did to him. No one is going to open this case back up just because that French woman wants to believe her father was a spy and not a drug courier. And you wanted a high-profile case, so you got carried away with her fantasies. Isn't that what's going on here, Avi? To pursue this with some Ben-Hayat guy who may or may not work for the Mossad is pointless.'

Avraham knew they might both be right.

He was not certain that Ben-Hayat worked for the Mossad, and if so, what his job and rank were. And since he wanted to catch Ben-Hayat by surprise, he'd avoided asking around. But he'd found no record of anyone named Yaakov Ben-Hayat in the police computer system. It was as if the man did not exist.

So when he called Ben-Hayat from his office at the station, he was prepared, but there were still many things he did not understand.

He wondered if the woman who answered the phone recognized his voice from the last call, when he'd posed as a delivery guy. She didn't reply when he asked to talk to Yaakov Ben-Hayat, and it was some time before he heard a man's voice.

Avraham introduced himself and asked if they could meet, and when he was asked what this was about, he said, 'I'd like to get your advice about a case I'm involved in. A police investigation.'

Ben-Hayat replied, 'I don't know how I can help you, but of course you're welcome to come over. Can you be here in a couple of hours? After eleven-thirty?'

Avraham quickly said yes, and wrote down the address. He put in a request to use a police vehicle because his Hyundai hadn't started that morning — that was one of the only two times he did not tell the truth that day.

When Ma'alul walked Avraham to the police car, he told him, 'I think there's a chance that after your conversation with him you'll know a lot less, Avi.'

But this time, Eliyahu was wrong.

BEING INVITED TO BEN-HAYAT'S home in north Tel Aviv on a work day in the late morning should have given Avraham an indication of Ben-Hayat's age. And yet he was surprised when they met. He looked completely different from what Avraham had expected. And he very much reminded him of his father.

Two dogs were grunting behind the stone wall. A large woman held their leads when she opened the gate for Avraham, preventing them from ripping him to shreds. One was a thin and sickly-looking German shepherd, the other a golden pit bull who dozed at Ben-Hayat's feet during their meeting and only occasionally, when Avraham's unfamiliar voice penetrated her slumber, craned her short neck up to look at him. The German shepherd was kept tied up in the yard, where he howled frantically for a long time.

Ben-Hayat was a head shorter than Avraham, stocky but supple looking. He was in his early to mid-seventies. He invited Avraham into a small living rom, which was dark, despite a large French window facing the yard. He wore blue jeans, a polo shirt and the same tattered plaid slippers that Avraham's father favoured.

The house that was revealed behind the stone wall was also surprising because it was different from the mansions Avraham had seen while driving around looking for a parking space. With its pomegranate and clementine trees in the small yard, it looked like an old farmhouse accidentally relocated to this upmarket suburban neighbourhood, or a guard hut left over from another era. When Avraham had got away from the dogs and quickly followed the large woman inside, he'd caught sight of a decaying tiled roof, and in the corner of the yard sat a wheelbarrow full of blackened pomegranates. A brown woollen blanket had been hung out to air on the railing of the small balcony on the second floor.

Ben-Hayat's head was completely smooth, like a cancer patient's, but he did not look ill. And his eyes, which did not miss a single move Avraham made as he sat down and took his notebook out of his bag, were blue.

'How can I help? What's the investigation you're working on? And one more thing – can you tell me how you got our phone number?' he asked, but Avraham could see in his eyes that he already knew the answers to all these questions.

'The investigation is over, so it would be more accurate to say that I *was* working on it,' Avraham said. 'I was looking into the disappearance of a man named Rafael Chouchani, who arrived from France in late August, and turned out to have been working as a courier in a drug deal. His body was found near the Rishon Le'Zion beach. Actually, in the water. In the sea. The cause of death was drowning, but his autopsy showed he'd been beaten before he died and had suffered broken bones and internal injuries. The case was transferred to the Central Unit's Narcotics Division, and a soldier in one of the biggest organized crime groups in Israel has confessed to assaulting Chouchani because he stole some of the drugs he brought into Israel for them.'

Ben-Hayat picked up one of the little statuettes that were scattered on the glass table in front of them and held it in his hand, as if gauging its weight. He did not take his eyes off Avraham. 'That was nice of him. A drug dealer with a conscience. I didn't know such a thing existed. So how can I be of help with this case?'

Avraham answered him directly, as planned. 'One of the witnesses I questioned suggested that Chouchani was working for the Mossad. I came here to rule out that possibility. Due diligence.'

'And why would you do that with me, if you don't mind me asking?'

It was too soon to put his cards on the table. And he remembered Eliyahu's warning.

In preparation for the meeting, Avraham had written in his notebook: *Ben-Hayat knows that Chouchani wrote his name on the window, there's no doubt of that. But does he know that I saw it before it was erased by the two men he'd sent there?* And on the next line: *Did he find out that I have information about the phone call between him and Chouchani?* His plan was not to reveal any of that. He said, 'Can I ask if you work, or used to work, for the Mossad?'

'You can ask, but I won't answer.'

'Why not?'

The pit bull put her head up, perhaps because Ben-Hayat touched her with his foot when he leaned closer to Avraham. 'I'm trying to understand: is this an official interrogation?'

Avraham answered calmly, 'No, not at the moment. If it was, would you answer me?'

'No.' Ben-Hayat's expression remained serious, but there was a hint of a smile in his eyes.

'Then I'll ask you again. Why won't you answer me?'

'Because I can't. Not privately and not officially. And because it's none of your business.'

'Then why did you invite me here? You could have told me this on the phone. You knew why I was coming.'

'I wanted to meet you. I've heard quite a bit about you lately. From various sources. I'm not sure you know this, but we have mutual friends. And I was curious to hear what you have to say.'

IT WAS OBVIOUS THAT Avraham would have moments of weakness.

Ben-Hayat used that secret language, in which things were not spoken but merely hinted at between the lines. Keren from the Prime Minister's office had used it when she'd told Avraham she understood he'd obtained information about 'why this man is pretending to work for us', without saying how she'd understood this, to make

262

sure Avraham knew someone was watching and listening. Then he'd heard it used by Idit Gerti, who had to know 'everything that happens in Paris and has anything to do with us', and who'd warned Avraham that they 'might lose you', in order to tell him that someone was watching him when he hung around places he wasn't supposed to be in and met people he wasn't supposed to meet.

And now Ben-Hayat.

He was prepared for these moments of weakness, and as he'd promised himself, he replayed the things Rafael Chouchani had told the border agent at the airport, and envisioned the picture of him with Sara Nuweima, to remind himself why he was there.

Will you remember me?

The large woman cleared space among the stone figurines on the coffee table and put down a tray embellished with red-roofed cabins dotting snowy mountains. She was fifty-five or sixty, with silver hair in a plait that reached all the way down her back, and when she stood by the table, Avraham could see her thick calves and her giant bare feet. On the tray were a metal jug and one glass, which was not meant for Avraham.

'I'm glad you're at least not denying that you work or used to work for the Mossad,' said Avraham while the large woman filled the blue glass with water and put it in front of Ben-Hayat. 'If you'd denied it, I would have left. But since you haven't, I'm going to speak to you as if you do work for the Mossad, all right?'

Ben-Hayat looked at Avraham with a bemused half-smile that gave him permission to proceed. Then he glanced at the woman, who put the jug back down and disappeared, after saying to Ben-Hayat, in German, '*Bitte*.'

'Let's say you did work for the Mossad. What would you recommend I do?'

'About what?'

'About the case I told you I was involved in.'

'I'm not a policeman, Mr Avraham, but I think I would advise you to make do with what you've found out. You solved the case, didn't you? Judging by what I read about the Israel Police, that doesn't happen every day. So give yourself a pat on the back.'

Avraham had been expecting remarks like this, too. And for a moment he thought he could grow to like this short, alert man who reminded him of his father before the stroke. And who did not stop lying to him.

You're not here to like him, Avraham reminded himself.

'I have a problem with what I found out,' he continued quietly, 'even though I'd be happy to make do with it.'

'What is the problem?'

'Too many things make me doubt that it's the truth. The testimony I mentioned, about Chouchani working for the Mossad, and some other testimonies and evidence that I can't share with you because you apparently do not and did not work for the Mossad, right? So, in fact, you have no connection with the incident.'

'That's true.'

'By the way, can you tell me where you do work, Mr Ben-Hayat?'

The smile on the stocky man's face vanished, and for a moment, there was something different in his eyes, perhaps anger, which he tried to conquer. He asked Avraham if now it was an official interrogation, and when Avraham said of course it wasn't, he said he'd prefer not to answer any questions regarding his personal life.

'That's fine. Then I'll continue with hypothetical questions, if you don't mind. Unless you'd like me to leave?'

Ben-Hayat waved at him to continue.

'Excellent. We spoke about what you'd advise me to do, didn't we? Chouchani, whom you also know by the name Jacques Bertoldi, and perhaps other names, has a daughter in France. He did not always keep in touch with her, but she does love him and she believes he was not a drug courier. She wants to know what happened to him. He had a girlfriend, too – a Lebanese woman, who has also disappeared inexplicably. She seems to have boarded a flight, apparently unplanned, with two men, on Transavia Air from Paris to Gibraltar, on August the eighteenth, and has not been located since. If she's alive, I'm sure she would also like to know what really happened to Chouchani.'

The expression on Ben-Hayat's face did not change, even when Avraham said the name Jacques Bertoldi or mentioned the details of Sara Nuweima's flight to Gibraltar.

'As I said, I would advise you to make do with what you have found out and let the matter go,' Ben-Hayat repeated. Avraham had not ruled out the possibility that this was what would happen in the end, but it was too soon to give up. But then, a moment later, he thought Ben-Hayat might have swallowed the first bait he'd thrown out because the conversation changed course. The bald man leaned down and stroked the pit bull on her belly, and she rolled over and put her stumpy legs in the air. He asked Avraham if he'd like a cold drink or some coffee, then called the woman, whom he later referred to as Esther, and said something to her in German that Avraham could not understand apart from the word *wasser*. Then he said, 'Look, Mr Avraham, since you're talking with me hypothetically, I'll do the same. I already told you that I've heard about you, right? One of the things I heard is that you like detective novels.'

'That's true.'

He hadn't had time to read since this case had begun, though. On his bedside table sat the book Marianka had given him, which he still hadn't managed to start.

'Very good. Then my sources are accurate. Our library is on the second floor, so you have no way to know that I also like books, although of a different kind, and most of our books are in German because Esther is from Vienna and reads mostly German. But I'll go along with a hypothetical detective conversation with you in order to help you make sense of what you do not understand. That's why you came all the way here from Holon, isn't it? You're from Holon, yes? I'm willing to play Hercule Poirot and . . . what was his friend called, Mr Avraham? Captain Hastings, wasn't it? Will you be Hastings?'

This might have been his way to get Avraham to like him. Or was he just trying to find out what Avraham knew?

You have no choice but to put some of your cards on the table now,

266

Avraham thought. *To keep him with you. But put them down carefully. And leave most of them in your pocket.*

'All right, let's play. What is it that makes it difficult for you to believe what you yourself found out? Explain that to me,' Ben-Hayat said.

Avraham told him that Chouchani's flat in Paris was burgled, that every single document connected with his life had been taken, as well as his laptop. 'And all that without leaving a fingerprint. It's hard for me to believe that Israeli drug dealers broke into a flat in Paris with that level of professionalism in order to steal a computer. Doesn't that strike you as odd?'

'I don't know. And of course you think the Mossad did it. Because it's well known that that's the sort of thing the Mossad does, right? Breaks into flats and steals laptops. What about jewellery? Was any jewellery taken?'

'I'm not the only one who thinks that.'

This was the first time Avraham saw surprise in the blue eyes.

Had he managed to transfer some of the fear to Ben-Hayat?

After a moment, Ben-Hayat said, 'To me it seems ludicrous. You think Mossad agents keep employee cards and log their jobs? Besides, you don't need to steal a computer to wipe its files. You know that, I would hope. I have a different explanation for you. A more logical one.'

'I'm listening.'

'What do you know about his daughter?'

Avraham wasn't sure what Ben-Hayat was getting at.

267

'If that old man fell in love with a younger woman, couldn't he have changed his will and left her some of his inheritance? Maybe even all of it? And if his daughter knew about it, she would have had a good reason to find the will and destroy it when she found out her father was dead. If there's no will, the daughter is the only legal heir. Do you remember if the burglary happened after the daughter found out her father was dead or before?'

Annette Mallot had searched the flat only after Avraham had informed her of her father's death. And when they'd met in Paris, she'd refused to go to the flat with Avraham. Frederick Glauser had walked Avraham to the door and stayed outside. The burglary was slick, not a lock or a window broken, and even though Mallot had said they did not have a key, that may not have been true.

But Mallot wasn't lying, of that he had no doubt.

He put his hand on the cards Ben-Hayat was trying to shuffle. 'That's an explanation from the type of detective novel I'm less fond of. It's a little old-fashioned: the classic twist in the end, and the motivation always being money. I don't find it convincing. I have no proof that there is or ever was such a will.'

Ben-Hayat smiled. 'You have no proof that he was with the Mossad, either. But I agree with you that it's likely something else happened to this man. Something far simpler. Almost obvious.'

'Go ahead.'

'You told me he was in love with a younger woman and that she's also disappeared, right? Got on a flight with two guys to Gibraltar. I assume, then, that you did not collect testimony from her and do not know much about her. Maybe she laid a trap for your guy? Stole money from him or transferred some of his assets into her name – this happens to quite a few older people, unfortunately – and then she left town. That could explain why he found himself in the financial adversity that forced him to work as a courier. And who knows, maybe it was she who lured him into that. She gave his name to the smugglers and pressured him, maybe even blackmailed him, to collaborate with them. You didn't consider that option, did you, Captain Hastings?'

Of course, he had considered the possibility that Chouchani's girlfriend, about whom he really did know too little, had guided him – perhaps even forced him – to go along with the drug deal. But he'd ruled that scenario out because the phone call Chouchani had made to Ben-Hayat told a different story, as did the name written on the hotel room window. But only during the conversation with Ben-Hayat did it dawn on him that this would be the next thing the short man and his proxies would try to fabricate. A soldier from a crime organization in France might come forward to testify that Sara Nuweima had seduced Chouchani, or it would turn out that she'd got her hands on some of his assets, and perhaps, if Nuweima was not located, a confession she'd allegedly written would turn up.

But he might still be able to stop them. And this was the time to do it.

He told Ben-Hayat, 'That explanation also suits the detective novels I don't really like. Forgive me for being so picky, but it comes from the American stories with a femme fatale, where, at the end, it's always the woman behind the crime. I've never liked those. Besides, the notebook Rafael Chouchani left in his hotel room tells me a completely different story. Detectives require not just brains but luck. Spies, too, isn't that right? And I got lucky this time. Because the two men who were sent to the hotel didn't search carefully enough, and they didn't find his notebook.'

That was the second lie of the day.

And it scrambled Ben-Hayat's plans. Avraham could see it in the way the pupils moved in his light blue eyes, even though the older man kept his cool and, in fact, broadened the smile on his face as he suggested that Avraham follow him upstairs.

Avraham wasn't sure who was waiting for him there, but he reminded himself that both Benny Saban and Eliyahu Ma'alul knew where he was.

Ben-Hayat led him along a grey rug into a small study crowded with books, where no one was waiting. After he took a black-covered book off a shelf, Ben-Hayat said, 'With all due respect to your detective novels, these are the books I prefer. Have you ever read *Don Quixote*?'

'Is this an official interrogation? Do I have to answer?' asked Avraham, and Ben-Hayat laughed and said, 'Touché. I'm glad we're finishing our meeting on this note. I wanted to remind you of a famous passage from the book. I'm sure you know it, even if you haven't read it – about Don Quixote's battle with the windmills. Are you familiar with it? The knight fights windmills that look to him like giants with mile-long arms. Listen: "Thirty or more monstrous giants present themselves, all of whom I mean to engage in battle and slay, and with whose spoils we shall begin to make our fortunes; for this is righteous warfare, and it is God's good service to sweep so evil a breed from off the face of the earth." That's what the knight says, yes? And what does his sidekick, Sancho Panza, reply — do you remember?' Ben-Hayat articulated the next line slowly, without taking his blue eyes off Avraham, as if he knew it by heart: '"What we see there are not giants but windmills, and what seem to be their arms are the sails that turned by the wind make the millstone go." So all I want to tell you, Mr Avraham, is that with us it's the other way around. Can I call you Avi now? With us, it's the other way around, Avi. Remember that. With us, people who look like windmills are actually monstrous giants with lethal arms that can reach very far.'

WHEN HE WALKED THROUGH the yard on his way out, the German shepherd almost himself free of his chain trying to reach Avraham and sink his yellow teeth into him. He looked up and spotted the woman bent over the balcony railing, her muscular arms holding a brush and a carpet beater.

Before he got into the police car parked outside the house, Avraham thought he had to do everything he could to find Sara Nuweima because if she was still alive, she might be in danger.

He drove onto the Ayalon highway. There were roadworks, and the drive to Holon took a long time, so he only reached the station on Fichman Street at twenty past two. He waited forty-five minutes, then went down to Ma'alul's office and asked if he could use his phone.

Eliyahu gave him a puzzled look. 'Of course you can. Is yours broken? How did it go? Did he deny or confirm?'

That didn't matter, but Avraham couldn't have told Eliyahu that before — and he still couldn't. 'You were right,' he said. 'He didn't say a word. I guess I never really stood a chance,' Avraham admitted. But what he did not say was that in this particular interview, words would not have helped. And he'd been better prepared for it than for any other.

Words could be erased from windows on which they'd been written in the dust. One could steal computers in which words had been stored or the paper on which they'd been printed. And above all, one could offer countless explanations for them. What Avraham needed now was clear proof, and he would only know in a few minutes if he had it.

He walked outside and sat down on the front steps of the station. Marianka picked up immediately. 'Where are you?' he asked.

'On my way home.'

'I can't believe it. They're already there?' he exclaimed.

He could hear the grin on her face when she said, 'Yep. Twenty minutes after you left, they turned up at his house. Just like we expected.'

'Did you get any pictures? Are you sure it's them? Did the pictures come out clear?'

Yes and yes and yes.

Ever since the investigation had begun, Ben-Hayat and his two men had always been one step ahead of Avraham. But this time, he'd turned things around.

'So what do they look like? Describe them to me,' he said to Marianka, too impatient to wait to see the pictures.

'They're just like in the photos you showed me, Avi. One is short and muscular and very blond. Shirt tucked into his pants, just like at the hotel. And the other guy is tall and thin. It's the same two men, there's no mistaking them. You'll see when we both get home.'

He felt as if he might burst into tears sitting there on the steps outside the station, though he couldn't understand why. He got up to release the tightness in his stomach and throat. It was neither happiness nor relief. 'Are you sure they didn't see you?' he asked.

'You're joking, right?' Marianka replied. 'Do you know how many men I've photographed going into houses without them seeing me? I told you, it's my expertise. He watched you drive away, and I was sitting in the car at the other end of the street, with the best telephoto lens on the market.'

This was the knockout he'd been hoping for. Proof that the two men who'd gone to the Palace to collect Chouchani's luggage had not worked for a crime organization but for Ben-Hayat and the Mossad.

Although he knew the battle was far from over, he couldn't possibly have foreseen how drastically everything would change that same evening.

'I'll see you at home, then. And drive carefully,' he said, because Marianka was still in north Tel Aviv, in his white Hyundai, and there was at least an hour's drive separating them. Perhaps also some monstrous giants posing as windmills, with lethal arms that could reach very far.

*

273

IT WAS TEN PAST six in the evening, and starting to get dark. Avraham's phone rang while he was sitting on the balcony.

He'd assumed he would hear from Saban, or perhaps even the district commander, but he'd not been expecting this call. Not today. He hesitated for a moment before answering, 'Gary, how are you?'

Gary asked if he was at home, and when Avraham told him he was, Gary said, 'You're on Alufei Tzahal Street, right? I'm outside. We found the letter Ilana left you and I was in the area, so I thought I'd drop it off. Can I come up for a few minutes, Avi? Are you alone?'

He hadn't expected anything of what was about to happen.

Avraham heard the lift stop on his floor, and then Gary knocked. He was holding the envelope Ilana had left. A plain, white, oblong envelope on the back of which she'd written in blue pen, in small, untidy letters: *For Avi*.

It was a crumpled envelope that should have been delivered weeks ago, but the touch of the paper surprised Avraham because it was not as soft as he'd expected.

They sat down in the living room opposite the television, which was turned off. As Gary looked at the bare walls and the sparse furniture, Avraham saw his flat through Gary's eyes, and through Ilana's, who had never visited it, and he felt embarrassed because it was so different from their home. Why, he wondered, had Gary come here with the letter instead of delivering it at the station?

'How did you find it?' Avraham asked.

'Uri found it, not me. I still can't bring myself to go through her things. Not the clothes, not anything. It's too soon for me. But it turns out she subscribed to all kinds of magazines and gets messages and has bills to pay, so Uri went through her drawers to figure out what needs to be cancelled and he found it. You remember we'd already found the envelope, right? She must have written the letter and put it in the envelope, then taken it out to change or add something, and she either forgot to put it back or didn't have time. That's why the envelope is open, even though she'd sealed it originally.'

Before Gary told him the real reason for his visit, Avraham thought it seemed somehow symbolic that he would read Ilana Lis' parting words to him on the day he'd managed to pull off what she'd told him he couldn't do. He'd climbed up onto the roof and looked down without getting vertigo, and without – so far – falling off.

But there was no symbolism here. Nor coincidence.

Avraham asked Gary how he'd been holding up for the first few weeks without Ilana, and Gary said, 'I never imagined it would be so painful. When she was sick, I thought things would be easier for us after she died, but that's not the case. I'd be willing to have her sick for many more years if she could only still be with us. She didn't want that, of course. So I'm throwing myself into work to avoid thinking about anything else, and the truth is that work is also the reason I came to see you.'

Avraham still had no idea what Gary meant.

'I'm sure Ilana told you I work for the Mossad.'

She'd never told him that. It was true that Avraham hadn't taken much interest in what Gary did, but he had asked Ilana at least once, and he thought she'd said he worked for a research unit at the Ministry of Foreign Affairs, and that was why he travelled a lot. He'd assumed there were other reasons why she rarely mentioned Gary when they talked.

'I'm surprised she never said anything. But that was Ilana, right? Secretive to the very end.' Gary smiled. 'So yes, that's where I work. And I'll be completely candid with you, Avi, because I see no reason to hide anything from you. Ilana loved and respected you, and that's all the security clearance I need. I'm head of a branch at the moment; I can't tell you which one – I hope you understand. And I'm here to explain something that you've been trying to understand. It's important for me that you know that I trust you one hundred per cent. If I didn't, I wouldn't be here. But I can't specify names and I can't go into details because there are confidentiality laws that I'm bound by. The people I will speak about are theoretical people, and if you go looking for them, you will find they don't exist.'

Avraham had left his phone on the bed when he'd gone in to get dressed, but he probably wouldn't have tried to record Gary even if the phone had been next to him. Instead, he would wait until after Gary left and write down what he could remember in his black notebook.

'You know that Israel operates agents in all sorts of places around the world. That's no secret. Both in friendly places and in less friendly ones. They carry out various assignments, some more important and some less. Sometimes they're exposed to a lot of information because of their assignments, and sometimes they're not exposed to any. There are all kinds of situations; I won't go into it. Alongside the assignments they do for us, these agents have their own lives. They have families and friends, and usually a job or a business, and sometimes, during the course of these ordinary lives, they forge relationships with people they are not supposed to have relationships with. People with whom such relationships pose a danger to the assignments they're doing for us. Do you understand me so far?'

Rafael Chouchani wasn't supposed to have fallen in love with Sara Nuweima. Just as he'd thought.

'In the event that an agent has a relationship with someone he is not supposed to be in touch with, it's my job to see that it ends. We especially dislike relationships between our people and individuals from enemy states. Relationships we do not control. Ones that were not created intentionally. Spontaneous relationships can endanger the agent himself as well as many other people, without him even being aware of it. That is why, sometimes, an agent in that situation must meet with his handler, who will spell out why he must cut off the relationship – unless he can convert it into one that is beneficial to us, of course.'

Is that what Chouchani was asked to do? To become a double agent and lie to the woman he loved? Had he refused to do it and paid with his life?

'When you say, "spell out why he must cut off the relationship" – do you mean by torturing him?' Avraham asked.

Gary smiled. 'I think you're confusing us with the bad guys, Avi. These are our agents, not people we torture.'

'Then how is it done?'

'The agent is invited here by the handler, who is a person who has worked with him for many years and whom he trusts, and rightly so, and the handler helps the agent understand the truth. What often happens – and I tell you this because I've seen it – is that the truth shatters them. They can't take it in. It's hard for them to accept that the person they thought was a friend or the love of their life was actually lying to them and only conducting a relationship with them in order to get information. And it's even harder to learn that because of your naivety, because of the information someone got out of you, people paid with their lives. People you know were tortured and executed or sent to prison in enemy states, all because you naively believed the woman you love. Do you understand how painful that can be, Avi? Imagine I discovered that Ilana had lied to me for all those years, or imagine you found out that your Marianka had married you for a reason you weren't aware of, to take advantage of you. And that your innocence had cost the lives of good people. Do you understand how tragic all this can be? People are broken by it. Because of the disappointment, but also because of the shame and the guilt. They can't handle the fact that they were entrapped, and they feel responsible for people having been hurt because of them.'

Sara Nuweima had obtained the information she needed from Chouchani and disappeared to Gibraltar. This is what Gary was trying to tell him. That this was why Chouchani had come to Israel. So that Ben-Hayat would inform him that Nuweima was working for an enemy organization or a foreign state when she was with him, and that the information she'd obtained about his work for the

Mossad had cost the lives of people in the organization. And because Chouchani could not bear the sorrow and the shame – he'd opted to commit suicide.

This is what Gary wanted him to believe.

'What about the beatings Chouchani suffered before he killed himself? And the drugs? Why did you make all that up?' he asked directly.

Gary smiled again. 'No one made anything up, Avi. You surprise me if that's what you really think. The Egyptian told me that you think everything you exposed about the drugs and the Bassisi family isn't true, and that surprised me. Don't be so binary. The world we live in is not binary. Agents do all kinds of things other than the assignments we give them, certainly after retirement. They can work as couriers for crime organizations because they're good at it and because they need the money. And for us, incidentally, it's sometimes convenient to work with people who have other things to hide.'

'The Egyptian' must have been Yaakov Ben-Hayat, who'd sent Gary to get hold of the notebook that didn't exist and to convince Avraham to believe what Gary wanted him to believe, and not to share what he'd discovered with anyone.

But the things Gary said made Avraham think of another explanation for what had happened to Rafael Chouchani – one he hadn't considered previously, and which now struck him as the most chilling. 'Perhaps it's convenient for you partly because, this way, criminal organizations and the police do your dirty work, without even realizing it,' he said, unable to hide how upset he was. 'For example:

the two men who work for the Egyptian steal some of the drugs Chouchani was smuggling at the airport and hide them in the hotel room, to frame him. When Chouchani delivers the drugs, the buyers suspect he's duped them, and so they torture him to try and find out where the stolen drugs are. But he denies it because he really didn't steal anything, and eventually they finish him off. And when a policeman like me – who is also essentially being operated by you without knowing it – finds the drugs in the room, the story seems clear to everyone. Couldn't that be what happened, Gary? That Chouchani didn't kill himself, but that you used both the criminals and me to get rid of him without getting your hands dirty because of what you thought he'd done or refused to do?'

In his mind's eye, he could see Chouchani at the moment of the drug delivery. Had he understood immediately who had stolen some of the drugs and why, and what this meant for him?

Gary smiled again before saying softly, 'I hope you don't believe what you just said, Avi. That you don't seriously think we could be that cruel or that manipulative. Because if you do, I find that very sad. Either way, I came here to tell you the truth because we trust you. And we're certain you will know what to do with it. You understand that's not a given, right? Me being here and telling you these things. Not everyone agreed that I should do this. I'm exposing you to a truth that almost no one knows because you deserve it. You've done some great investigative work and proved you're worthy of it, but in order to keep being part of the small circle of people who know the truth, you will need something other than your insights as a detective. You will need to show loyalty and know how to keep the truth to yourself.'

AVRAHAM OPENED THE ENVELOPE on the balcony, shortly after eight.

Marianka sat on the brown sofa next to him.

He'd told her that Gary Lis wanted him to believe that Rafael Chouchani was a Mossad agent who'd found out that the woman he thought was his lover had betrayed him – that she'd extracted secrets that had cost other people's lives, then fled to Gibraltar. That Chouchani had come to Israel at Ben-Hayat's request and taken advantage of the trip to do a drug delivery and fleece the buyers because he needed money, but he'd been caught and beaten to death. Or that he was so devastated by Sara Nuweima's treachery and its toll that he'd committed suicide.

The story did explain why Chouchani had come to Israel after countless attempts to talk with Sara Nuweima and after his conversation with Ben-Hayat. And if Ben-Hayat had told Chouchani on the phone that Sara Nuweima had betrayed him, as Gary wished Avraham to believe, that might even explain why he knew he was going to die.

When he had asked the border agent at the airport, 'Will you remember me?' he hadn't been assuming he'd be murdered; rather, he had known he was going to commit suicide.

They embraced on the dark balcony, and Marianka put her hand on Avraham's leg while he read in the faint light coming from the living room and then translated the letter into English for her.

Avi,

I'm writing to explain why we haven't talked for a few months and why I asked you not to come here. I know it hurt you and possibly still does, and I want you to understand, in the hope that when you do, it will be less painful.

Since the day I met you, more than a decade ago, in my office (do you even remember that?) I felt that you treated me like someone who was supposed to solve your doubts, to decide for you what was right and what wasn't. And I suppose I took on that role you gave me because it flattered me and perhaps because no one before you had treated me that way. Over the years, I also felt the burden it placed on our relationship. Perhaps you felt it, too. When I got sick the first time, I didn't want to talk or think about work. But whenever you visited, you insisted on telling me about cases, so that I'd let you know if you were getting close to solving them. Remember?

But these are my final months. Maybe my final weeks. And I don't want to know. You may not be able to understand, and maybe it can't be understood, but I don't want to know what's going to happen to me. How much longer I'll live. How many days I have left to open my eyes in the morning and see Uri and Na'ama and Gary, and whether I'm going to a place where I'll meet Amir, whom we lost ten years ago and might be there to welcome me. I don't want to know if my life was good, or right, and I definitely don't want to know anything for anyone else. I also hope you understand that you don't need me. You know the right thing to do. It's not complicated. You've always known. You're a man who knows what the right thing is. You just didn't trust yourself enough.

We had some wonderful years together, and if there is memory in the place I'm going to, you can be sure I will not forget you.

Ilana

Avraham might have believed the lies Gary told him about Rafael Chouchani and Sara Nuweima, if he hadn't recognized that the handwriting was not Ilana Lis'.

EPILOGUE

THE PICTURES MARIANKA TOOK were on a flash drive, along with the detailed report that Avraham had written in mid-October and not shown anyone, as Gary had demanded. Inspired by a detective story he liked, Avraham was at first planning to hide the drive in plain sight, connected to his office computer, where no one would think to look. But eventually, he buried it in a pair of old socks in his underwear drawer in the bedroom. Another copy of the files connecting the Mossad with Rafael Chouchani's death was stored in his mother's email inbox, both because she never opened it and because the thought of her unknowingly possessing confidential and compromising information gave him some pleasure.

In the secret report, Avraham laid out the possibilities between which he was still debating, in a language that even he himself recognized as overly lyrical: *It all hinges on the question of love*, he wrote. *If Sara Nuweima did not love Chouchani, but was misleading him, and that was what he discovered here, then Gary might be right. On 18 August, Sara boarded a flight to Gibraltar, then continued to another country, with the information she'd obtained from Chouchani in her possession. Ben-Hayat asked Chouchani to come to Israel for an inquiry, and when Chouchani learned the truth, he decided to commit suicide, after being beaten by Bassisis' men, because he no longer had a reason to live. But there is another possibility: Gary was lying. Nuweima genuinely loved Chouchani and was not an agent, but Chouchani's Mossad handler still frowned upon the relationship because Nuweima was a Lebanese journalist. In this case, there are two possible scenarios: one is that the Mossad kidnapped Sara or lured her to Gibraltar, to avoid hurting her in Paris, and since Chouchani insisted on finding his lover and threatened Ben-Hayat to expose what he suspected had happened to her, he became a risk that had to be neutralized. The second scenario is that Chouchani himself organized Sara's flight to Gibraltar, to protect her before he came to Israel. Either way, when Ben-Hayat realized that Chouchani was not going to give up on Nuweima, and that he posed a threat, he instructed his people to get Chouchani into trouble with the drug buyers — namely, to steal some of the cocaine he'd smuggled into Israel and plant it in his room, so that they would suspect he'd tried to cheat them, and they'd eliminate him — effectively working on the Mossad's behalf without knowing it.*

Marianka asked what Avraham was going to do with the information he'd found out and the photographs she'd taken, and when he said he still didn't know, he was telling the truth.

For now, he was simply waiting.

For Sara Nuweima to suddenly turn up, alive.

For the people who did not exist to do something that would help him understand what to believe and how to proceed.

In the letter Gary had given him, which he refused to reread, Ilana had supposedly written that Avraham *knew the right thing to do* and that it was *not complicated*. But that was not true. At times, he suspected he must be inventing things or hallucinating – like the grotesque knight in the passage Ben-Hayat had read to him, who imagined he was fighting monsters. But at other times, he realized that what other people considered paranoia was the only way to break free from truths that were held as axiomatic.

WEEKS GO BY THIS way.

He doesn't hear from Gary or from Ben-Hayat, nor from the district commander or Benny Saban. Even Annette Mallot doesn't call to find out if he's learned any new details about her father. It's as if the story is over and done with. Every day on his way home, he drives along the promenade in Bat Yam, past the Palace Hotel, as if there's a chance he might spot Chouchani walking in or out, alone or with the woman who had breathed new life into him. He sits in his white Hyundai with the window open, watching passers-by, trying to imprint every person's face in his memory. Walking along the beach in the dusk, he might appear – if someone were watching from above – as though he is waiting for something to be spat out of the sea.

One weekend, he finally manages to start and finish the detective novel that's been sitting next to his bed since September, and he comes across a passage he feels was written for him: *Your profession, my dear friend, has become absurd,* says one of the characters to the detective. *It presupposes the existence of the individual, and the individual does not exist. It presupposes the existence of God, the God who blinds some men and enlightens others, the God who hides . . . It presupposes peace, and there is war . . . That is the point: war exists, and dishonour and crime must be restored to the corpus of the multitude . . .*

OUTWARDLY, AVRAHAM GOES BACK to his routine work.

He questions under warning the suspect in the fake Viagra smuggling, who has recovered from surgery. He signs the investigation report submitted by Esty Vahaba in the baby case, which ends up with serious charges filed against Liora Talyas; the charges against her daughter Danielle and Amir Souen are dropped due to lack of culpability. He meets with Chief Inspector Orna Ben-Hamo, from Yiftach Precinct: she is convinced that a lawyer murdered two women and staged their deaths as suicides, but when three more women are found to have died under similar circumstances and the lawyer could not have murdered them, the court releases him.

There are days when he doesn't think about Chouchani at all, and days when the man's grey face will not leave him alone, and various inconsequential insights about the case emerge even in his sleep, waking him before dawn. It occurs to him, for example, why

Chouchani resolutely refused to take the taxi driver's business card: he didn't want the Mossad to find the card on him and hurt the driver to prevent him from testifying that he'd met Chouchani.

Winter is in the air, and Avraham knows this makes Marianka happy.

On a Friday evening in early November, he accompanies Vahaba and Ma'alul to look into the attempted assassination of a man who ran an illegal gambling business. It's a rainy evening, the first of four days in which it pours constantly. The would-be murderer skidded on his motorbike a couple of miles from the scene, suffered severe injuries and was hospitalized at Wolfson, two rooms down from the man he tried to kill.

Even when Benny Saban asks Avraham in to inform him that he's going to be offered a new job, as requested, Avraham does not mention Rafael Chouchani, as if the two issues are unrelated. 'What's the job?' he asks.

Saban admits he's jealous: 'I can't understand how you're being offered this. Actually, I can, but still . . .'

The proposal is for Avraham to be appointed the Israel Police delegate to Europol, the EU's law-enforcement agency, based in The Hague. 'You probably got it partly thanks to Marianka. They thought it would be good for you to live in the Netherlands, and that she could help you fit in. It comes with a promotion to Chief Superintendent, the salary is in Euros, and you get a car and a driver. Let me say right now that you should expect me to visit. It's not official yet, but that's the offer, and I think it'll come in later this week. If you take it, I'll probably have Esty replace you. What do you think?'

Was this to reward his loyalty? Or a way to get him out of Israel?

Avraham walks back to his office, planning to phone Marianka and tell her about the job offer, but sitting in the hallway outside his room he finds a man who, at first glance, he has no doubt is Rafael Chouchani.

The man is waiting for Avraham on a white plastic chair, wearing the brown suit. His face is wizened, as if he hasn't eaten since the last time Avraham saw it, the day his body was pulled out of the water.

When they sit down across from each other in his office, Avraham can see that the man is a few years older than Chouchani, but the shock of the resemblance stays with him throughout their conversation, and perhaps also dictates the way he treats the old man.

Hassan Souen explains that he is the grandfather of the boy investigated on suspicion of deceiving and raping Danielle Talyas. He's been waiting for Avraham for half an hour. 'The reason I came to you is the baby,' he says, and when Avraham explains that the case against his grandson has been closed, he replies, 'I know. But we wanted to ask what you're going to do with the baby when she's discharged. Can I talk to you for a few minutes?'

Avraham is still thinking about Europol. He wonders if Marianka has ever been to The Hague, and although he doesn't know what the city looks like, he imagines a flat with a picturesque balcony cascading with flowers overlooking a canal with a bridge.

Souen looks at the shut window and asks if he can smoke. Avraham says no, but then he changes his mind. 'You know what? Okay,' he says, putting a plastic cup with a little water on the desk, and then getting up to open the window.

It's stopped raining. The sky has been cleansed of its clouds, with an autumnal glimmer of light, and there is a warmth in the office that seems to emanate from the visitor and the connection between them.

Avraham does not yet know that he will soon sense that this is the conversation he's been waiting for. Or that afterwards, he will understand that the two cases are related, not only because they began on the same day and both led him to Paris, but because one will help him decide how to act in the other.

Hassan Souen looks surprised when Avraham says he has no idea what will happen to the baby. As far as he knows, she'll stay in Wolfson Hospital for another few weeks. Vahaba continues to visit her and reports that the baby has a name – Emunah – given to her by the young nurse who has cared for her since the day she arrived. Danielle Talyas approved the name, and she's been to visit the baby once with her older sister. When Avraham suggests that Souen contacts the welfare authorities, he replies, 'We did. But we thought maybe if the police put in a good word it could help.'

Avraham still does not understand what Souen is asking. Does he want his grandson to visit the baby?

'No, not Amir. He doesn't know anything, he's just a boy. Do you know how old he is? Barely sixteen. Even younger than her. The mother.'

Then who wants to see her? Amir's parents?

'His parents, yes. His mother wants to visit. And so do I. We tried to see her at Wolfson, but they wouldn't let us. I don't know why – after all, she is my grandson's daughter, isn't she? Even if he didn't treat her mother well and didn't help when she needed him to. He was scared we'd be angry or ashamed. I was angry at how he treated her, but that's not his fault. Kids today do a lot of wrong things.'

Avraham recalls the moment in Paris when he asked Danielle Talyas what she wanted to do with the baby. *I wanted the baby to die*, she'd said, and that must be what Amir Souen had wanted, too.

'Why didn't he help her when she contacted him?' Avraham asks.

'I think he got scared that she wouldn't want him if she found out who he was. That's why he disappeared. He was afraid she wouldn't want him. That's what I believe.'

'What do you mean, you believe? Didn't you ask him?'

'I did, but kids say a lot of things and they don't always know what they're saying. Grown-ups do as well, of course, but kids even more. He won't say that he liked her because he's embarrassed and maybe he thinks it'll embarrass him in front of his family. That might be what she thought, too, you know? Kids can like each other regardless of what the grown-ups say they should or shouldn't do.'

Avraham briefly recalls a picture of Chouchani and Nuweima at the beach restaurant. He promises Souen to try and help the family visit the baby, and the grandfather says, 'But not just visit. We want to help her.'

'What do you mean? Help her how?'

Souen lights another cigarette and offers one to Avraham, who hesitates before turning it down.

'How old do you think I am?' the grandfather asks, and he laughs at Avraham's reply, which is probably coloured by his resemblance to Chouchani. 'Sixty-two? Thanks, pal. You're too nice. I was born in nineteen forty-nine. Do the maths. I have four children and ten grandchildren. How many children do you have?'

Instead of answering straightforwardly, for some reason Avraham says, 'None yet. But I will.'

'*Inshallah*. And your mother? How old is she?'

'Around your age. Born in forty-seven.'

'Can I tell you a story about my mother, so you'll understand why I'm here?' Souen asks.

Avraham nods. And it's possible that as he listens to the grandfather, he imagines that he is hearing not only Chouchani's voice but his own father's, a voice he has not heard for a long time, not since his father used to tell him stories. And this, too, makes it easier for him to decide what to do.

'When I was born, in forty-nine, as I told you, my late mother felt alone. Her family had fled to Gaza in forty-eight because of the war, and they couldn't ever came back to Jaffa. Only she and Father and her older brother stayed here to look after the family's orchards. The other flats in our building had belonged to the family, but they were taken over by Jewish families – one from Iraq and one from Bulgaria. New immigrants. And the mothers, like my mother, had little children. Babies. My age. My mother was only eighteen or nineteen, just imagine that, and she missed her family terribly and was sad about staying in Jaffa without them, and she couldn't give me milk. It's sad to admit, but that's what happened. She told me this, not anyone else. She wasn't ashamed to tell me. She tried very hard to nurse me, but she couldn't do it. So who nursed me? The Jewish neighbour from Bulgaria and the Jewish neighbour from Iraq. For a few months they took turns, one day this one and the next day the other one, breastfeeding me with their own babies, until I grew enough. That's what I wanted to tell you. I never forgot what happened before I was born, and what happened afterwards. I never forgot any of it. Lots of bad things have happened to my people and to your people. But God has given me a chance to close the circle. Do you believe in God? You don't have a choice if your name is Avraham, right? Avraham was the first believer. Even when God told him to leave his father's home, Avraham believed in Him and did what He asked, right? So you have no choice. I believe that before God takes me, He is giving me this chance to repay Him. Not the Jews – Him. For the life and the strength He gave me when I was a baby and my mother couldn't. That's why we want to care for the baby and give her a good life, and I'm sure you can help make that happen. It won't be Amir raising her; we will raise her as a family, and the mother can visit if she wants. Can you help us convince them to let us have her? Maybe it's the welfare department that makes the decisions, but police officers have long arms that reach far, don't they?'

And that is how it ends.

The die is cast.

Avraham phones Saban and tells him he'd like to stay on in his current job for now, without explaining why. When Marianka asks why he's changed his mind, he says he's decided to stay on the ground floor because from the rooftop you can't see people's faces.

He drives home and retrieves the flash drive. He could use

Marianka's phone, or his parents', but he decides not to hide, so he drives back to the station and dials the Paris number from his office phone. First, he puts on his blue jacket because the wind is blowing in through the open window, and he picks up the wooden pipe that Marianka bought him in Jerusalem.

When he hears the pleasant voice answer, he says, 'It's me, Superintendent Avraham. Can you talk?'

He knows Jules is not a senior officer in the Paris Police but just a clerk at the information bureau, and that he's not speaking from Quai des Orfèvres, but Avraham nevertheless likes to picture Jules next to a blazing fireplace in the old police building overlooking the Seine. *And if that helps you do the right thing*, he says to himself, *then why not?*

'I would like to share with you some information that the Paris Police must look into,' he begins. 'Yes, it's about Chouchani and his girlfriend. No, it's not over yet. Why not? Because the score isn't settled until we decide it is, Jules. And it will not be settled until we punish the murderers. In short, I plan to keep doing everything I can at my end to bring them to justice, but I'm going to email you a photograph soon, and I will tell you who the people in the photo are and who operates them and what they did to Chouchani. All right? And I would like you to forward this information to Chouchani's daughter, Annette Mallot, and to your supervisors, as soon as possible. Because Rafael Chouchani was not murdered by drug dealers, and his lover, Sara Nuweima, did not just get on a flight from Paris to Gibraltar. May I start telling you the true story, my dear friend? Are you writing this down?'